WEEDING OUT THE LIES
Love and Loss on Mackinac Island

ALSO BY W.S. SIMONS

Losing August

A Second Look

Stone by Stone

WEEDING OUT THE LIES
Love and Loss on Mackinac Island

By W. S. Simons

Copyright © 2023 by Wendy Simons
All rights reserved.

For information about permission to use or reproduce any part of this book in any manner contact info@wssimonsbooks.com

This is a work of fiction.
Names, characters, places and incidents are drawn from the author's imagination. Any resemblance to actual events, persons, living or dead, or locales, aside from Mackinac Island, is coincidental.

Cover Design: WS Illustration
Photo credits: AdobeStock,
Dustin Thibideau/SHUTTERSTOCK

ISBN: 979-8-9893594-6-2

*This book is dedicated to my dad
who maintained our
annual sojourn to the island
for nearly forty years.*

Ralph was a story teller.

CHAPTER 1

Enigma

"I don't know what to tell you. I am nobody of note who's done nothing of interest."

It was the fall of 2017 when Janet Marie Granger delivered this statement to the stout woman standing on the porch of Baldwin Cottage, then turned her back, stepped inside, and shut the door hard behind her.

Mrs. Cecelia Coventry, left outside alone, mouth agape, lost any sense of what should come next. No one had ever, in any manner, directly or accidentally, closed a door on her. She pushed up the scarf around her neck and waited, the chilly reception outdone only by the bite of an early cold snap. Certainly, it had been a mistake and Ms. Granger would reappear with sincerest apologies.

It had not been Janet's intention to shut Cecelia out. She had, in fact, meant to simply go in ahead of her, reluctantly invite her to follow, and offer some clarification concerning her perfunctory self-deprecating description. But the door closed directly behind her with a solid thunk leaving Janet as stunned as Cecelia. She tried the doorknob, but it was frozen in place, not even a jiggle.

"It's stuck," she said through the door. "We'll have to do this another time."

"There's a side door," Cecelia instructed. "Let's try that."

"Oh, let's try it on a return trip," Janet said. "Next summer."

"But it's the last issue of the season," Cecelia countered, dumbstruck. When she was met with silence, she turned abruptly, stumbled on the runner of a green wicker rocker, regained her footing, and exited the porch in a huff, the screen door smacking closed behind her.

She had ventured onto Janet's porch that afternoon seeking answers concerning the enigmatic new owner of an historic cottage in Hubbard's Annex. This endeavor was not out of idle curiosity, but for the season's last issue of *The Island Times,* the weekly paper of Mackinac Island. She was a journalist, a term loosely applied to her activities as the writer of *The Scoop*, the less-than-profound commentary on who was doing what with whom among the island's summer homeowners and shopkeepers.

Cecelia's computer search on Janet had exposed others who bore her name with web-worthy lives: One J.M. Granger had a medical practice; one wrote self-help books; another had two children who were outstanding soccer players; one had a blog about being a painter in France for a year. Cecelia, however, left this J. M. Granger's property, still knowing nothing about the Annex's newest resident.

Janet heard the thuds and the clap of the screen, and rushed upstairs to look out a window to make sure the woman left and was not prowling around. There she was, Mrs. Cecelia Coventry, walking away, her short, choppy stride carrying her around a corner out of sight behind the cedar hedgerow. Satisfied, Janet took in the view through the trees down to the Mackinac Straits, a narrow waterway connecting Lake Michigan and Lake Huron. Sunlight glistened on calm waters.

The description offered to Cecelia was not out of character or overstated. At fifty, Janet had no delusions about herself, having lived firmly ensconced in mediocrity without any accomplishment of record except for her recent purchase of a 130-year-old white clapboard Victorian house on Mackinac Island, a spit of land between Michigan's lower and upper peninsulas.

Her grandfather used to bring the family up to spend a couple nights on the island every August. It was the highlight of her year. They always stayed at the Grand Hotel, where she felt like a princess wearing a nice dress and white shoes for dinner, taking carriage rides, swimming in a pool where Esther Williams filmed a movie in the 1940s. It was all very posh.

Her dad continued the annual sojourn after Grandpa Max died, though they went in June instead of August and no longer stayed in the Grand. He found a smaller hotel down in town. The Windward was an old building with big but sparsely furnished rooms and tiny bathrooms. There were no more expensive carriage rides but she and her dad biked around the island every time, no matter the weather. They ate breakfast at the same place every year, sang in the piano bar every trip, and toured the historical sights. What her mother deemed monotony, Janet and her dad found reassuring. Each night, her dad opened the window to hear Taps played from Fort Mackinac in the center of town. He never missed it.

He arranged a summer job on Mackinac for Janet right out of high school. Maybe he thought it would be a fun experience for his daughter. It was just as likely he wanted to get her out of the house, away from her mother, a woman whose sole purpose in life seemed to be to make Janet's life miserable. Whatever his reasons, working for the park service imprinted the four-square-mile island into Janet's DNA.

Janet spent most of her free time that summer wandering the woods alone, exploring the lacework of trails tourists didn't know about or bother with. She liked the high ground of Fort Holmes. Little more than a mound of earth and a wooden gate, in its prime, it was once occupied by the French, then the British, and eventually the Americans. From its vantage point in the Straits of Mackinac, she could see east into Lake Huron, west into Lake Michigan, and south beyond Round Island to the Lower Peninsula. Mackinac Island had been the fur trading capital of the upper Great Lakes. It became a national park in 1875, the second behind Yellowstone. Magnates of industry arrived and built grand summer homes on the bluff overlooking the straits. The federal government turned it over to the state in 1895, becoming Michigan's first state park. It was a history Janet knew by heart. As a park guide, she used to rotate a circuit of historical markers, reciting facts and anecdotes to tourists.

Her favorite aspect of the island was the quiet. With no motor vehicles, transport was accomplished by foot, bicycle, horseback, buggy or dray. There was a peacefulness about horse-drawn carriages, rubber-shod hooves clomping pavement in town, plodding along gritty dirt roads through the woods and Annex. From June to September, tourists on foot and bicycles filled the main street of town, bathed in the aroma of fresh fudge, caramel corn, road apples, and horse urine.

She made a point of biking the eight-mile shoreline once a week, each time finding some wildflower she hadn't noticed before, some view she hadn't appreciated yet. Each evening, after the last ferry left for the mainland, she sat in the broad grassy park overlooking the marina, listening to errant clanking of sailboat rigging as gulls screamed overhead. She reveled in the quiet streets peopled only by the overnight guests and summer locals who made their way out for late suppers, arriving in elegant horse-drawn surreys and buggies. Then came the bats, darting about, their swooping aeronautics a sideshow. Each night, she listened for Taps and thought of her father.

Her daily walks always took her through the Annex, originally called Hubbard's Annex to Mackinac Island National Park. It was named for Gurdon Hubbard. After losing everything in the Great Chicago Fire, his land on the island was all he had left. Subdividing the acreage, he sold lots, rebuilding his fortune before his death in 1884. Unlike the massive old homes on the island's west bluff, Annex houses were smaller, less ostentatious, and considerably more private, enclosed by a tall, dense hedgerow. Janet recalled it all from her guide tour rotation in the Annex.

Baldwin Cottage was a house Janet knew well, if only from the outside, with its steep-pitched, cross-gabled roof, intricate wooden grillwork, and its wrap-around screened porch. She'd been drawn to Baldwin Cottage all her life with a kind of yearning she never understood. Year after year, she'd pause at the gap in the hedgerow, looking in, never seeing anyone. While other houses in the Annex had people coming and going, Baldwin Cottage remained quiet. There was no laughter from the porch, no bikes in the yard, no chairs scattered about. She often thought it appeared to be lonely, if a house could be capable of emotion.

Standing in the largest of four bedrooms, Janet took in every detail, from white wainscoting walls peppered with framed prints of wildflowers and birds, to moss-green rag rugs on the gray-painted floorboards. There was a pale blue chest of drawers and a white rocker. The gable carved out of the wall had two large multi-paned windows. An overstuffed chair with threadbare floral upholstery nestled in its cubby.

She sat on a straight-back chair with a woven cane seat, imagining herself years ahead when every floorboard, knob, and windowsill would be familiar. In the corner of the room sat a small potbelly woodstove.

She wandered through the other three bedrooms, one blue, one green, and one yellow, all with iron scrollwork beds. Each had a painted dresser, nightstand, and an odd collection of small table lamps. Rag rugs of every color lay scattered about. Each room had a washstand with a large pitcher and bowl, all antiques, but possibly useful since there was no bathroom upstairs. She wondered how one used a washbowl. Was it just to wet a facecloth? Did one spit toothpaste in it? Did one pour drinking water from the pitcher?

There was little about the furnishings or fixtures to indicate whether it was 2017 or 1887, the year it was constructed. There was an art deco clock in the hall from the 1920s and table lamps from the '50s. The original gaslights had been retrofitted for electricity with wires running up walls.

Looking out a southern window, she watched a horse-drawn dray pass by, a large flatbed loaded with boxes and furniture. Two Clydesdales walked at a slow, steady pace, their work for the season nearly done. Soon they would be taken off-island to winter on the Upper Peninsula.

Back downstairs, Janet walked the well-worn hardwood floors of the spacious living room, large enough to accommodate a big family, something she did not have. Straight ahead along the back wall in front of two large windows was an oak dining table for ten. She stood at the head of it, her back to a large sideboard, wondering who had eaten there, what they talked about, if they'd been happy. Her condo crew would visit at some point, but even they were not enough to fill it. Opening one of the doors of the sideboard, she saw it chock full of tableware, vases, and candlesticks. "For another day," she said aloud, closing it up.

Glancing about the room, she presumed the large windows lining its three walls would let in enough fresh air to stave off the hottest summer swelter. She brushed her hand along an old lumpy couch and addressed an assortment of chairs and occasional tables as though they were inhabitants, people she would get to know.

She presumed the potbelly stove in a corner could do little more than take the chill off the room. It would be no match for winter's bite. Not that it mattered. It was a summer island. Only a contingent of local families lived there year-round on the island's interior.

Feeling a chill on her back, she glanced to the front door, the one that had closed on poor Mrs. Coventry. It was open again. Wide open. Cold air spilling in. Janet inspected the door jam, closed and opened the door again without hindrance. She wrote its behavior off to eccentricities either in the structure of the house or her brain.

Stepping to the porch, she pulled her jacket tight to her neck.

She remembered the two massive lilac bushes out front weighed down each June with heavy, deep purple clusters. They not only provided shade to the porch but offered privacy from nosey tourists snooping through the cedar hedgerow. She once told her parents she remembered being a small child, wandering onto the Baldwin porch on a warm summer afternoon, finding a pale green fairy fly on a chair, letting it crawl onto her finger, its large shimmery wings slowly opening and closing as it clung there. "Impossible," her mother barked. "Never happened." Yet the vision persisted.

In her fondest daydreams, Janet never imagined owning this house. Now it was hers, a realization so overwhelming she gasped, as though a rush of events had swept her away and dropped her there, a sudden halting that left her breathless.

Crossing the yard, she waded through fallen leaves to a small four-stall stable. All the historic houses on the island had stables for their horses and carriages. Unlocking the door with one of her two keys, she flipped on a light, a bare bulb flush to the ceiling. Stalls were empty, the hall packed with lawn chairs and porch furniture. The carriage room was empty except for a few scraps of moldy tack hanging on the wall. Climbing narrow steps, she discovered the dark, empty loft, partially open to below, with a wide door on the wall facing the yard.

Closing it up, she went back inside, glancing into the kitchen, thinking for the size of it, it offered no more working space than her small condo. The floor was covered with linoleum, uneven floorboards underneath leaving little ridges from years of wear. One bank of double cabinets and a pale green Hoosier pantry offered little storage. An old fridge stood next to the bathroom door. A freestanding electric stove occupied the opposite corner. She liked the vintage white enamel cast iron sink with the drain boards on either side, its black nicks adding to its character. Beneath it she found pots and pans, an odd assortment of bowls, and mason jars of all sizes. A quick inventory of everything suggested she'd need to bring very little with her.

Back upstairs she was drawn yet again to the white bedroom, the one she decided to make hers. Late afternoon sun poured through windows, long angular mullion shadows spreading out across the floor. She nestled into the overstuffed chair. Cold room. Warm sun. She closed her eyes, and without any intention to do so, slipped into a nap.

⌘

A warm summer breeze sifted through open windows waking her. Sunshine made her squint. Outside, dense green-leaved branches reached just shy of the window ledge. Someone called from down the hall. A lilting voice, it beckoned as if speaking to a child. Janet went to investigate and saw a young woman at the top of the steps, her hands outstretched, smiling at her. Janet, now a small child, ran to her. She giggled as she was carried down through the house to the bathroom off the kitchen. A yellow rubber ducky floated in the big white cast iron tub. Janet raised her arms, and the woman gently slid the nightgown off over her head and lifted her high over the rim of the tub, holding her over the water, just high enough so her toes dipped into its warmth, then up again and down, teasing, laughing. The bath was delightful, the warm, soapy washcloth gliding along her back and her legs, soft hands caressing every toe. It was a simple experience, nothing noteworthy except that even as she dreamed it, Janet was aware nothing so loving could have come from memory.

⌘

When she woke, she found herself not in the chair upstairs but standing in the bathroom downstairs next to a cold claw foot tub. Thunder rolled in the distance, and rain began tapping windows. She closed up the house and hiked down to town, cold and soaked through by the time she made it to her room in the Windward.

After a hot shower and a change of clothes, she found a small café. The rain had abated by then, moved off to the east. Skies were clear as dusk settled in. She devoured a supper of a hot beef sandwich with mashed potatoes and gravy before the nearly empty streets drew her outside. With her wet jacket still in the room, her sweater was no match for the cold night air. She stopped at a clothing store where a couple was packing up their stock. They sold her a warm jacket and hat for the cash in her pocket. "Won't need it in Florida," they said in unison, laughing at each other. The wife told Janet they spent winters at their shop on Sanibel Island. "Any cold weather gear left from here goes to a liquidator," she said, taping up another box. Her husband tossed Janet a long-sleeved tee-shirt emblazoned with the name of the store. Janet thanked them and wished them a prosperous winter.

With a few street lamps and a full moon to light her way, she walked silent backstreets, wind snapping branches above her. Two drays made their way toward the docks, piled high with boxes, furniture, and a surrey. The thud of rubber shoes was comforting as it ambled by, two men up front nodding as they passed.

She wandered up to the Grand Hotel, where a handful of guests sipped brandy nestled under blankets in rockers on the long porch. She walked the length of the hotel, over six hundred feet, arriving at the West Bluff to the row of magnificent homes with their spires, gables and towers, their windows all shuttered. Gardens, such a spectacle in summer, were trimmed back and mulched high against the coming freeze. From here, there were no more streetlamps.

Circling through dim woods, Janet arrived at Baldwin Cottage expecting to feel tentative. Yet, as soon as she cleared the hedgerow, she had the sense of coming home. Stepping onto the porch, she slipped her key into the lock. The door opened easily and stayed open. It did not suddenly close on its own as it had earlier in the day. Once inside, she stood in the cold darkness, faint moonlight softening edges. What should have felt unfamiliar somehow felt very familiar, as if she'd lived there in some other life. Suddenly aware of someone behind her, she jumped.

"Didn't mean to startle you," a man said from the steps, his face aglow in the half-light. "Checking things out again, are you?"

"You scared me."

He smiled. "I'm Mr. Harris. Sort of a caretaker around here. I noticed the open door and came to check on it. Wouldn't want anyone in here who didn't belong."

"I see," she said, comforted by his advanced age and gentle demeanor. "It's just me. I'm Janet. I'm the new owner."

"Good, good," he said, clearly pleased.

"It all looks so lonely now," she sighed.

"That it does."

"I'm looking forward to the spring," she told him.

"It will be here waiting for you. I'll see to that."

She shivered, and he suggested she get back to town and warm up. Taking one more glance around, she turned back to ask if he would put the last rocker in the stable with the others, but he was gone. She pulled the chair into the living room and locked up.

Walking back down to town, she thought how she'd become an owner in Hubbard's Annex through no accomplishment of her own, not by pedigree or heritage, not through connection within local or affiliated society. She was an alien among esteemed property holders, the purchase having come about through a serendipitous string of unlikely events.

CHAPTER 2

Condo Crew

Janet lived in Edgewater, a small lakefront town downstate. When local dentist Dr. Bodine died earlier that spring, his daughter Karen found an old box of legal documents in the office basement. The building had once been a law office. Sorting through the musty old papers, she found an envelope stuffed with stock certificates and recognized the name on them.

Janet was surprised to see Karen walk into Doc Kelsoe's office without any of her five kids in tow. Doc was one of two pediatricians in Edgewater, and Janet managed his practice.

Karen handed over the envelope, explaining how her dad bought the building from a dead attorney ages ago. "God only knows what else got thrown away when he cleared out all the boxes left behind, all except one I found crammed in a corner marked Dormant. It's stocks. Worth a *shit load* of money if they're valid," she said, turning heads from a waiting room full of mommies with children.

Janet retreated to her office, closed the door, and emptied the envelope. Without letter or note, she was left to presume the stocks came from her grandfather. Her father had always said there was money put aside, but her mother's years in a nursing home depleted any funds Janet knew about. As her mother was raised in Edgewater, it made sense they would have had a lawyer in town. But it didn't make sense that such an important envelope would be stuck in a random box of dormant files. If Janet believed in fate, she might have experienced a little thrill. But, as fate had not been kind to her so far, she was more prone to doubt. More likely than not, these sheets of paper were as worthless as the envelope they came in. And if they weren't, if they were legit, Janet could not fathom what she'd do with the money. She liked her simple life. She wanted for nothing but more time. And money couldn't buy it.

If she took after her father, Janet would be dead before she hit sixty. If she took after her mother and a long line of women on that side, she was on the precipice of developing dementia. No matter what path her life took, for over twenty years Janet had lived with the assumption her future was arguably non-existent. Such a perspective inhibits ambition to such a degree she never felt any true calling beyond doing a good job on a daily basis. Yet, even before she knew her parents would die young, before she learned she might, too, there was a hesitancy about her. Aside from her tight-knit circle of friends, she seemed incapable of bonding. Romantic relationships had nowhere to go with her. The condo crew was enough. She'd known most of them since moving to Edgewater after college.

The condos were originally a small apartment complex on Lake Michigan. It resembled a motel with parking in front. Two small brick buildings overlooked a pool and the beach. When it turned condo, Janet bought in with a little help from Doc Kelsoe. It was the only bonus he ever gave her.

Life at Lake View Apartments - the name never changed - was, and continued to be, as inbred as a college dorm. Marriages, affairs, and divorces played out within its confines, making for a lot of turnover. The units were small. For some, the partying got old. People tended to last two, maybe three years, except for a core group, Janet's crew. The place became a little run down and too retro to attract a new generation. While the average age had once been under thirty, it was currently pushing sixty with a constant stream of Boomer divorcees.

Janet had always been the youngster of her crew. Carmen, Mike, Mattie, Janet, and Sam were among the original renter-turned-owners. When Janet moved in, Sam, a veterinarian, was newly divorced from Carmen, who'd left for a year and moved back in two doors down with her next husband who couldn't accept partying with the ex-husband every weekend and eventually left her. Sam was, however, no threat since he was having an affair with Mattie, who was married to an electrician in building two. The electrician had no idea what Mattie was up to because he was too busy schtupping the high school football coach's wife. Mattie divorced the electrician, married Sam, and bought a kitchen shop with her divorce settlement. Carmen married a third time, a man named Jack, who'd given up drinking and lived in a huge country house. Carmen insisted she keep her condo and they spent their summer weekends there. Jack took up drinking again and eventually died of liver failure. Carmen sold Jack's house, moved back to the condos full-time, and happily bid adieu to teaching algebra and geometry to hormonal teenagers. Content in widowhood, she swore there would be no husband number four.

Stock certificates in hand, Janet left work and got home to find Carmen rummaging around in her cupboards. "Where's your balsamic?" Carmen asked. "I thought you brought some home last week."

Janet dropped her satchel on the table and told Carmen to text Mattie. "She can bring some from the shop."

"We're grilling tonight," Carmen said while texting. "Mike is picking up the steaks. I was going to do my crostini but not without balsamic and I'm out."

"I'm sure you'll figure something out. What's the occasion?"

"What do you mean? You're the occasion. Your windfall is the occasion."

A cell phone dinged as Mattie appeared in the doorway. "Way ahead of you," she said, handing over a bottle of 25-year-old balsamic vinegar. "Sam's on his way. He had to put two dogs down today, so he might be a little moody."

"I don't know how he does it," Carmen said.

Janet rolled her eyes. They had the same discussion all the time. Mattie would say people should be so lucky to be put out of their misery, and then Carmen would remind her of all the ways somebody could take advantage of euthanasia to off some wealthy uncle.

"But it's just so sad," Carmen said. "All those sobbing people. How does he do it? All the time we were married, I could never get over how he was so casual about killing all those animals."

Mattie shook her head. "Let's just let it rest this time, OK? He's been putting animals down for over thirty years. I think he's figured out how to cope." On her way out the door, Mattie took a call on her cell. "The order was short this month. I asked for a dozen ML285s and got four…"

Janet went in to change her clothes while Carmen began chopping cherry tomatoes. When she came back out, Carmen was gone, and Mike was at the table looking through the stock certificates. "Debbie closing up today?"

"Yeah," he said. "She's waiting on the charters to come back in to get them fueled up for the morning. Steaks are on the counter."

"Must have been a good day if they're coming in this late," Janet said, unwrapping a stack of New York strips.

"Steelheads are running."

Janet sprinkled the meat with salt, pepper, and garlic powder, rubbing it in.

"She's right," Mike said.

"Who's right?"

"Bodine's daughter. I'm looking up values. If these are valid, they're worth a shitload of money."

"How big a shitload?" Janet asked.

"Ever been by a stock yard and see those huge mounds of manure with the tarps held in place with tires?"

Janet stood mute.

"I'll take them over to my lawyer tomorrow," he said. "… have him dig into it."

By the time Debbie made it home from the marina, dinner was being prepped at the picnic table.

With her cell phone crammed between her jaw and shoulder, Mattie took a serrated bread knife to a loaf of hot garlic bread, nearly slicing her finger as she talked to one of her employees, explaining that they did indeed need to show up for work the next day no matter who showed up out of the blue to visit.

Sam nursed a beer, checking steaks on the grill. "Talk or cut," he scolded Mattie.

Carmen poured frozen margaritas.

Mike set the table, calling out to Janet to bring down the hot sauce.

She was already out the door with a salad. "I'm not letting you ruin a perfectly seasoned cut of beef with hot sauce."

Debbie grinned and hollered to her. "You tell him. He won't listen to me."

Once they all got over the shock of Mike telling them what Janet's stocks could be worth, they all speculated as to the best use of the money.

"You could buy us out of the marina," Debbie joked.

Janet assured her she didn't want a marina.

Carmen suggested Janet take all of them on a trip around the world.

"You hate traveling," Mattie sniped.

"Well," Carmen whined, "I can change."

Sam said it would be enough just to know the money was there for any eventuality. "You don't have long-term care insurance," he said. "Now, you're covered."

Janet cut him a look, and Mattie elbowed him.

"What?" Sam said. "She might need it if she goes the way of …"

"Sam, really," Debbie said. "It's going to skip a generation, and she's going to live a long, mentally fit life."

"Enough," Janet said. "Enough."

Mike, quiet to that point, spoke up. "This is life-altering kind of money. The kind that can fuck with your head if you're not careful."

Janet said she'd do her level best to not let it fuck with her head. "All this is a little premature. We don't even know if the certificates are valid."

Mattie opened a bottle of Prosecco. "I don't understand where they came from, or did I miss something?"

"That, my friend, is the million-dollar question," Janet said.

Debbie corrected her. "You mean the one-point-six-million-dollar question, don't you?"

CHAPTER 3

Dreams

Like the delivery of the envelope, the purchase of Baldwin Cottage was a thing with its own momentum. Janet took her traditional June sojourn north with no intention of going up again. But at the end of September, she got a wild hair and hit the road, landing on the island, checking into the Windward, and walking her normal route through the Annex. It was a chilly evening, and she almost turned around, but decided to make the loop past Baldwin Cottage. Seeing a FOR SALE sign in front of it, made the hairs on her neck stand up.

Walking the perimeter of the cottage, she took in every nook and flaw with a peculiar sense of ownership. One word, almost audible, came to mind: Finally.

She tried texting a photo to the crew. It wouldn't go through.

The next day, she learned there was a signed offer on the table. Discovering the price was considerably less than her windfall, Janet put in a backup offer, having no expectation of ever getting the call. It was the first inherently impulsive thing she'd ever done in her life.

After the trip, she made light of the incident, never believing she had a real shot at the property. Mattie called it a close call. "What would you do with a Victorian cottage? You hate to clean one bedroom. It has four!"

Carmen couldn't wrap her head around there being no cars. "You have to take a boat to get to your car? What's the attraction? I don't get it."

Debbie tried to be diplomatic, suggesting it was Janet's first foray into imagining what to do with the money, but fortunately, this property was already taken.

Sam said as long as there were enough bedrooms for all of them, he was fine with it.

Mike waited until he was alone with Janet. "You've never lived alone. Ever. What the hell are you going to do up there with all that house and only you bouncing around in it? You said it yourself. Cell reception sucks there. No internet. No cable. I just don't see it, Janet. I really don't."

"You just can't imagine life without me," Janet joked.

"You're right. I can't. Thirty years."

"More like twenty-eight, but who's counting."

"You know what I mean. What if things go . . . sideways?"

"If I lose my mind, I lose my mind. Nothing any of you can do about it."

"We're your family, your support staff. We're all you've got." His bluntness stung.

"It's not like I'm going to get to buy it," Janet said. "But I don't know why, it felt right. Bone deep kind of right." A wave of melancholy washed over her. "You don't have to worry about me."

"Someone has to," he said and gave her a hug. Her body stiffened the instant her face hit his chest, and she pulled away. "That never gets old," he said.

"If you two are done smooching down there," Debbie called from the balcony, "I can use a hand up here."

"He's worried about me," Janet told her.

"That's never going to change," Debbie said. "I got used to it ages ago."

Back in the beginning, Mike tended bar when he wasn't fixing boats. He and Janet had a tentative off-and-on relationship status. They were always friends, sometimes lovers, but something always lacked. She never asked for more than she was willing to give, and Mike wanted more. He wanted to be on top once in a while, but she wouldn't let him. He wanted to hold her in his arms, but she'd pull away. He wanted to sleep with her after sex, but she always made him go back to his own place. He wanted normal, and she couldn't give it, not to him, or anyone.

Over the years, they became each other's fallback when other relationships fizzled out. Then Debbie came along. She bought the unit next to Mike. She was bright, funny, and solid. He fell hard. Janet readily relinquished any claim on him. Mike and Debbie were married on the beach. They bought Casper's Cove, a run-down upriver marina carved out of a marsh. Together, they built it into a thriving little business.

In early October, Janet got a call telling her Baldwin Cottage was Janet's for the taking. Prior to closing, the original buyers rented the cottage for a week. After spending only two nights, they backed out of the deal.

The crew tried to talk Janet out of going through with it, but by the end of the week, she was on the island signing papers and wiring funds, after which she had her awkward encounter with Cecelia Coventry.

Janet's ferry ride off the island the next morning was brutal. A front had moved in overnight. Waves roiled from multiple directions, pushing the heavy ferry around like a toy. Back on the mainland, she was pelted by sleet getting back to her car.

She headed home from Up North feeling strangely empowered. She owned a cottage on Mackinac Island, fulfilling a childhood fantasy. Yet, approaching Gaylord, not even an hour into her six-hour drive, she became overwhelmed with a sense of doom. It passed, leaving a knot in her shoulder that tightened until she was cocking her head to compensate. She heard echoes of everyone telling her it was a mistake. Soon, she was in the full throes of buyer's remorse. A couple hours later, navigating the S-curves through Grand Rapids, she came around, making peace with the purchase. If it didn't work out, she could always sell it.

Arriving home at dusk, she unlocked the door to her condo and dropped her bag on the floor. A ribbon-festooned bottle of Malbec sat on her counter with a note: *Congrats, the crew.* After a singular group text saying she was too exhausted to actually talk to any of them, she threw a frozen pizza in the oven and took a long look at Lake Michigan from her window. For nearly thirty years, she'd looked at that view, the water never the same color as the day before, the sky always new. It was like living on the edge of the world where nothing beyond was conceivable. She got into her PJs, settled into bed with her remote, and made her way through half the bottle, half the pizza, and half a movie before calling it a night.

When she was a child, Janet suffered night terrors, waking her parents with her screams. The doctor said she'd grow out of them. She didn't. The nightmares persisted into adulthood, though with less frequency and severity. She never remembered the dream itself, only the terror and a sensation of suffocating. The purchase of Baldwin Cottage triggered a new dream cycle.

There were good dreams, too. She woke more than once that winter expecting to be on the island, sunshine spilling through windows, only to hear the cold wind howling outside her condo, and wake to sleet snapping glass. Over the winter, she kept track of the dreams in a small notepad, whatever snippets lingered momentarily, recording the date and how a dream felt, drawing a small triangle in the upper corner of the page if it was a bad one. There were a lot of triangles.

In early March, as a heavy spring snowstorm raged, Janet dreamed she was standing in the living room of the cottage mid-summer, surrounded by people who loved her. When her grandfather stepped in from the porch, grinning at her, she woke up. She lay there, images like memory sifting from the dream to waking, wondering who was real, feeling those who peopled her dream were as known to her as her friends, or were her friends the dream? One minute, she was in Baldwin cottage painting a wall pale pink, admiring it, and the next, she was transported to her bed three hundred miles away, her mind stirring. There was a peacefulness to this drifting, eyes not yet open, understanding in that moment like an epiphany that reality is subjective, and if this sensation was what her future looked like, an existence of comfortable uncertainty, if this was what dementia felt like, if there was no struggle to get it all straight, maybe it wouldn't be so bad. She opened her eyes. Outside her window, a delicate ice cycle glistened in morning sun. She watched a single drip form and fall.

She pulled out her notepad. *Saw Grandpa Max.*

Her grandfather represented the only love she recalled from her childhood. Her parents, Howard and Ellen, were incapable of filling the void left by his passing when she was ten.

CHAPTER 4

Howard and Ellen

In photographs, Janet was the striking one in the back of the pack. The camera loved her large eyes and full mouth. It was the kind of face that usually belonged to vital, vivacious flirts who understood the advantages of beauty. But Janet was neither a flirt nor aware of her beauty.

She was never one to wear flattering clothes. She rarely wore makeup. Her shoulder-length chestnut brown hair was usually pulled back to get it out of the way. Her eyes were intelligent and quick. They could size a person up in a heartbeat and dismiss them just as quickly. A person knew where they stood with her. She carried herself with a confidence few people possess.

Janet Marie Granger was the only child of Howard and Ellen Granger. Howard had understood all too well the lure of the condos for his daughter. He saw in those people the family she never had. After she moved there, he did his best to keep her mother at bay, but sometimes he failed. Ellen would call Janet in the middle of the night railing on and on about how Howard was spying on her and how Janet was a thankless daughter for not sending her a birthday card. Of course, it wasn't Ellen's birthday, and Janet never sent her mother any obligatory greeting cards. Ellen was a terse woman seemingly incapable of showing affection. Janet learned early on to reciprocate in kind.

Janet used to call her dad at his office to ask how he was getting along, which was code for *how wacko is Ellen these days*. Howard never complained and he never asked Janet to come home. He visited her occasionally and partied with her friends. Janet used to think he'd have moved there himself if he'd been younger, single, unencumbered, if he was anyone but who he was.

Like most young people, Janet had no idea who Howard was aside from being her dad. She hadn't thought to ask about his childhood, his aspirations, his disappointments, and then it was too late. He died before she was thirty.

If Howard had been inclined to answer any of his daughter's questions, should she have asked, Howard Granger might have admitted to being an invention. He was born Howard Lund, though his mother would later admit, as if it would have no impact on her son, that she wasn't sure who his father was. She'd made up the name. It was the kind of wound she inflicted regularly when she drank too much, leading to little leaks of brutal honesty.

As a kid, Howard dreamed his life would take a certain path. He'd go to college, find a job, get married, buy a house, and raise a couple kids. He had no reason to believe any of these things would happen for him. It was just a life he grew up coveting.

His childhood had been an endless procession of unsavory affairs. His mother went through men the way some people go through used cars, always looking for the newer model and ending up with another clunker. All her men drank to one degree or another as they'd all met Marjorie in a bar, either with her current man, or on the prowl for the next. Marjorie always put the men first, pushing Howard to the background. "Keep out of his way," she'd say. "Don't do anything to scare him away or piss him off." Her favorite line of dismissal was always delivered with a chuckle, a private joke between mother and son, something he was supposed to find humorous: "Be a good boy." Loosely translated, it meant 'bring us a couple of beers and make yourself scarce'.

Marjorie lived in a constant state of expectation with the futile belief someone would step in and save her, take over all the decisions, pay all the bills. The men, however, rarely contributed and usually walked off with some of her stuff. Furniture, TVs, even a coffee maker disappeared. Changing men came with the added benefit of changing towns. Marjorie was convinced the man of her dreams was out there somewhere, in the next town, or the next.

Marjorie rarely went without a man except for the stretch when Howard hit fifteen, and nobody was willing to put up with him. Just as he was about to enter his sophomore year of high school she moved them to Brainerd, Minnesota. She took a job in a hospital cafeteria. "You just watch," she told her son. "I'm gunna get myself a doctor."

Marjorie met Mr. Clark at a back-to-school night, and she began dating him, reluctantly on her part, as he wasn't a doctor. Brad Clark wasn't like her other men. He didn't go to bars. He didn't get drunk. He didn't spend the night. And he didn't put up with any crap. He walked in one evening on Howard yelling at his mother, throwing stuff, and calling her a whore. Mr. Clark grabbed him by the neck, flipped him to the floor, and pressed his knee into Howard's diaphragm. Mr. Cark was the wrestling coach. He invited Howard to try out for the team and Howard turned out to be a fast learner. He won matches.

Mr. Clark's presence in their lives was healthy and positive. He was the first person to ever care about Howard. He taught him how to study and take tests. He encouraged Marjorie to be a better mother, to actually cook a meal instead of relying on packaged food and take-out every night. But she couldn't keep up the front. "I have needs," she told Howard as a one-nighter skulked through the kitchen in the morning.

Once Mr. Clark discovered Howard was right about his mother, he broke it off with Marjorie and she went on the prowl for a new Mr. Wrong. She found her first mean drunk, a man who swore a lot. And hit. Howard turned his frustration at home into aggression on the mat earning a college scholarship.

Mr. Clark showed up to all of Howard's college tournaments until he dropped dead of a heart attack during high school state finals. When Howard went back to Brainerd for the funeral, his mother had a new man in the house, a man who made it clear the kid was only staying the night. "One man's enough in any house," he said and Marjorie was too pathetic to dispute it.

Howard did not sleep that night, too preoccupied taking mental inventory of every slight and rejection his mother ever imposed on him. He counted the men who'd lived with them, assigning a name to each finger leaving only one thumb unclaimed. He didn't count the one-nighters. There weren't enough digits for that tally. He pushed away any gentle moments with his mother, the few glimpses of affection he sometimes caught in her eyes, the soft grazing of her fingers through his hair when she passed behind him at the table, her quiet laughter when they watched TV. He was steeling his heart against those rarities, careful not to give them any weight. He wrestled with an idea throughout the night, imagining Mr. Clark coaching him from the edge of the mat, hearing his mantra *Make good decisions. Make good decisions.* The next morning, Howard Lund walked out of his mother's apartment before sunrise and disappeared from her life.

He gave up his scholarship and transferred his credits to a small college in Michigan. He legally changed his name to Howard Granger, after a character in *Fahrenheit 451*, the first book Mr. Clark ever gave him. The Granger character believed the wonderful thing about man is that he never gets so discouraged that he gives up. "Words to live by," Mr. Clark had said. Howard got a job, rented a room and earned a degree in accounting.

Deserting his mother had been the easy part, a physical act of negation, a choice made every day to not make contact. Walking away from the person she'd made of him felt impossible.

Placing all his hopes in the new name, Howard aimed for a life he believed Mr. Clark would be proud of. Instead, he missed the mark completely when he met Ellen Crawford, a woman who would dictate his life much as his mother had, denying him in new ways, destroying any possibility he might become the better person he thought he could be. She was the first woman to show any interest in him and for a moment or two let him believe he might actually achieve his dream of a happy family life.

By the time he realized Ellen was not the key to happiness, it was too late.

The flirty, kind, supportive woman he married changed almost as soon as she vowed to love, cherish and obey. It was as if she flipped a switch and he suddenly had no value at all. She griped when he read the paper or a book because he wasn't paying attention to her. She accused him of having an affair if he wore one of his nicer shirts to work. She pouted when he didn't praise her cooking or thank her for clean sheets. Nothing he did appeased her. The litany of his flaws grew by the month, until he found himself right back where he started, living with another miserable woman. It had taken every ounce of gumption he had to free himself once. It wasn't in him to do it again and he succumbed to a life of less.

Over the years, he sometimes wondered where his mother was, if Marjorie was even alive. He would find himself attempting to rationalize his motives for leaving her and come up short. She had abandoned him as a child repeatedly and in so many small ways that his one act of exclusion could not compare. The difference between them was intent. She was mindlessly neglectful, ignorant of the damage. He, on the other hand, knew exactly what he'd done. Self-awareness, he came to understand, was a curse. Intention carried accountability, leading inexorably to guilt, which led him to believe he didn't deserve to be happy. Whether he deserved to be as miserable as Ellen made him was a question he was better off not asking.

Janet was at work when she got the call from a hospital in Ann Arbor. Her father had suffered a heart attack in a restaurant. Her phone number was in his wallet. She called her mother but Ellen hung up on her. Two hours later, Janet sat in an empty emergency room bay waiting for her father to come back from a scan. She called her mother. Ellen hung up on her again. They brought Howard back. She didn't need any test results to see he was failing. He opened his eyes and raised his fingers. She took his hand and held on.

"Your mother," he whispered, breathless.

"She won't take my calls."

"She's sick," he said before falling asleep.

When Howard was settled into a room, Janet was given the prognosis. There was nothing more to do for him. He would probably sleep through the next several hours. Janet went to collect her mother.

Dinner was on the table, two aluminum trays with compartments for Salisbury steak, peas, mashed potatoes, and apple crisp. Ellen did not rise from her chair when Janet came in. "You're not Howard," she barked.

"He's in the hospital. I've been trying to call you. He's had a heart attack."

"So, he's not coming home." Ellen's hands turned to fists.

Until that moment, Janet had no idea what her father had been putting up with. "No," she said. "He's not coming home. He's going to die. Soon. He's going to die soon."

"Why did I cook dinner if he's not coming home?"

"I don't know," Janet said without compassion. "Do you want to go see him?"

"I'll see him when he gets home," Ellen said as she scooped a spoonful of cold potatoes and flung it at Janet.

Janet dodged it without much effort. "Right. So no trip to the hospital then," she said and left the house. As Janet had never been a priority for Ellen, Ellen was not a priority for Janet. She spent the night at her father's bedside.

He rose to consciousness only once. "I didn't live up to my potential," he said. Janet asked what he wished he'd done with his life but he lost the thought, drifted off, and died before dawn.

When Janet went to the house to tell her mother, the TV dinners were still on the table, one of them untouched. Ellen sat in the living room with a blank stare. Ellen startled, bolted up and shouted at her. "Get out! Leave me. Leave me like that asshole Howard did!"

In an indifferent tone of voice, Janet told her that Howard hadn't left, he died. But Ellen saw no distinction. The shouting stopped when Janet left the room. Ellen resumed her silent staring. Janet didn't pay enough attention to see her mother wore the same clothes as the day before.

After tossing the TV dinners, Janet stood out of sight in the hallway to the living room, and asked if Ellen wanted a funeral for Howard.

"Get out!"

"You got it," Janet said. She left Ellen alone and went back to Edgewater. She arranged for Howard's cremation. Less than two weeks later, on the same day her father's ashes were delivered to her home, she got the call from Ann Arbor police. Ellen had been found sitting on the riverbank, naked, covered in mud.

Ellen was hospitalized. Yet again, Janet made the drive to Ann Arbor to deal with a parent. Her mere appearance in Ellen's room brought on such a fit of rage Ellen was sedated. Janet's indifference was on display for all to see as she heaved a heavy sigh and with a slight shoulder shrug walked away. She had an appointment to discuss her mother's care.

Janet's indifference gave way to shock when she walked into her parents' house. There was a pile of poop on the kitchen floor. TV trays of food in various stages of spoilage were scattered about the house, as were clothes and dirty towels. It looked as though every item in every closet and cupboard had been pulled out. The curtains were drawn closed in every room. Only then did she realize what Howard had been doing to manage their lives. He'd done everything for Ellen. Without him, she was entirely unhinged.

Janet made a run for cleaning supplies and heavy-duty trash bags. Wearing a facemask and rubber gloves, she threw everything into garbage bags. She cried as she scrubbed floors, imagining what her father's life had been like. While she held no sense of anything but responsibility toward her mother, she wished she had been more attentive to her dad. What he'd done to protect her from his hell was more than any parent should have had to do.

"Your mother was diagnosed with behavioral frontotemperal dementia nine months ago," the doctor told Janet. "It's progressive. In your mother, it presents in behavior and executive functions. According to the file, in your grandmother, it presented with language and mild behavior issues. We don't know how your great grandmother or great aunt presented, but they were both institutionalized before the age of fifty-two, and died within two to three years."

Janet heard his words but nothing registered.

"I gather you were unaware of any of this."

"I was not."

The doctor, a man in his early fifties, gave her a moment to center. "It's a lot to take in."

"Yes. A lot."

"Your father never . . ."

"No. He never told me. Ellen and I never got along. I guess he was protecting me."

"How old was my grandmother when she . . ."

"I never knew her."

He scanned a page. "Ah. Fifty-six when she died."

Something about his demeanor made Janet think he was waiting for something. Then, suddenly, it hit her. "It's genetic," she said.

"Yes."

"So, I'm going to end up like them. Like my mother. An angry bitch who can't remember shit." She apologized for her candor. He shrugged.

"I'd be pissed, too. But to be clear, you have a 50/50 chance of having FTD. I'd focus on the 50% chance of not having it if I were you."

"You're not me."

Janet went home to Edgewater that night and gathered the crew. "I'm fucked. I wanted you all to know that. I am, right now, most likely already over halfway through my life. All the women in my family go insane and die by their mid-fifties. It's called FTD and I'm not open to any jokes about the flower deliver service. It is what it is, and I don't feel like talking about it. Just thought you should know."

Carmen, Sam, Mattie, Debbie, and Mike sat stunned.

"Sucks to be you," Mike said.

"You can all leave now," Janet said.

"Fuck no," Mattie said with a cockeyed grin. "Alcohol. Lots of alcohol." With that, everyone dispersed and returned moments later with many bottles of alcohol. Carmen called it a midlife crisis party. By the end of the night, they'd given the dementia a code name: Flowers.

Not yet thirty, Janet faced what was likely to be an abbreviated future. On top of that, she was legally responsible for the woman who never showed her one ounce of love or affection. She sold the house and planted Ellen in a nursing home in Ann Arbor. There had always been a distance between them. Janet saw no reason to change that.

Unable to recognize her daughter, Ellen shouted *Sissy! Sissy!* when Janet came into her room. According to an attendant, sissy was Ellen's preferred insult for everyone. For the first few months, Janet made a point to make the drive to visit Ellen once a month. It was what she thought was expected of her. Then visits whittled down to once every other month, mostly to gauge Ellen's decline. There was no joy between mother and daughter, no fond memories, nothing but obligation and a lot of spite. There wasn't a visit that Ellen didn't shout at Janet to get out, spit at her, slap her, or throw something against the wall. Janet watched people visit the memory unit, a place she perceived as little more than a lockup for dementia patients in various stages of physical decay. Some went through ridiculous emotional gyrations just to get a hint of recognition from a loved one. It always looked like a little slice of hell for both parties.

"You have the right idea," a nurse told her. "You never try to break through. I hate to see people try so hard. There's nothing in it. And honestly? Your mother doesn't care either way whether you're here or not. It isn't about who she is anymore, or who you are. It's about what reality she's living in at the moment. And her reality? It's always unpleasant." That observation granted Janet permission to stop visiting.

Eight months later, Ellen was moved to a facility capable of managing cases like hers. She'd become violent. Another year in, Ellen settled down as the disease took over. Every year she clung to her miserable life, money in the family trust circled the drain.

When Ellen started to fail, Janet was there, watching her fade every day for nearly a week. Somewhere in that silent sleeping woman was a mother she had never been. Janet imagined that Ellen might wake, and say, *Good morning, sweetie. What are you up to today? I love you.* But such moments were a fiction. Life with Ellen had never been kind or loving or good. Only after her mother's death did Janet realize how much her life had pivoted around thoughts of her crazy ass mother. Ellen Granger's death released Janet to the light. At 34, she was free.

CHAPTER 5

Spring

Anxious to settle into Baldwin cottage, Janet headed to the island in early May. She went over on a cargo ferry full of construction materials, furniture, and half a dozen Clydesdales. Despite of the sunshine, it had been a cold crossing from Mackinaw City. The last of the ice on the straits had only disappeared a week earlier.

She thought she might feel like an outsider arriving so early, an intruder in the workings of the place. Instead, she felt connected, united in pre-season activity. There were no tourists yet, just people with jobs to do. She met the ferry pilot, Captain Leronge, when he flagged her to come into his control cabin. "You're new," he said, and by the time they docked at the island, she knew he had lived in the area all his life, and he knew she'd been an island visitor all of hers.

Disembarking, she saw Mr. Harris wave from the street, his lazy smile peering out from under the shadow of his cap. His presence gave her a sense of coming home. Weaving her way through stacks of boxes, furniture, and crates, a loud beeping alerted her to a forklift hauling a stack of drywall behind her. A table saw whined from inside an adjacent shop as men came out to collect 2X4s from a pile on the street. Meeting up with Mr. Harris, he told her the livery captain would see her luggage and boxes were sent up to her cottage. He asked if he could walk with her, and she was happy for the company.

Up a block, they hit Market Street, bustling with people hauling boxes from the curb into shops and small inns. A bicyclist pulling an empty handcart alongside flew past them back down to the docks. Two blocks further, they were on Caldotte Avenue, a wide street leading up to the Grand Hotel. Beyond lay the core of the island where locals lived, where the Grand kept its carriage teams. And just beyond that was the airstrip used by charters and private planes.

Passing the little stone church, she watched three big mowers snake their way around sand traps on the Grand Hotel golf course.

Flowerbeds and planters held row after row of tightly packed daffodils, their green rapier shafts not yet budding, and scores of tulips with pointy leaves just beginning to emerge. Up at the Grand, drays lined up three deep, waiting to unload. Crews swarmed stacks of boxes, case after case of wine and liquor, linens and condiments. She texted a photo. It went through.

Walking the road in front of the Grand's long porch, Janet saw a roll of red carpet leaning in the main entryway where guests would soon step from shiny black carriages to begin their glorious stay. Below them, rimming a vast green lawn, undulating flowerbeds were being prepared for the multitude of colorful annuals that would be planted in the coming weeks.

Past the Grand, along the West Bluff, Mr. Harris cataloged each magnificent house they passed. A meat packer from Chicago built one. A senator from Grand Rapids built another. One made his fortune selling hops to the brewing industry. Another was a lumberman. All self-made men, boasting their wealth with their summer homes resplendent with shingles and spires, turrets and porches, covered verandas, and colorful awnings. As multiple crews of gardeners planted, trimmed and raked, other laborers painted trim, took down windscreens, and washed windows. From in and around these structures rose a cacophony of saws and hammers, even a chainsaw out back somewhere.

Turning onto Grand Avenue, the narrow road turned to gravel as it slipped into the woods. A quiet settled in. Birdsong filled the trees. A cardinal calling for a mate, a titmouse, a robin, and several goldfinches sounded out. Two juncos darted by like fighter pilots, white tail feathers flashing.

Janet kept an eye out for wildflowers, knowing it was too early for jack-in-the-pulpits or lady slippers, but mayapples had emerged, their umbrella like canopies still coiled around sturdy thin stalks. And trillium, like little spear heads, rose up, leaves curled in a tight twist. Walking in silence, she almost forgot Mr. Harris had tagged along.

Nearing the Annex, she heard rhythmic hammering and other more staccato pounding, and the clap of lumber dropping, and rotary saws. A dray passed loaded with hay bales and sacks of grain. She texted another photo. It took a minute but went through.

"Abbott Cottage," Mr. Harris said, his voice startling Janet. "Put a boiler in that one there. Dries her out something terrible when they use it."

"Charles Caskey built it, didn't he?" she asked.

He smiled. "No stranger to the place, I see. Know your history, do you?"

"I know he built Baldwin Cottage. One of nine he built that year."

A clutch of women rode by on bicycles, their large baskets loaded with cleaning supplies.

"This one," Mr. Harris said. "Well, she's had a few facelifts over the years. First, it was adding a shower to the bathroom downstairs, then they sliced up one of her bedrooms and made half of it a closet and the other half an upstairs bathroom. That one there, Pink House, can't seem to keep her shingles on, always patching her back together in the spring."

As if on cue, a tapping came from Pink House where a worker replaced a section of shingles. Not far away, another section was getting a coat of pink paint.

"That Gothic Revival there, with the round living room? Had a hell of a time replacing that glass when the old sugar maple came down on her." Mr. Harris filled Janet in on all the cottages they passed as if they were old people with quirks and moods. "The floors in that one were milled from the trees they took down to build her. Red oak downstairs and white pine up. Beautiful wood. Just beautiful. A stonemason from New York State came over to do the stonework on this Queen Anne and ended up coming back and working for another ten years. A good portion of the best stonework you'll see here is his. And this one, poor old thing. She settles a bit each year and has a tough time with her doors and windows. Always sticking. Some of them won't even open anymore. Old joints. Like mine." He told her he'd been tending Annex cottages since he was a boy helping his father. There wasn't anything he didn't know about any one of them. He did not, however, speak of the people inhabiting them.

Only half listening, Janet was more taken with the business of things, so many people making the most of the last few days before the island opened its arms to the world. In all these endeavors, she had yet to see an owner, only those who made sure all was ready for them. In this observation, she realized perhaps she was not meant to see behind the curtain, and in doing so had broken some unspoken law, or at the very least, tradition. Her arrival was premature, and in this, she felt pedestrian, of a lower orbit than her fellow Annex occupants.

"And there, my dear, is your new home. Baldwin Cottage. Good bones, that one. Solid pine beams. Mortise and tenon joinery. You keep those windows open, and you'll have ventilation a plenty all summer. She alone stands unchanged, proud in her old age. Oh, she's got a mind of her own, but you'll get to know her."

Following her to the steps, Mr. Harris told her how to build a fire in the small potbelly stoves. "Just stuff some newspaper in with the kindling. It's all the local rag is good for," he said. "Fire starter. There's a stash of firewood by the back porch."

Mr. Harris continued his tutorial from the steps while Janet collected twigs from the yard. "Slowly add some larger pieces until you have a full blaze. Don't overfire 'em. Just give 'em a little time to warm, and then keep 'em stoked. You treat 'em right, and they'll keep you nice and toasty." He wandered off, saying he had tasks a plenty. "Don't forget to plug in the Kelvinator."

"The what?" she called after him, but he was out of earshot. She texted a selfie in front of the woodstove, but it wouldn't go through. She went out into the yard, to the road, and it still wouldn't go through. Baldwin Cottage was indeed in a dead zone.

It wasn't long before Janet sat cross-legged in front of the little firebox downstairs, watching the flames grow. She was amazed how quickly it took the chill off. She had just prepped the stove upstairs when a dray delivered her luggage, boxes, and groceries. The driver asked for ten dollars and she gave him a twenty. "Keep it. I used to work here," she said as if that might explain her generosity. He thanked her and moved on to his next delivery. She hauled everything into the kitchen.

Her first few hours were hectic. She unpacked groceries to the refrigerator, only to realize it was not plugged in. "Ah," she smiled, looking at the logo plate on the door. "The Kelvinator." She filled it and plugged it in.

She dug through boxes for linens to make her bed, then dusted and swept the master bedroom. It wasn't until she tried to make a grilled cheese sandwich that she realized the stove, too, needed to be plugged in. When it still didn't work, she discovered the fridge was not cooling. She tried a light switch. Nothing. In a small room off the back porch, she discovered not only the fuse box, but a washing machine and dryer she hadn't noticed on any of her walk-throughs. Flipping the main switch, she heard a hum from the fridge and water filling a small tank in the corner. By the time she ate her tomato soup and grilled cheese huddled at the stove in the living room, the sun was setting.

After dinner, with dishes in the sink and half unpacked boxes cluttering the kitchen, Janet opened a bottle of wine, poured a glass, and stoked the fire. Sitting on the couch, she talked to the house like a new friend. "I hope you don't mind my intrusion. I'm staying for the summer. I'll take good care of you. From the looks of it, it's been a while since anyone did that." There came a thunk from somewhere in the house, and Janet smiled. "We understand each other then. Good."

It reminded her of the old house in Ann Arbor. It used to creak a lot, stretching with the heat, retracting with the cold as if complaining. Something was always going bump in the night, or skittering across the ceiling above her in the attic, or scratching in the wall. Squirrels used to litter the attic with acorns until Howard cut down the oak tree in the backyard. When she was a kid, Janet amused herself with the idea that the house was aware of her presence. She talked to it, imagining drafts from leaky windows were incoherent whispers, and warm air slipping through the register was the house sighing. She never understood what it was saying, but she thought it probably couldn't understand her either when she would try to comfort it on stormy nights, whispering her thanks for its sheltering walls.

She believed every new sound in Baldwin Cottage would bring her closer in kinship with it.

Before turning in for the night, she stoked the fire one last time, hauled firewood up to her bedroom, and closed doors upstairs to conserve warmth. She lit the fire she'd prepped in the bedroom potbelly. The room slowly warmed as she lay in bed, the activities of the day still with her like a vibration that would not settle. When she finally turned off the bedside lamp, she snuggled in and spoke aloud to the dark, empty house again. "I'll pick up after myself tomorrow, get it all put away. Don't worry."

The fire died out. The room grew cold. Two in the morning found Janet digging through drawers in the hallway, hoping to find a blanket the old owners might have left behind. Pulling out a quilt, she noticed the bedroom doors were all open. Presuming she had forgotten to close them earlier, it was too cold to bother with them, and she hurried back into the bedroom where the fire was ablaze again. She smiled, put more wood in, and unfolded the quilt she found. It was too small to cover the bed but would have to suffice.

The cottage rewarded her that night with a delightful dream of music coming from downstairs, a man quietly playing a piano and singing. His voice was gentle and clear, full of longing. *Skylark, have you anything to say to me? Won't you tell me where my love can be? Is there a meadow in the mist . . .*

She tried to get out of bed to go downstairs but instead woke up to darkness and rain pattering the roof. She fell back to sleep. In the morning, she recorded the dream in her notepad. Pulling the small quilt up around her shoulders, she noticed an intricate hand-embroidered sunflower on a corner of it. When she made the bed, she tossed the quilt on the chair. A woman's voice, indistinct words, drifted from behind the house. Looking out, the lane was empty. She went downstairs to start a fire and make coffee.

Coming back up for heavier socks, she found the quilt folded on the foot of the bed. *This is how it starts,* she thought. *Small stuff. Imagining you did things you didn't. Forgetting the things you did.* She put the folded quilt back on the chair. "Stay there."

After her second cup of coffee, the day's work began.

"What's all this?" Mr. Harris asked at the screen door, looking at a heap of furniture in the hallway. Janet's head bobbed up from behind it, her hair tied back with a scarf.

"I was just giving the room a thorough cleaning," she quipped. "Pretty dirty, actually. Giving it a good scrubbing. Already did the woodwork and baseboards. Now it's the floor's turn."

"Ah, I see," he said. "Good work. Don't want to interrupt."

"Please! Interrupt!" she said, standing up, stretching with a wince. "I can get a bit carried away sometimes. I could use a breather."

Mr. Harris stood on the steps, hands in his pockets, watching her. "Thinking of rearranging things, are you?"

"Why would I rearrange?" she said. "Everything has a place as far as I can tell. Why mess with it?" Hearing vague voices behind her, her eyes darted about.

"Why indeed," he said. "Why indeed. Everything has a place."

"Did you hear that, Mr. Harris?"

The voices stopped.

"Hear what?"

"Yup. This is how it starts," she grumbled. "Great."

"How what starts?"

"Nothing. Just acoustics." She stepped out to the porch, unaware the rain had stopped. A breeze slid by like a breath and just as quickly dissipated. A rustling drew Mr. Harris's attention to the arbor overflowing with its budding wisteria tendrils. "Where did you find that?" It was almost an accusation the way he said it and Janet bristled.

"What?"

"That chair. Under the wisteria. Where'd you get it?"

"Oh, that. I found it in the stable."

"I'd be careful. Could be dangerous up there."

"Looked solid to me. I thought I heard something when I was out there. Like singing, so I went up to look."

"You heard singing, eh?"

"Yeah. An old Johnny Mercer tune. Or Hoagy Carmichael. I can never remember. It was a man's voice. Sounded sad."

"And did you find someone up there?"

"Just that chair. I thought it would look good sitting over there."

Mr. Harris looked at her and smiled. "So, you're doing OK here then?"

"Yeah. Thanks."

"Well, that's good, good to hear," he said turning to leave. He told her there was an oilcan under the sink in the kitchen. "Give it a shot in those hinges. The back door. Squeaks." Janet watched Mr. Harris saunter across the yard. He looked at the rocker under the wisteria as if it could return his gaze.

Later in the day, she made a trip to the island's only grocery store across from the ferry docks for a few supplies, more pine cleaner, floor wax, sponges, and potato chips. Any more, and she wouldn't be able to carry it all. She was in and out quickly, no lines, no tourists.

Her cleaning continued over the next few days, moving every table, chair and dresser, scrubbing floors, wiping window trim and shaking out curtains. She washed every pan, plate, glass, and dish in the kitchen. She scrubbed cupboards and waxed the kitchen linoleum. She polished wood and washed lamps and vases and knick-knacks, her hands intent on touching every square inch of the place to make it hers, a statement of arrival. Upon going to bed bone tired on the fourth night, she heard a woman's voice again, only not from the road, but as if someone stood beside her. *Gathering* it seemed to say but was too faint to make out. Janet froze to stillness on the edge of the bed. *Gathering*, it came again.

"I'm not ready for this!" she shouted, and flopped down clenching the pillow, wondering how long she could keep a grip on her remaining sanity.

Giving up on sleep, she went downstairs, poured a bit of bourbon into an old Depression glass goblet, stoked the fire, and curled up on the lumpy old couch with a blanket. She left the firebox door open so she could watch the flames. She downed the last of the bourbon and dozed off.

⌘

Janet stood in the middle of the living room, people moving around her, little more than blurs. There was talking and laughter. She heard her grandfather's voice and saw him, clear and solid, standing next to her. He looked just as she remembered him. "You have nothing to worry about," he said. Then he shook her by the shoulders. "But you need to wake up!"

⌘

Janet woke to silent darkness except for a pulsating ember glowing on the floorboards. She scooped it up, returned it to the firebox and closed the door. She woke the next morning in bed without recalling how she got there. She went downstairs and checked out the floor, finding a small black spot where the ember had burned. She remembered dreaming of her grandfather, and suddenly felt a deep longing for him. She missed her father occasionally, but it was Grandpa Max she wanted back. He'd been gone forty years, yet this day her grief felt fresh.

CHAPTER 6

Betsy

Max and Betsy Crawford had one child, Janet's mother Ellen. Janet was the only grandchild and Max was devoted, above anyone else, to her.

When Max met Betsy, he was part of a team designing one of the first electric clothes dryers for Hamilton Machine Company in Edgewater. She was pretty with wavy brown hair, shapely hips, and a smile that always looked sincere, even when it was little more than a prop. Her mother had died of cancer a year earlier, and Betsy latched on to Max. Her father was only too happy to marry her off.

She was very complimentary in the beginning. Pleasant. Agreeable. You are so talented. Hamilton Machine is very fortunate to have you. You're a better engineer than anyone they've got. You will take that company into brave new territory. If they've got a brain in their heads they'll see you're management material. You'll be promoted in no time. She laid it on thick. But within weeks of their wedding, the praise stopped.

Just as her daughter would turn on her husband years down the road, Betsy turned on Max. She didn't like the face he made when he shaved. She chastised him for dunking donuts in his coffee. She complained he didn't compliment her enough, or thank her enough. Her parting words to him out the door each morning were *Try not to make any mistakes.* It was as if marriage negated everything good she'd seen in him. He wrote it off to her youth. She was only twenty-one. She was right about one thing, though. When the dryer went into production, Max was promoted to project director.

Betsy gave birth to Ellen in 1939. Max presumed fatherhood would generate an automatic bond but the baby screamed every time he tried to pick her up. No matter how he approached her, she cried, and Betsy always rushed in, scooped her up, and reinforced the infant's fears. "Of course you're afraid of him," she cooed. "He's a man. But mommy loves you." Max's attempts to play with his daughter, dress her, or feed her were always met with Betsy's criticism. "Daddy doesn't know what he's doing, does he? Bad daddy." Max let it go on only so long before he told her to stop saying *Bad daddy.* "I will," she said, "as soon as you start being a good one." Little Ellen learned quickly to ostracize her father and was well on her way to replicating her mother.

Max worked under Carleton Post at Hamilton Manufacturing. They became good friends. After Pearl Harbor was attacked, they both enlisted and landed in England. Carleton worked on planes and flew non-combat missions. Max joined the Army Corps of Engineers teaching soldiers how to blow up bridges. When the war ended, Carleton came home to a loving wife and a three-year-old daughter he'd never met. Max came home to a wife he no longer knew and a five-year old daughter who cried at the sight of him and ran away. Betsy had done nothing to keep his memory alive for her.

Max presumed all vets were having difficulty assimilating back into civilian life, and given enough time, he would adjust.

"No one made you go overseas for years on end," Betsy told him in what became a barrage of malcontent.

Max could do nothing but wait for her diatribe to extinguish itself.

". . . and raising our baby in your absence on less than half what I was used to, mind you. No one could have held it together as well as I did. And I'll have you know I never complained, even though I had plenty to complain about. You try living on that pittance and see how far you get. Ellen loves me more than anyone ever loved their mother. People constantly tell me what a wonderful job I'm doing with her. Ask anyone and they'll tell you I was the best chairperson they ever had for the toy drive last Christmas. And I did all that without once complaining about the hardship I endured. People say I'm a saint. They all say it and you should be grateful."

Max had no idea what to say or how to react. He stared at his wife, her face a vision of expectation. He took a breath to speak. Her eyes grew wide. He gave her a half smile and walked out the door.

For the first few weeks after he came home, she let him have sex when he wanted it, though she did not feign even a modicum of enthusiasm. It was the only time she touched him, but never below his waste. Sex was nothing more to her than an obligation of the marriage contract. Six months later, she went on strike.

Max wanted to go back to war. Any war.

At a company party that first Christmas home, in the presence of his boss, other coworkers and their wives, Betsy held his hand, smiled lovingly, and told anyone who'd listen how happy she was to have him home again. She carried on about all the fun she had with little Ellen, how bright the child was, how she could already read. She told the president of the company, Bert Hamilton and his wife about a snowman they'd made just the day before and how Ellen loved to be pulled around the yard on a sled. They were delightful words. But they were all lies. Ellen couldn't spell her own name. There was no snowman in their yard. They didn't own a sled. On their way home, Betsy again showed nothing but disdain for Max, telling him to shut up when he thanked her for her performance.

It was at his father-in-law's funeral that Max accidentally found an unexpected shred of enlightenment. Betsy's uncle told him her mother had not died of cancer as everyone had been told. She'd been institutionalized and died in a mental hospital about a year into the war. "She was my sister," the uncle said, "but there was no getting around it. She was a hard woman to love. An impossible woman. Just plain impossible."

There it was. Betsy came by her personality naturally and in all likelihood, would never change. Max did not tell Betsy about her mother as it could have served no purpose.

Ellen had her mother's full attention growing up but it was not loving attention. Betsy showered the child with gifts, but demanded gratitude in return. If Ellen's smile was not big enough, or her kiss to Mother's cheek not fast enough, the gift was summarily withdrawn. Thus began Ellen's tutelage as a manipulator, learning to get what she wanted with disingenuous displays of affection. Max was not immune.

"Daddy," she said one spring with a demure smile. "Can I go to Westchester Camp this summer? Pleeeze? It's where all the best girls go. They have horses and sailboats and I'd love you forever." She went to the camp. Four days into the three-week session, she came home spouting a litany of complaints. There was no refund.

For their tenth anniversary, and at Betsy's request, Max made dinner reservations at a restaurant that someone in her bridge club raved about. He came home on the night to an empty house. He showered. Betsy was still not home as he dressed. The reservation was for eight. At five after, he poured himself a scotch. At quarter after, Betsy and Ellen came through the door, Ellen dressed in a lemon-colored tutu.

"Where have you been," he said. "The babysitter should be here any minute. Our reservation . . ."

Ellen interrupted him as she scuffed her way through the kitchen. "Thanks for showing up, Dad."

Betsy did not make eye contact.

"Did you forget about our dinner tonight?" he asked.

"We ate at five. She had to be there by 5:30."

"Had to be where?"

"Her recital. I told her you were coming this time."

"What recital?"

"I told you about it."

"No you didn't. You begged me to make reservations at The Nest."

"On recital night? Really? You're so inconsiderate. So sorry our plans interfered with yours."

"Not that I much care, but it's our anniversary."

"Your daughter is heartbroken. I told you her recital was tonight."

"No. You didn't tell me. You never tell me. You do everything you can to sabotage my relationship with her!"

Ellen looked at the bottle of scotch on the counter. "I'm not speaking to you when you're drunk." She left the room.

Max poured another shot, took a small box from his pocket, dropped it in the trash, and retreated to his den. There was no getting past the level of defeat he felt in every encounter with his wife. He was a man who understood detail and logic and Betsy was beyond all comprehension. No matter what he did, he was wrong. She was unhappy. They were all unhappy.

Betsy appeared in the doorway. "What's this," she asked holding a gold bracelet in her fingertips like holding a dead mouse by its tail.

"Happy anniversary," he said without looking at her.

She dropped the bracelet, making a little scraping thud on the hardwood floor.

"You can't buy love," she said, walking away.

He came to a realization in that moment. If he felt any love for his wife, it was little more than an invasive vine, tendrils insinuating themselves into the carpet and floorboards so thoroughly the two of them were bound together by a tangle of twisted knots. He used to blame himself, believing his shortcomings were responsible. If he was more involved, more sensitive, more loving, Betsy and Ellen would respond in kind. But Betsy, and possibly Ellen as well, were incapable of compassion. He decided there was something inherently wrong with them, like faulty wiring, and he wondered then what mental instability had sent Betsy's mother to a mental hospital. There was no one left to ask.

Max had not gone into marriage expecting to be happy every day. But he never anticipated the profound emptiness of it. It was as if he'd been built to be lonely and so far had lived up to specs.

As the years passed, Betsy did everything expected of the perfect housewife to the extent that her house was impeccably clean. She made sure Max always came home to a freshly prepared meal. His clothes were clean, pressed, and put away. This endeavor, however, had nothing to do with consideration for him. It was her job. Nothing more.

Ellen found a husband, and as always, Max was little more than the wedding's financier.

Betsy used the occasion to buy twin beds and gave their double bed to a charity.

Betsy had no friends. Max, however, had Carleton Post. They golfed nearly every weekend all summer, played Bridge every other week with Bert Hamilton, CEO and chairman of the board, and bowled in a league all winter. Their wives, however, were not friends. Though they traveled in some of the same circles, Jeanne Post and Mrs. Hamilton were of the executive strata in town. Betsy was relegated to the middle strata, women whose husbands were middle management. Edgewater was a company town.

Betsy made a point of always looking her best even when going to the market. Her handbag matched her shoes, her earrings matched her necklace. Her hair was never out of place, cropped short and curled each night in tiny bobby pin spirals. She played Bridge every Friday and belonged to the Women's Hospital Auxiliary, the

Children's Aid Society and was on the Wednesday Musical committee. She belonged to these organizations only in so far as she showed up to meetings and events. Betsy was not one to be counted on for anything due to the immense responsibility of her wifely duties. She had never chaired a toy drive, in spite of bragging she'd done so.

Max could, however, count on Betsy over the years to maintain the pretense of happy family at company functions and the rare occasions they were invited to Carleton's. Given the opportunity, she would praise Max and feign adulation of their daughter and son-in-law. Beyond that, she was adept at standing near conversations without ever engaging.

Max had no concept of her growing reticence toward social activities, or that her routine had grown tighter and tighter. Shopping on Monday. Laundry on Tuesday. House cleaning on Thursday. He wasn't aware she dropped out of Bridge club and all her committees. Their meals, simple as they were, were eaten in silence. They did not celebrate his promotion to vice president.

It's impossible to say what keeps a marriage together in the throes of such disconnect. The thought of divorcing Betsy occasionally floated to top of mind, but paying for separate homes and facing the scrutiny of others quickly pushed it back down. Divorce was not a word bantered about lightly in the 1960s. Whether he stayed with her out of obligation, convenience, or some semblance of habit was irrelevant. He stayed. Period.

CHAPTER 7

Midlife Crisis

Something happened to Max Crawford when he hit fifty-one. He'd been so stoic about facing fifty that fifty-one blindsided him. The pervasive discontentment always hovering on the horizon began to swell and blew in like a hurricane, overtaking him at a rather inopportune moment in the middle of a board meeting.

Carleton stood up front explaining to the board the prospects for a new washer drum Max had designed. It was about to revolutionize the industry. As Max listened, Carleton's words turned to gibberish. Max began to sweat. He couldn't catch his breath. He loosened his tie. He felt the room closing in. He pushed back from the table, stood up, and keeled over. He was suddenly on the floor surrounded by a gaggle of gray suits. Somebody was straightening his legs, another undoing his tie, another putting something under his head. "Leave me the fuck alone!" flew out of his mouth, but they paid no attention. He tried to get up on one elbow, but Bert Hamilton pushed him back down.

"You're having a heart attack, man! Stay still!" Bert's heart attack the year before made him an expert.

"Give him some room, boys," Carleton said calmly, clearing the men away. "He's OK."

Max sat up.

"What have you had to eat today, Max?" Carleton asked. "Nothing, right? Just a low blood sugar thing I'll wager."

The men stood off to the side, but did not take their eyes off the man on the floor. Perhaps they saw themselves there one day. "Give him some air," Carleton insisted. "Come on. Move out. Just go back to your offices."

"The ambulance will be here soon," a secretary hollered as she hung up the phone.

"Just hang on," Bert said, short of breath, right before his knees buckled and he fell into a chair. By the time the ambulance attived, Max was already in the elevator with Carleton. Bert Hamilton was the one requiring medical attention.

"What was with that blood sugar stuff?" Max asked, pushing the button for the ground floor.

"Heard it on TV last night. Ben Casey." Carleton chuckled. "Hey. It worked, didn't it? Got you out of there."

"Damn, I can't take this place," Max grumbled.

"Yes, you can. You're just realizing you're finally at the party you've been dying to get into all your life. And now that you're here, it's not what you thought it would be."

"Well, that's just a fucking disappointment."

"Yeah. It is. Been there. You'll get over it. Spend some money. Do something spontaneous. Buy new underwear."

"What the hell?" They both laughed but Carleton was serious.

"Jeanne is always buying new lingerie and it's not to make me happy, it's for herself. She says it makes her feel fabulous knowing she's wearing leopard spots under her proper Channel suit. So, I went out and got me some silk boxer shorts with horses on them, and Viking shields, and clowns."

"Clowns? Are you nuts!"

"Yeah. They are comfortable as hell and it's my little secret all day long. I recommend it. Really. It's hard to let things get to you when your ass is covered in clowns."

They walked out onto the loading docks, and both men stood with the sun on their faces. "Anything I can do for you, Mr. Post?" asked a man approaching from an office.

"No, Nick. We're good. Everything OK down here today?"

"Smooth as silk, sir. Smooth as silk."

Max and Carleton laughed out loud, and Nick walked away, shaking his head.

Carleton took a deep breath and spread his arms wide, stretching his chest open, buttons almost popping. "I'll walk you to your car."

"I must be falling apart," Max said as they both jumped off the platform.

"What? Look at yourself," Carleton laughed. "You're in great shape."

"For a guy my age?"

"For a guy any age. You haven't changed a hell of a lot in twenty-five years. I bet you could still fit in your old uniform. I sure as hell couldn't!"

"Next thing you're going to say is my gray makes me look distinguished."

"At least you still have a thick head of hair and not a shiny dome like me."

Approaching his car, Max stopped. "What the hell *was* that in there?"

"A warning, my friend. A warning to change your life while you still have time." Carleton pulled a tobacco pouch from his jacket pocket and filled his pipe. The aroma of vanilla surrounded him.

"And what makes you such an expert?" Max asked.

"Like I said. I've been there. Remember that trip Jeanne and I took five years ago?"

"When you turned 50?"

"Yeah. Eight weeks. We traveled the world. We saw the pyramids, Incan ruins, the Taj Mahal, the Amazon. Jeanne and I woke up each day and asked ourselves where we wanted to be, and we went. And somewhere in there, we realized this life is a fleeting moment. Everything we saw was a monument to some dead civilization. And since we, as a species, a culture, had recently barely managed to not completely annihilate ourselves in the war, we owed it to ourselves to really *live* life. By the time we got home, we were exhausted but rejuvenated. Life is in the small stuff, my friend. It's in the moment. Even your moment in there. Spectacular! That was fucking spectacular!" He slammed Max on the back and opened his car door for him. "Go find it, Max."

"Find what?"

"Whatever it is, you need to find."

"Right."

Max got into his car, closed the door, and pulled away. Normally, he would have turned left toward home, but fat bud clusters on the lilac hedge distracted him, and he turned right instead. It was late April. Things were just coming to life after a long Midwestern winter.

A few miles out of Edgewater, he drove past Spirit and Miller lakes and pulled into the county boat launch at Baldwin Lake. He slowly approached the far edge and stopped just shy of the shore. He sat there, engine idling, looking out over still water, a single white ribbon of sand encircling it. In another couple weeks, docks would go in, jutting out from every cottage along the shoreline. Then boats would be launched, families would invade, and a buoyancy of life would return. Max suddenly felt as if he'd missed out. On everything. On life. Overcome with a familiar melancholy, he backed up and drove out, away from the perception of missed opportunities for happiness.

Heading east, he crossed a river and passed a field carpeted with new shoots of brilliant green, so fresh and full of promise he wanted to run through it barefoot as if it held regenerative powers. He opened all the windows wide. He felt a surge of something wonderful as he pushed the pedal to the floor and sped down a road dissecting a field of corn shoots, little more than green flecks in the rich black soil. He wanted his Lincoln to lift off and fly over the approaching house and barn and silos, then saw a truck approaching from the right, and he slowed down in time to stop easily at the intersection. The truck pulled past and Max pulled forward, cruising at the legal limit, traversing a countryside dotted with small inland lakes, farms, and swaths of forest, ever farther away from home, from Betsy, from his life.

Disillusion and disappointment weighed heavy on his heart. He began to think his life was nearly over, and he'd wasted it. He wondered how he'd ever allowed Betsy to manage their lives into such a tedious routine. Dinner on the table at six. TV from eight to eleven, the same shows each week. Lights out at eleven-fifteen. Even dinner, every Monday, the same meal as the Monday before, and on throughout the week, except for Friday. Max hit the Sandbox Grill, a hole-in-the-wall bar on the river for a beer and a burger every Friday because it was Betsy's bridge club day. She didn't cook on bridge club day. Such was the routine to which Max had long ago surrendered.

Cruising through some innocuous small town, he thought of Ellen and the kind of parent he'd been to her and hoped she would one day forgive him if it ever crossed her mind to feel shortchanged. She'd been kept safe and was given everything she needed, but there were no daddy-daughter dances, no piggyback rides, no snuggles or cuddles. He was a hands-off kind of father, a distance Betsy regularly reinforced. In hindsight, if he'd stood up to Betsy, maybe Ellen wouldn't have been such a difficult child, excelling at absolutely nothing except pouting. Maybe she would not have become a carbon copy of her mother. Whether Max could have done anything to alter that outcome was the question he pondered as he rounded yet another small lake.

He'd been disappointed when Ellen came home from her freshman year of college with Howard Granger in tow, a senior majoring in accounting and economics. Max considered him a milquetoast kind of man, but probably the steady sort. It seemed to be Ellen's idea to marry, though they didn't act as if they were in love or even infatuated. They seemed, above all else, happy to settle for each other. Max was certain there would be no surprises, that their lives would plod along, an exercise in tolerance and boredom. Heaven help any kids they might have. With parents as unimaginative as they were, they'd surely turn out to be grocery baggers or homicidal maniacs.

Ellen dropped out of school to marry Howard, leaving Betsy incensed when they moved to the other side of the state. Thanksgiving in the Crawford house became an annual day of reckoning when Betsy informed Ellen of her most prominent failings. Year one, Betsy reprimanded Ellen for putting on fifty pounds. Year two and subsequent years, without fail, as soon as Betsy took the masher to the boiled potatoes, the scolding began. "What purpose is a woman if not to raise a child? I know it's repulsive, but you've got to get on it." She hollered loud enough for Max and Howard to hear her over the football game in the living room. "It's up to you," Betsy insisted. "Do something. Get that man riled up." Her cheerleading was nothing short of nagging and did nothing to improve the situation.

There was, of course, no mention of Betsy's refusal of intimacy with Max.

Without being conscious of his route, Max accidentally landed at Michigan State University. From somewhere deep within, a heady *Yes!* rose up, and this surprising remnant of what had once passed for enthusiasm intrigued him.

He parked near the engineering building and walked in feeling a little pathetic, like a kid coming back to his high school to visit a favorite teacher, someone who might have told him life did not come with endless possibilities, so he'd better figure out how to focus on what he wanted before all opportunities were spent. No one had said that to him, but he wished they had.

He stepped into a lecture hall listening to some grad student lecture about stress equations. Suddenly, a hand landed on his shoulder and a familiar voice spoke behind him. "Well, I never thought I'd see you back here, Max. Come about the position?"

Max turned to find a rosy-cheeked man who seemed pleased to see him. "Dr. Grayson, how the hell are you?"

"Good. Too damn old, but good."

"Aren't you the dean of the school of engineering now?"

"Now? Going on a decade. What about you? I hear you're a vice president at that firm you're with. Good work, Max. You like it?"

"I do," he said, and it wasn't a lie. He'd simply suffered a moment of doubt about his life, but standing in that old building reminded him of the kid he'd once been and how far he'd come.

Dr. Grayson took Max down the hall and outside. The fresh air suddenly felt different to Max, sweeter, livelier. The two men sauntered over to the dining room reserved for tenured professors.

"So? Are you here about the position?" Grayson asked again. "We have someone in mind, but I'd love to bring you in. I think you'd be better than anyone we've looked at so far."

Max had no idea what Grayson was talking about and assured him he had no ambitions of coming back to school. But over a late lunch the dean explained what the job entailed. "Experts coming in straight from the field. Non-academia types. Real people. Like you, Max. That's what we're looking for. Somebody who excelled while they were here and kept it up once they left. Max! I want you here. Join us. What do you say? It doesn't start until August. We'll work out the details over the summer. You in?"

In the time it took Max to drive home, he decided to take an adjunct professor post at Michigan State for a one-year stint, one day a week, with a select group of students. He felt energized again, ready for what came next. He didn't know what it might be, but the anticipation was palpable, something he hadn't felt in decades, if ever.

CHAPTER 8

Weeding

Janet stood at the steps of Baldwin Cottage on a damp day wearing two layers of fleece. She did not recognize this new life in a big house on a tiny island. It made no sense to her, and yet again, she felt swept up by the peculiar circumstances that led her there.

With a small hand rake in her grasp, she stepped to the grass and surveyed the border garden within the hedgerow. The last time she'd seen it was in the fall, when all but the mums were finished for the season. Standing in the sunshine, wet soaking through her shoes, she felt intimidated. Knowing what to weed out of any garden can be tricky, but it's daunting in an unfamiliar landscape. The previous night's rain dripped from budding branches above her.

Janet had helped take care of the flowerbed at the condos but that was a simple task. Each spring they pulled all the old annuals out, raked it clean, and put in new ones. Nothing was allowed to linger from one season into the next. She liked that it was a clean slate every year.

Glancing down, she observed green shoots working their way through leaf litter and mulch. White trillium bloomed under a lilac in the corner. Tightly coiled reddish-green fiddle neck fern nubs pushed their way through mounds of last year's dried fernage. She looked to the pattern and spacing of any new growth to decide if it looked intentional or not. If it didn't seem to fit the symmetry of the space, she presumed it was a weed.

In hopes of attracting a new owner, or more to the point, to keep the property from looking as abandoned as it was, the annex co-op hired a landscaper to maintain the yard. The same co-op paid to repair the roof.

The landscaper left sturdy metal plant markers throughout the garden to identify various spots of empty ground where hosta and bleeding hearts had not yet erupted. This left the unmarked shoots suspect, but she was not ready to declare them weeds.

She knew that given the slightest opportunity, a weed will overtake the flowering plant. Proficient at mimicry, what appears to belong often doesn't. Janet knelt beside a small aluminum nameplate stuck into the ground: *Papaver Orientale*. The area behind it was full of hairy new growth that seemed to belong. Yet within that area, there were other leaves with similar hairy features. Which was weed and which was poppy was a mystery. Until she knew for certain, she would let them co-exist.

There were other intruders she recognized like dandelions, crabgrass, and creeping little vines she felt confident deserved extraction. She reached down and pulled a dandelion. The moist ground made the long root give way easily and each subsequent tug on other dandelions met with equal success. Feeling a palpable sense of satisfaction, she settled onto her knees in the cold wet soil and worked her way front to back, pulling and raking only those things she felt certain were weeds. She liked the tidiness of the fresh, clean soil between supple new growth. As she moved down the hedgerow, clearing away leaf debris and dead foliage, she left little piles on the grass, remnants of her accomplishment.

"I can take care of that if you like," Mr. Harris said.

His voice startled Janet. She hadn't noticed him watching. She put down the hand rake and stood up, attempting to brush away the dirt from her jeans only to smear mud instead. She laughed at the futility of it.

"I'll take over from here. Weeding is kind of Zen, don't you think?" she asked.

"You know what you're doing? Wouldn't want you yanking out any of the good stuff."

"I'm being careful," Janet said, trying to hide her doubts.

"See that you are," he grumbled, and turned to walk toward the stable. "I need to stow the storm windows." They'd been taken down before Janet arrived. Mr. Harris turned back to ask if she needed anything else while he was there.

Janet shrugged and reached for the hand rake, about to rake out some sturdy, fat-leafed seedlings she thought needed to be yanked before they became unmanageable. But the hand rake wasn't there and she nudged a pile of weeds to see if it was buried within, then another, and another, before scanning inch by inch everywhere she'd been. "God damn it!"

Mr. Harris bellowed from the stable. "No need for foul language. And you want to be careful not to bother those young sunflowers. They can be mighty pretty come August." Seeing her blank expression, he came over to show her and pointed to the fat sprouts. "I wouldn't thin them out. Rabbits will do that for you," he told her.

"Got it," she said, relieved to have not raked them all away. "I'll leave them alone for now." Mr. Harris walked off and she looked for the hand rake again, finding it next to her foot. Anger rose fast, fear racing right along with it, as it had, no doubt, for her mother and grandmother and all the poor wretches before them. "Things don't just vanish," she yelled. "And they sure as hell don't just reappear!"

Noticing the storm windows still leaning against the wall, she glanced about for Mr. Harris and saw a pale gray horse walk behind the stable. Thinking someone would certainly be looking for it, she went to retrieve it but there was no horse. The stable door was closed. She looked down the road. Nothing. She opened one of the double doors thinking maybe it had swung open and the horse had stepped in, the door closing behind it, but the stalls were empty.

"And now I see things that aren't there," she muttered. "Fine!" she shouted, slamming the big door, and it waffled and bounced. Hands shaking, she went to the utility room off the back porch and stripped out of her muddy jeans, throwing them into the washing machine. Looking at her muddy hands, she had visions of her mother, naked, caked in mud at river's edge. *I didn't know it would happen so fast*, she thought, her heart cracking a little.

Janet knew very little about her mother's decline. Howard had protected her from the worst of it. Had Ellen heard things? Seen things? Was she aware of her failings?

She recalled the Thanksgiving she went home uninvited. She hadn't been home for any holiday all through college. Holidays had never been warm or cozy affairs in the Granger household, but a couple years after graduation, she decided to surprise them. She walked in carrying a pumpkin pie, expecting to smell roasting turkey. Instead, she found Howard making a ham sandwich.

"What are you doing here?" he said. "Your mother isn't feeling well."

From the front room came Ellen's familiar shouting. "Who the hell is at the door?"

"It's just me," Janet said, stepping into the living room.

"What the hell are you doing here," Ellen said.

"I brought a pie for Thanksgiving, but I see we're not doing Thanksgiving anymore."

Ellen mumbled something unintelligible and turned back to the TV show she was watching.

"Go home," Howard said without compassion. He was too tired to stumble around the truth. "She's better when you're not around."

There it was. The whole of Janet's life reduced to one simple statement of fact. Nothing cut so deeply as the truth.

She left. There would be no more visiting the folks.

As with any self-perpetuating fear, once Janet was told about the family history, she began to see corroborating evidence that she, too, was following in familial footsteps. Every little slip of the tongue or lost thought proved it.

In preparation for the inevitable, Janet became a list maker, thinking that when all else failed, she would be able to fall back on her record of everything: schedules for the day, week, month, and year; where she put things like winter gloves and summer tank tops; monthly and quarterly bills to be paid; financial information like insurance policies and bank accounts. There were small spiral notepads in her purse, on her bed stand, in her car, on the kitchen counter, all full of random thoughts, lists, and extended continuations of lists, each with a symbol or number or some indication of other lists related to it, symbols cryptic to anyone but her - until such time even that knowledge would evade her. She rarely referred to these lists but kept them with pragmatic regularity. On the way to the market, she would run in her head all the items she'd written on a list, organizing them in terms of grocery aisle, categorized by dairy, produce, canned goods, coffee, paper, and cleaning supplies. She was good at it, rarely missing anything. But when she did forget something, even a single item, she took it as a sign of the coming battle she was certain to lose. She wondered if being obsessed with maintaining one's mental acuity was a sign of losing it.

The cottage cleaning progressed to the bedrooms. Janet shook out rugs, aired curtains on a line outside, swept the floors, dusted the dressers and nightstands, and finally washed each of the chenille bedspreads. She opened the new pillows and distributed them to all the beds. The old ones were stuffed into garbage bags to throw out, disintegrating feathers lofting in the process. She would leave the mattresses to breathe before putting new sheets on. In the meantime, the unopened packages laid in respective dresser drawers.

She gave the upstairs hallway a once over and inspected the oversized drawers under the bench where she'd found the little quilt her first night. She found several disintegrating feather pillows, which she immediately removed to a trash bag. Another drawer held blankets and quilts. The last big drawer was full of sheets, on top of which lay three perfume atomizers and an ornate silver-handled hairbrush.

She lifted one of the atomizers, marveling at its beautiful cherry-red, multi-faceted cut glass. The little rubber bulb was covered with gold netting. Giving it a squeeze, there was nothing but a slight waft of residual scent. The other two were equally fascinating, one round and royal blue with fine glass ribbing, the other tall, its frosted glass cut to resemble climbing flowers. Its squeeze bulb had a gold silk tassel attached.

A shaft of late afternoon sun spilled from the green bedroom to the hall. Janet smiled wide and took the atomizers to a nightstand at the west window. The glass lit up, each one casting its colorful light to the floor beyond. She put the silver hairbrush on a small table in her bedroom.

Tired but still curious what else she might find, she pulled everything from the sideboard downstairs, filling the big table with place settings for twelve, glassware, silver-plated serving pieces, crockery platters, serving bowls, and a small collection of antique majolica vases of all shapes and designs. She took four favorites and put one in each bedroom.

The next day, as she placed the clean, folded bedspreads in each room, she noticed the atomizers were no longer in the green room where she'd put them. They were in the yellow bedroom on the dresser, along with the hairbrush she thought she left in her room.

Ever the rational pragmatist, Janet thought two things: Either she was too exhausted the day before to recall where she put them, or she forgot because her mind was crawling toward dementia. As she ruminated over which was the more likely option, she glanced out the window. The first daffodils had begun to bloom in the far corner of the yard. They felt like a gift in the moment, a reminder to not sweat the small stuff.

She went down and picked a handful, deciding the blue and white majolica vase would be perfect, but it, too, was not where she'd put it. Going down to the sideboard to look for it, she found it sitting mid-shelf. Once again, she rationalized the incident, and put the flowers in it, placing them in the center of the table. Doubtful of its noteworthiness, she consciously did not record it in her notepad. Yet, as days went on, Janet found herself recording other incidents of equal and lesser interest.

She wrote about doors she'd left closed being open and lights she'd turned off being on, and voices, never quite audible or recognizable, just whispers on the air. She thought maybe one day, her record of progression might prove interesting to anyone researching her family's form of dementia.

She headed out for a walk mid-afternoon. Inherent in her realization of impending insanity was a gift of sorts, a heightened awareness of each moment, and a driving urge to be present in her life. Three women surged past her on the road, babbling to each other, barely noticing their surroundings. Janet veered off onto a narrow trail, sauntering, taking in the smell of wet cedar. A squirrel far above gnawed on a nut, bits of hull falling down to the forest floor. A beetle slowly crawled over moss on a decaying tree stump, mandibles outstretched, A red and black ant drank from a dew drop. Such attention almost became too much and she had to force herself to not see every little thing, to just walk the path for the sake of the walk. Even then, she was aware of the tension and release of her muscles, and her breathing, and the feel of the soft earth beneath her shoes, and the dull snap of a twig soaked from the week's rain, and her skin tightening as a breeze touched her face, and its release in the warm sun. She didn't want to miss a thing. She wanted to imbed all the things she loved about her life into her brain, to hang on to them for as long as she possibly could until it all, one day, without warning, disappeared forever.

Over her shoulder she heard Grandpa Max telling her to relax. She'd been hearing him recently, just one more element to make note of upon returning to the cottage.

CHAPTER 9

The Spark

In early June, not long after Max's visit to MSU, Carleton invited Max and Betsy for a weekend on Mackinac Island with the Baldwins. Max had reservations about spending that much time with James Baldwin. They'd golfed together once at the club and played cards at Carleton's a few times, but they'd never had a real conversation. He found Baldwin to be a drill sergeant sort of man, always in charge. Yet, Max could hardly refuse the invitation. The weekend was a respite for Carleton. Bert Hamilton's episode at the board meeting in April turned out to be his second heart attack, forcing him into retirement. Carleton scrambled to take over as CEO until the board decided on a permanent replacement.

Max had never put Betsy in such a position before, yet had no reason to think she would be uncomfortable. She had her lady's groups, after all, and committees, and social endeavors. He had no idea the prospect of sudden immersion into the executive circle of women terrified her, that she'd be fearful they would scrutinize what she said, how she looked, and everything she did.

He didn't know she spent three days packing and unpacking before going shopping, buying four new outfits, three pairs of shoes and two new brassieres.

Carleton flew them up in the corporate plane. It was a good day for flying, and he made a perfect three-point landing on the island.

Betsy was a little rattled in the air but settled down once she felt pavement under her feet.

"If you think this is hair-raising," said Carleton's wife Jeanne, "you should have been with us in the Australian outback. We flew straight into the bush country, no roads, no landing strip, just a Land Rover waiting for us in the middle of nothing. I was horrified!"

"Yup," Carleton confirmed. "Especially when the plane took off again after depositing us there with two aborigines who barely spoke English."

"James and Trixie Baldwin are tame compared to that!" Jeanne laughed, even though Trixie was known to chair committees with a whip.

A horse-drawn taxi pulled up to the landing strip. Painted bright orange, the hardtop buggy had bench seats for six and a shelf in back for luggage. A charmingly handsome young man jumped off. He had a fresh-scrubbed look that made him seem much younger than he was. "Jimmy!" Jeanne hollered with a huge smile. "We didn't know you'd be here. How delightful!"

"Just for a couple days," he said, giving Jeanne a big hug. "I'll grab your bags. My folks are waiting for you."

Sensing a bit of trepidation, Carleton slapped Max on the back. "It's OK. We're always looking for new blood up here. We get a little stale sometimes. Come on. Let's get to some serious drinking!"

Jeanne's slacks made for an easy climb up into the carriage, but Betsy was having difficulty in her straight skirt. Carleton pulled her up by both hands while Max pushed her from behind.

With all the bags loaded, Jimmy sent the foursome on their way.

"Not coming with us?" Jeanne asked.

"Nope. Anna is meeting me here and we're walking back together."

"Excellent!" Jeanne called out as the carriage pulled away. "See you soon!"

The buggy ride through the woods was delightful. The silence of the woods and the rhythmic thudding of hooves lent a nostalgic air to the journey. "Wow," Max sighed with a soft smile.

"Yeah," Carleton said quietly. "I love it up here. I really do. I'm anxious for you two to see our Anna. How long has it been?"

"Since I've seen her?" Max asked. "Oh, maybe five or six years. She came to the office to gather you up for lunch or some such. Beautiful child."

"That she is. She's been up here with the Baldwins for a month already."

"We've been coming here since before she was born," Jeanne explained. "James and Carleton went to school together. Roommates all four years. Even started at Hamilton together."

"He's the one who got me into Hamilton Machine but ..." Carleton started to explain, until Jeanne finished his thought.

"But James had bigger plans."

Max interrupted. "Baldwin went off on his own just after I got there, didn't he?"

"Yeah. Before the war," Carleton said with a slight wisp of envy. "He went into aeronautics in '38. I had no interest in it. Big mistake."

"Could have made a fortune," Jeanne added.

"How long have they had the cottage up here?" Max asked.

"Don't really know, actually," Carleton admitted.

"Yes, we do, dear," Jeanne corrected him. "The late 1800s. His great, great something or other built it."

"So, he came from money, then," the first words out of Betsy's mouth. "You know my Max would be nothing without me. I keep his life in tip-top order, don't I, dear? Everything you need right at your fingertips." She took his arm in an expression of devotion where none existed. "Tell them, dear. We'll have to have you all over for dinner sometime. Wouldn't that be nice, dear?"

Jeanne smiled and complimented Betsy on the fine job she was doing with Max.

Carleton looked at Max, whose gaze was as far from his wife as possible.

Carleton said he couldn't remember where the Baldwin family money had come from originally, and Jeanne said it was timber. "It was all that rebuilding in Chicago after the great fire, wasn't it?"

"Maybe," Carleton said, patting Jeanne's hand. "Sounds right."

"Anyway," Jeanne sighed, putting her head on Carleton's shoulder, "we've been vacationing here for nearly forty years."

"Thirty-five, Sweetie," Carleton whispered.

"Baldwin Lake is named for them," Betsy announced. No one responded.

As the carriage pulled up to the stable behind Baldwin Cottage, James Baldwin Sr. was waiting, chest out, hands in his pockets. He was a stout man of stern expression. His statements were demanding and pointed. "Trixie, dear," he called into the cottage. "Our guests have arrived." Trixie, a tiny, perky woman with perfectly quaffed hair, stepped to his side. She wore her make-up like a mask, her mascara, eye shadow, and lipstick perfect in every stroke.

"How delightful to see you," Trixie said to Jeanne, putting her arms around the woman but barely touching her.

The others disembarked except for Betsy, who was having difficulty navigating the step from the carriage to the road. Carleton and Max finally grabbed her by the elbows and lifted her down.

Trixie stood in front of her, chin high, straight-backed, waiting. Carleton finally spoke up. "I'm sorry," he said. "I thought you two knew each other. Trixie Baldwin, this is Betsy Crawford."

"Yes," Trixie said with a disingenuous smile. "Welcome to Baldwin Cottage."

"Max and Betsy," James Sr. barked. "We're delighted to have you as our guests. Your room is at the top of the stairs to the left. Carl, old friend, and Jeanne dear, your room awaits. We'll have cocktails on the porch in half an hour, then we'll walk down to the Grand for dinner. Jimmy will tend to your luggage later." With that, he marched into the cottage. Trixie and Jeanne scurried off together, disappearing around the corner.

Carleton stretched and smiled. "I'm off for a constitutional before cocktails," he said. "See you later."

He headed down a path into the woods, leaving Max and Betsy on their own.

"I need my suitcase now," Betsy whined. Max grabbed both bags, and together, they went in through the side door where James had entered. "This can't be right," Betsy muttered, walking into the kitchen. "There must be another door."

Baldwin stepped into view. "That is the back door. The front is off the porch, that way," he said, pointing. Pointing to a door in the corner, he said, "There is the bathroom."

"We all share?" Betsy said, appalled.

James looked at her as one might look at an insolent child. "Yes."

On their way up the steps, laughter carried from the porch where Trixie and Jeanne sat sipping iced tea.

Finding their room, Betsy shut the door and began unpacking, stewing about where to put her toiletries since they had to share a bathroom with everyone. "Did you see this?" she asked, incensed, staring at a pitcher and washbasin. "What are we supposed to do with this?" She hoisted the full pitcher and poured some water into the bowl. "Well, I never. Do they think I'll use this?"

Max sighed. "Use it. Don't use it." As Betsy puttered, filling drawers with her undergarments, spreading her make-up and lotions on the dresser, he stood under a gable looking out to nothing but woods, feeling penned in.

Betsy pulled dress after dress out and hung them up, disgruntled by the wrinkles, wondering how she'd be able to wear any of them in such condition.

Max watched her, his face placid.

"What!" Betsy snapped.

"Nothing."

"How was I supposed to know what to bring? You don't tell me anything. You want me to look like a fool in front of them."

"Not at all. You know these women from your committees, don't you?"

"Of course I know them," she said, but she only knew of them. She had a passing acquaintance with Jeanne through Max's friendship with Carleton. But Trixie Baldwin was perched too high to associate with the likes of Betsy Crawford.

"You'll be fine," Max said, clearly indifferent. "Just get dressed. I'm going down."

"It hasn't been half an hour yet. Hasn't even been fifteen minutes."

"I'm going down."

"So now I can't tell time? Fine. You go make a fool of yourself."

He left her to stew.

Max was halfway down the stairs when a young woman appeared below him, crossing the hallway from the kitchen to the living room. Her white Bermuda shorts revealed tan slender legs that made Max want to chase her around the yard like a kid. She wore the kind of top Audrey Hepburn often wore with not so much a neckline as a simple slit from shoulder to shoulder. A crescent of neck peaked through it under unruly waves of sun-tinged auburn hair.

Her eyes lifted to his. She smiled. His heartbeat faltered. He felt a twinge in his gut. His sudden inhalation of breath felt as if he'd awakened from death itself. He smiled back, an honest, warm, heartbreaking smile.

Carleton came in from his walk, ripping her attention away.

"Daddy," she chirped. "I'm so glad you're finally here." She looked back up to Max. "Mr. Crawford! Come on down here. I heard you were coming. How nice to see you again."

Carleton hugged and kissed his daughter, then looked up to Max. "You remember my daughter Anna, don't you Max?"

But Max couldn't speak. He forced himself down the steps, trying to remember who he was, feeling like he'd stepped into someone else's body. Carleton went into the living room, where Jimmy was mixing drinks. Anna followed behind him. Max followed Anna, forgetting entirely about his wife waiting in the room upstairs.

The first round of Tom Collins highballs broke the ice for the weekend. James mellowed out. Carleton brought Max into the conversation, reminding James that Max had been there almost from the beginning. "That dryer really put Hamilton on the map," he said. "And Max was a big part of getting it off the ground."

"I remember Max, all right," James said. "Bright young man. Fresh out of State, weren't you?"

Max was only a few years younger than these two but felt like a child in their presence. "Yes," he said. "You two had a plane together, didn't you?"

"Oh, my dear man," Trixie chimed in. "That open cockpit scares me half to death."

Jeanne laughed in agreement. "Every time they go up in that thing, I'm sure they'll fall right out of the sky."

"Timm M-150 'Collegiate," James said. "Love that plane."

"It belongs in a museum, Daddy," Anna laughed.

"All you old guys," Jimmy joked. "In a museum." Anna gave him a mock elbow jab, and everyone chuckled.

Max was taken with both Anna and Jimmy, so young, so beautiful. Their smiles danced. Their voices lilted through the air. He couldn't remember the last time he'd even entertained such lighthearted thoughts.

James looked at Trixie, then his watch. Trixie looked at Jeanne, who took it upon herself to retrieve Betsy.

Jeanne was the picture of restraint laying eyes on Betsy dressed for a ball in a shimmery evening gown, wearing elbow-length lavender gloves. All she needed was a tiara to complete the rhinestone necklace and bracelet ensemble. When she saw Betsy's feet stuffed into three-inch spiked pumps, silk, stained to match the dress, she asked with a smile if she had any more comfortable shoes. "I'm afraid you won't make it in those, dear. We'll be walking to dinner. It's a ways. You'll ruin them, and they're so pretty."

"But they match," Betsy whined.

Jeanne Post was not the chair of multiple committees because she was bossy. She was favored for her generosity of inclusion and her tact. "Well," she said with a smile and a shrug. "I guess we'll have to find the best shoes and pick the dress to go with them. What do you say about that?" Jeanne went straight to the closet and sifted through the six dresses Betsy brought for their three-day visit. "We're a pretty casual bunch here," she said. "Perhaps we'll take a carriage to dinner tomorrow, and you can wear this outfit. Would be a shame to let it go to waste."

That Betsy was entirely at a loss was evident by the tears welling in her eyes, but Jeanne was quick with another smile, pulling out a bright blue dress. "This is perfect," she said. "And this shoulder cape will be handy if a chill sets in later. Where did you get this?" she asked, taking it off the hanger. "I might have to see if they have another. In a different shade, of course." She retrieved a pair of black, thick-heeled pumps.

"Not those," Betsy griped. "I can't possibly."

Jeanne assured her black and blue were a classic combination as she began to unzip Betsy's dress, at which point Betsy yanked away in shock.

"Oh," Jeanne quipped, "just pretend we're in a dress shop and I'm your assistant."

Betsy relaxed and let Jeanne slide the fluffy dress down and hold it as she stepped out of it. When Jeanne raised the blue dress to slip over her head, Betsy snapped as she might have with a shop-girl. "Be careful of my hair."

Jeanne closed her eyes, took a long, deep breath, and handed the dress over. "Yes, you'd best do this yourself." She then went rummaging in Betsy's jewelry box, pulling out a colorful strand of beads. "These are delightful."

"But they don't go with this dress," Betsy moaned.

Jeanne removed Betsy's rhinestone necklace and wrapped the beads twice around her neck. "Voila! Gorgeous! Let's go to dinner, shall we?"

Betsy followed Jeanne downstairs, having just been entirely rearranged.

No one but Trixie saw Jeanne's eye roll.

Walking the road through the woods, the three men sauntered together, ladies ambling behind, Jeanne and Trixie yammering as good friends do, bouncing from one thing to another, rarely finishing a whole thought before they were on to another. Betsy walked silently, trying not to trip on gravel and stone.

Arriving at the Grand Hotel, James apologized to the maitre d' for their late arrival. At was their ritual, the maître d' assured him their table awaited. The Baldwins had never been on time for a reservation.

Max asked if Jimmy and Anna were joining them. "They make a good-looking couple."

Carleton said kids don't want to hang out with their parents. "They're good pals," he said. "Best friends since they were kids, those two."

Taking their seats, James said Jimmy was a doctor. "Junior is going to be a surgeon. I have no idea how he got the time to come to the island. He's doing his residency at John Hopkins. Baltimore. His schedule is grueling."

"Congratulations," Max said.

"We gave him the opportunity," James responded, almost arguing the point. "What he did with it is all his accomplishment."

It was a point not lost on Max. He saw the merit in it, and looked to his own life for confirmation. He was the first in his family to get an education, the first to have a profession, to become vice president, to accomplish anything beyond subsistence. James was right. Whatever a man's kids do or don't do is up to them. His daughter, Ellen, had opportunities. What she'd chosen to do with them – drop out of college to marry Howard – was up to her. He was not responsible for her bump-on-a-log little life. This revelation suddenly freed him from guilt or responsibility, and he had pompous James Baldwin to thank for it.

If the rest of the weekend landed in the crapper, it was worth it for that nugget. And, for Anna. In one glance, she'd re-ignited his pilot light. It wasn't her, specifically, too young, his best friend's daughter. It was what she represented: Life was still worth living. He could still rise to the occasion.

Betsy never wore the gown she brought or the other fancy dresses, choosing to stay in the simple blue dress Jeane had chosen. She came away from the weekend with new vigor. She asked to rejoin her Bridge club, but had to settle as a substitute. She showed up at a Children's Aid luncheon, speaking to a clutch of ladies about the Baldwins as though they were close, personal friends. "Certainly, you know who I mean," she said. "James and Trixie. From Baldwin Aeronautics. Lovely people. Why, just a few weeks ago, Max and I flew up for the weekend . . ." Jeanne Post, sitting at the next table, did not contradict Betsy. She knew there would be no more invitations to the island for Betsy Crawford.

CHAPTER 10

Anna

Anna had no earthly idea what she wanted to do with her life. In her twenty-three years, she'd found life far too predictable to be interesting. She loved literature. In stories, the most unlikely things happened all the time. This gave her hope for her own life, as she had yet to encounter her own plot twist.

Unlike most of her friends, she graduated Michigan State with a degree but no husband, as did her best friend since childhood, Colleen Jennings. Their singlehood was by no means a failure but a step in the right direction. They wanted something more than marriage, a house, and kids. More what, they hadn't figured out yet. The Russians had just sent a woman into space, so anything was possible, but not if they were shackled to a man.

They considered joining the Peace Corps but decided it might be too messy, and it was such a serious commitment to be so far from home for so long. They opted instead to stay in familiar surroundings, sharing an apartment on the edge of campus as they pursued advanced degrees.

Anna was working her way through a Master of Arts in Comparative Lit. Coleen was working on her Masters Degree in Cultural Anthropology. Across the river on the other side of campus, Max was working his way through a midlife crisis.

On the first cold, blustery day of the season, Anna powered past Beaumont Tower on her way to the library. With her face buried in a scarf wrapped about her neck, hair whipping everywhere, her eyes fell to the pavement, thinking how much colder 38 degrees felt in October than it would in January.

The wind whipped Grand River into a froth as Max crossed the bridge, his collar turned up, shoulders tight to his ears. Must get a hat, he thought. And a scarf. With a brisk pace and wide stride, he charged up the walk to the library anxious for the silent warmth of radiant heat.

Anna spilled in through the library doors with a cluster of students, all clattering about the cold, complaining it arrived too early, surmising it did not bode well for the rest of the winter. Had she not dropped her scarf, had she not bent down to retrieve it, Max might have walked right by without noticing her. It could have been weeks or months before another chance meeting would present itself. When she stood up, she saw him standing not six feet away, smiling at her.

"Well, hey there, Max," she said with a broad grin. "Daddy said you were teaching here. It's about time we ran into each other." She stepped over and hugged him, an innocent impulse. His response was tentative, a half hug. Any closer, and she might have felt just how happy he was to see her even through their bulky coats. She asked him to go for coffee, and he said yes, blowing off an appointment with one of his students.

Anna had seen something behind Max's eyes up on the island, a sort of lost boy expression. Over coffee, she discovered he wasn't lost, just lonely. Watching him laugh reminded her of a kid with a new toy he couldn't put down.

Their conversation seemed endless. They talked about Mackinac Island and campus life and places they wanted to visit like Venice and South America. They talked about books and art and movies. They argued Nietzsche's proposition that what doesn't kill you makes you stronger. She said it did. Max assured her it didn't. "Sometimes it just makes you numb."

Anna felt as if no man before him had really listened to what she had to say. None of them had ever been present in the moment, always caught up in their own thoughts, making of her what they wanted, what they expected. But Max seemed to hear her and offered thoughtful responses, even challenging her to go deeper, to look from other perspectives if only to solidify an original premise. She thought maybe he was the first man she'd ever had an honest and meaningful conversation with.

Max made her feel alive, important, and grounded. She didn't see the difference in their ages. All she saw was a man, ageless, spontaneous, and deeply moving. Afternoon coffee turned into drinks and drinks turned into dinner.

She didn't let him leave without promising to call her next time he was on campus. He agreed with an expression in his eyes that made it absolute. Watching him drive away, Anna knew her life had found its twist.

Up to that point in his life, Max had slept with two women, one in college, then Betsy. He'd taken things slow on their wedding night, dancing in the hotel room, caressing her back, kissing her neck and mouth. She hadn't shown any particular resistance, but she hadn't shown any interest either. She had no idea what to do in bed, and he did his best to introduce himself to her gradually, gently trying to arouse her without affect, climbing on top, urging her, reassuring her. She yelped a little when he entered her, accepting his gyrations as one would a painful dental exam. After he grunted a few times, finished, and rolled over next to her, she asked if that was what it was supposed to feel like. When he said yes, she asked how often they had to do it. In their entire marriage, she never warmed to sex and he'd never seen his wife naked. He'd long since resigned to a life without pleasure beyond what he could give himself.

Anna, however, had him thinking about sex all the time. He dreamed about sex. He woke up aroused. He jerked off in the shower every morning, thinking about the curve of her back, the crotch of her jeans.

They met up again the next week, and the next. On their fourth Wednesday together, Anna invited him to her apartment where Colleen cooked Indian curry. Anna had no idea how overwhelmed Max was by every aspect of the evening: the aromas and tastes, the independence of these two young women, so certain of who they were, so confident and casual, and the fact that Colleen was as eager as Anna to engage Max in conversation. Anna had no idea that the touch of her hand on his created such a deep impact. She was erasing the whole of his life and rewriting it.

The evening became a delicate journey. Both Anna and Max knew where it would lead, but the path was a mystery. Anna brushed her hand across Max's shoulders as she sat down to the table. He brushed her hair behind her ear when he couldn't see her eyes. During dinner, they began to finish each other's sentences. After dinner, Colleen left for the night. Max put plates in the sink. Anna reached around him to turn on the water, pressing her breasts against his side. He turned and kissed her. She kissed him back and felt his heart pound.

If Max had shown any sign of loving his wife, Anna wouldn't have been able to be with him. But she had seen him with Betsy and thought the woman was void of heart. Their movements were not as a couple but as unrelated creatures forced to share the same space. In that observation, Anna found permission to step in.

"It's OK," she said, and held his face in her hands, looking into his eyes, reflecting his gentle smile with her own. He kissed her again, long and slow. When she said she wanted him to spend the night he pulled away. "It's OK," she said again, and took his hand, leading him to her bedroom.

Her smile, a cross between confidence and temptress, lured him on. Her bedroom was cozy with books stacked everywhere, clothes draped over a chair, her dresser cluttered with books, jewelry and cosmetics. Her robe and a collection of scarves hung from hooks on the back of the door which he saw as she stepped around him to close it. She pulled off her shoes. He stepped out of his loafers.

He watched as she moved to the bedside, slowly pulling her sweater over her head, her white bra cupping firm round breasts. He was in awe of her, so confident and comfortable with her sexuality. He did not budge, just smiled with delight.

"Your turn," she teased.

"Not yet," he said, pointing to her slacks.

"So that's how it is," she laughed, slipping them off, revealing bikini underpants.

"Knee socks," he said.

She pulled them off and stood shivering while Max unbuttoned his shirt, dropped it to the floor and unzipped his trousers, letting them fall. His boxers stood at attention.

"This is going to be fun," she said, and with that, Anna yanked out of her underwear. He slid out of his boxers and their bodies met, hands groping, mouths meshing. Belly to belly they fell to the bed. He could hardly believe how willing she was, how eager her kiss was, how his heart pounded, how he was inside her so quickly, how her legs wrapped around him, how they held on so tight, how she moaned with his every thrust, and he held out as long as he could, but it was all too much, too strong, too erotic, and he finished too quickly, like great crashing waves, feeling like he'd never really had sex before, not until this time, with this woman.

Afterward they crawled under the covers. Max wrapped around her, holding her close, catching his breath. He said he could do better.

Anna grinned. "Why do men always think we're grading them?" She rolled to face him.

Max couldn't stop looking at her, her eyes so relaxed and soft. Betsy's features never softened. She was a tense creature with hands like restless insects, a mouth that twitched with any effort to smile, and eyes never inviting, or forgiving, or loving.

Lying with Anna, his body temporarily spent, he felt a peacefulness he didn't think possible. It was contentment. When she smiled at him he knew he was in love for the first time in his life.

She pushed her pillows up against the headboard and sat up. The sheet and blanket rested against her hips, exposing her breasts to the chill of the room.

Max sat up on the edge of the bed, the sheet tight to his groin. Glancing over to Anna's nakedness, he stood, letting the sheet fall off his body, and walked to the bathroom. He hadn't exposed himself to Betsy after the wedding night, after she turned her face in disgust. Returning to Anna, the covers now tight to her shoulders, he walked tall and proud, pleased to watch her watch him. He climbed back in next to her.

"You're in great shape," she said.

"I'm just lean. There's a difference."

They made love again, this time less frantic.

He asked Anna how Jimmy would take this transgression.

She laughed out loud. "Jimmy? He's gay. Didn't you know? He's been my closest friend since we were little, and the sweetest person I've ever known. We pretend to be together. James Sr. is such a shit. The pretense keeps him at bay."

Max tried not to look uncomfortable. "He's a homosexual?"

"Yeah. If Senior knew the truth, well, like I said. He's a real shit. And we only call him Jimmy around family. To everyone else, he's James. He hates being called Jimmy – or worse, Junior."

"I see," he said, but he didn't. Not really. "I should be going. I'm already late leaving."

"No sweat," she said, kissing him quickly before getting up, walking across the room, and slipping into her robe. "Next week, you stay the night." She grinned before disappearing down the hall into the bathroom.

As Max got dressed, he suffered a momentary lapse of confidence, like what they'd just done was wrong, a mistake, one he'd be made to pay for at some point. He wouldn't allow himself to believe freedom was real. Then Anna came back, leaned on the door jam, and grinned.

"Do you believe we just did that?" she said. "Are you OK?"

"Do I not look OK?"

"You look a little, uh, shell-shocked maybe?"

"Do I?" Her acknowledgment of his feelings, that he even had feelings, was enough to calm his anxiety. "I'm good. More than good."

Max forced himself to leave Anna's apartment. The smell of her on his skin almost made him turn around and go back to her. He thought about the way her hips rose to meet him, how she sighed and whimpered and shouted his name, how her mouth had been so eager to meet his.

Back in Edgewater, he stood in the hall watching Betsy sleep. Unable to settle down, he showered in the guest bath with thoughts of making love to Anna. He couldn't stop smiling. He felt young.

Unwilling to sleep in the same room with his wife, Max sprawled out on the couch downstairs. A photograph on the mantle caught his eye. Ellen and Howard looked straight at him from their sterling silver frame. He turned off the lamp but could still see them in the ambient light. He got up and turned the picture. He didn't need to be reminded Anna was two years younger than his daughter.

In the morning, he told Betsy he added an evening class and he'd be staying in East Lansing every Wednesday, at least during the winter when weather might make roads dangerous. And he may also have to go up on Saturdays. Betsy didn't protest.

Up to that point in her life, Anna had slept with a handful of men, all young and enthusiastic. The experiences had nothing to do with love so much as experimentation. As lovers, they'd been rambunctious and in a hurry, leaving her disappointed. Unlike them, Max was kind and patient, aside from their first time when neither of them showed any restraint. She understood finally why having sex was called making love. He made her feel cherished.

Over the course of the winter, Anna introduced Max to other intimacies, showing him that sex was not relegated to the missionary position. Such primal, raw passion was all new to him. Her gasps and moans brought a satisfaction he'd never known. Sex with Anna was like being reborn. Every time.

CHAPTER 11

The Affair

Max and Anna were together every Wednesday and weekend throughout winter and spring. There was no talk of future. No plans or complications. They were happy, something Max still couldn't get used to.

He felt like a fraud around Carleton, pretending not to know Anna was about to finish her Masters. He was certain Carleton, more than anyone else, would notice a change in him, sense his buoyancy. But Carleton, by then officially CEO, was stressed out over union negotiations and other problems Bert Hamilton left behind when he so abruptly retired. Carleton dropped out of the bowling league and rarely made the bi-weekly bridge night. Though Max missed him, it was easier not seeing him. Fewer chances to slip up.

In mid-April, Colleen moved out to take a job in Cleveland. Max offered to pick up the rent to keep Anna there. She refused.

When Max showed up the following Wednesday, Anna thought he seemed distant. He didn't take his tie off.

Didn't even loosen it. He was quiet all through dinner He didn't reach for her as he usually did. There were no soft glances.

Max felt the static as soon as he stepped through the door. Anna's movements were quicker, her shoulders were high, her voice pinched, her eyes tight. Dinner was excruciatingly silent.

"When were you going to tell me?" he finally said. "Or was I just supposed to come up here next week to find you gone?"

Her eyes would not meet his. "Daddy told you."

He hated when she called Carleton daddy. It sounded childish, reminding him how young she was. "He mentioned something yesterday. Before he left for the airport."

"Do you trust me?"

"What kind of a question is that?"

"When Mom and Dad come up for my graduation . . ."

"When did you decide to walk for your Masters?"

"Seemed important to them, so I'm doing the graduation thing. Again."

She said it with a coy grin, like a child telling a lie and Max was again reminded of her youth.

"And they're going to move me out," she said. "Back home to Edgewater. For a little while."

"How's your dad going to do that? He's on the West Coast for two weeks."

"He's flying back and . . ."

"Of course. He's flying back. I get it."

Max was dismissive. Anna bristled.

"So, this is over then," he said. "Whatever this was, is, it stops. That's what you're saying."

"No," she snapped. "But the way you're acting, it may as well be. Nothing has to end. I love you. Don't you know that?"

"I don't think you know what real love is."

"That's just mean."

"Look, Anna. I'm not going to go sneaking around Edgewater to see you." Max stood up and looked at her with a contempt he didn't know he was capable of toward her. "I don't know how to do this anymore. Not until this moment. Here. Now. Did I feel we were doing anything wrong. I was wrong. We were wrong."

"Max! Don't say that."

"I'm not built for this," he said, grabbing his coat and duffle, walking out her door. If anyone else had done what he did, lie to his family and best friend, sneak off every week to sleep with a woman half his age, he'd have passed judgment on the man with harsh recrimination. Yet he had held himself above reproach until this moment in which all his joy, exposed as delusion, became tawdry and shameful.

"Max!" she called after him. "Don't leave now. Let me explain." He kept walking. "Max! Please!"

Unwilling to turn back to her or respond, he strode to his car and drove off feeling a fool to think anything with Anna would last. For a few months, he'd felt young again, vibrant. Now he'd been slingshot back to reality. He would go home. To his wife. To his sobering, pitiful life. He made it as far as Kalamazoo and got a room for the night.

Anna flew to Baltimore the next day, surprising James outside the hospital. "You look exhausted," she told him.

"I've been on shift for thirty-two hours straight. What's your excuse?"

She wanted to walk to his apartment, but he hailed a cab. "Been on my feet long enough," he groaned.

As they arrived at the apartment, Martin was just leaving. A handsome man in his late twenties, he swept Anna up in his arms and kissed her on the cheek. "Lovely to see you, darling, but I have places to be and people to charm." He kissed James on the mouth and disappeared down the hallway.

"Love you," Anna said.

"I love you too," Martin hollered from the elevator as the doors closed.

"Are you sure your parents still don't know?" Anna asked James.

"Of course they don't. And I intend to keep it that way. Can you imagine Senior explaining a gay son?" James laughed it off, but she could see the resentment simmering behind his bloodshot eyes.

Anna scrounged around for something to eat while he took a shower. Over a plate of scrambled eggs, she told him she had something to help with his parents. "You won't like it," she said. "but we can both benefit. It can get your folks off your back about there being no girlfriends in your life and I …" she stopped short. "Well, I need a husband. Pretty quick, actually. Interested?" She looked at him with a pleading smile.

"I thought so," he said with a wide grin. He traced the length of her arm with his index finger. "You're pregnant, aren't you? I can see it in your capillaries."

"You cannot," she laughed.

"Well? Who's the daddy?"

"You can't ask me that. Promise me. No questions. Not yet."

He shook his head and lit a cigarette. "Christ, Anna. I don't want to get married. I don't."

"I know. Either do I. But think about it. You can live your life the way you want to, and I'll be your cover." She scowled. "You really should stop smoking. Nasty habit."

"See? You're already nagging me." He took an extra long drag, then snuffed it out. "And what about Martin?"

"Nothing has to change."

"Everything will change. He lives here, Anna."

"Technically, he lives next door. He does still lease the other apartment, doesn't he?"

"Yes, but…"

"Look. We'll figure it out." She leaned in, forcing him to look her in the eyes. "I'm not going to mess up your life with Martin," she explained. "You and I have been best friends forever. I hold no expectations of you. I'll make life at home pleasant while you finish your residency. I'll cook and clean."

"Martin does that. At least he pays for that."

"Fine. I'll just lay around and read and grow fatter by the week. We'll work it out. I'll have the kid, and one day, when you feel like telling your parents who you really are, we'll get a divorce. Like I said. We can both win."

"They won't buy it. Mumps, remember? No sperm."

"Don't you see? That's our ace in the hole. They will believe because everybody wants to believe in miracles. And what are they going to do, try to prove you wrong?"

"And the father? You're cutting him out? That's not like you."

"It's complicated."

"Oh, fuck all, Anna. He's married, isn't he."

Anna rolled her eyes. "It's so much worse than that," she said, about to tell him everything, but he stopped her cold.

"You're out of your fucking mind. I'm going to bed," he said. "To sleep. For forty-eight hours till I have to go back on shift. You can take all this up with Martin when he comes back." He went to his bedroom and closed the door. Hard.

"It doesn't have to be a big affair," she hollered to him. "Hell, we can elope."

The next week was the first Wednesday in months that Max was not out of town. Coming home from the office, he found Betsy at the kitchen counter strewn with boxes, cans, and jars. She jumped when he came in.

"I forgot what to cook on Wednesday," she said.

He couldn't comprehend how something so simple could be such a problem. "We can eat out."

"I eat a peanut butter sandwich on Wednesdays because you're gone on Wednesdays," she said. "You go out."

"Don't be silly. Come on. We'll go out for a nice dinner."

"I'm not silly! And I'm not going anywhere!"

Happier without her than with her, he headed out to the Sandbox. The first beer was for washing down the grease bomb of a burger. The second and third were to help get the thought of Anna out of his head. She was at Carleton and Jeanne's, less than a mile away. The shot of bourbon was to keep him from going up to their front door. He couldn't call her. She hadn't called him. As mad as he was at her, he needed her. He wanted her. He couldn't comprehend how she could so summarily toss him aside.

When he found his way back home, Betsy was watching television. His presence startled her and she shouted at him for scaring her. He reminded her he wouldn't be staying in East Lansing anymore. She turned her attention back to the TV.

When Wednesday rolled around again, Betsy told him to eat somewhere else. The bartender at the Sandbox put a beer on the bar as Max walked through the door. "Had a hunch," he said as Max sat down. "So, it's Fridays and Wednesdays now?"

"Fridays and Wednesdays," Max said.

"I got a nice rib eye in the back. Sound good?"

Max nodded and pushed the beer aside.

"Goin' straight to bourbon, eh? You got it." He poured Max a shot. Max threw it back. He poured another. Max threw it back and slid the beer back in front of him.

"Well, alrighty then," said the bartender, heading to the kitchen.

A week later, after eating his steak and downing two shots and a beer, Max went home to find Betsy lying on the couch in front of the television. His presence startled her yet again, and she shouted at him yet again. He reminded her he wouldn't be staying in East Lansing any more. She turned her attention back to the TV.

Max picked up the day's mail and went into his den. One item in particular blindsided him.

Carleton and Jeanne Post
request the honor of your presence
at the wedding of their daughter
Anna Eileen Post
to
James Carson Baldwin II
June 4, 1966
Little Stone Church
1590 Cadotte Ave, Mackinac Island, MI
Reception to follow at the Grand Hotel

He poured a glass of bourbon, hoping to dull his rage. And another to drown his confusion.

CHAPTER 12

The Wedding

Baldwin hijacked the wedding. He made it big. Mackinac Island big. It became a three-day event for some, two days for others, depending on where they fit into the food chain. Baldwin paid for it all.

Max had no intention of participating in the charade until Carleton insisted. "Max," he said. "Come on, I need you there. It's going to be crazy town with Baldwin running the show. You'll be in charge of my sanity. You're in my foursome the day before the ceremony so bring your clubs."

He could have refused his friend easily and without animosity. And it would have been the better thing to do. But Max craved sight of Anna. Under any circumstance. He needed to hear her voice. He needed to touch her. His heart raced just thinking about the possibility. He had to know why she quit him, why she was marrying James. There was something behind it. He knew as much. Probably some scheme to protect James, a ruse for Senior's sake. That was as much as he could come up with. She chose helping James over loving him. Maybe it wasn't over. Maybe there was a future for him after all. He had to know. He had to go.

June can be a tricky month weather-wise in Northern Michigan. It's just as likely to snow as hit seventy. But James Baldwin Sr. would not tolerate ill-behaved weather for his big affair. The sun shone bright. It was a comfortable sixty-seven degrees.

Carleton begged off the golf outing and sent Max out with strangers. They were coming off the ninth green to board the carriage to the back nine when Max saw Anna through the woods waving to him. He told the others his shoulder was bothering him and to play through without him. When their carriage was out of sight, he went to her.

"I'm so glad you came," she said with one of her huge smiles. She reached out to hug him but he stepped away.

"What the hell?" was all he could come up with.

"I'm pregnant, Max."

"You're what?" His brain tripped.

"Max, darling? We're having a baby."

"You and Jimmy? But you said . . ."

"No, silly. You and me. We're having a baby."

Max's eyes welled up. His arms automatically pulled her tight to his chest. "We'll leave right now. I'll get you off the island. We'll leave everyone behind and . . ."

"No," she whispered. It slipped out too quietly to be heard. She pulled back. "No, Max. We have to think about the baby."

"I am thinking about the baby."

"Oh, don't you see? So many people would be hurt. Think of my parents, and Betsy. James. And Ellen."

"What the hell, Anna?" Max shouted.

"I tried to tell you at the apartment, but you shot out of there so fast..."

"How hard could it have been? Two words. I'm pregnant!"

"Don't yell at me!"

Max had never been so torn by anything. "All I care about is you. You can't get married. I'll take care of everything. It will work out. I'll . . ."

"No. We have to be patient," she pleaded.

"What do you mean? You can't go through with this wedding."

Anna laughed at him. "But the wedding is *how* we manage this. Patience, my love. I have a plan."

"A plan?" Max asked, his temper rising. "This is a plan?"

"Trust me," she said, placating him. "You'll see. It will be fine."

"What's fine about you getting married and moving to Baltimore? You'll be so far away."

"You'll come see me. Whenever you can."

"How . . ."

A whistle pierced the air and Anna bolted away. "I have to go," she said. "Someone's coming. I love you!"

In a heartbeat, she was out of his arms, disappearing through the woods. Max followed her until Martin stepped out from behind a tree to block his way. "No, Max. She's right. She has a plan. You have to let her go."

Max tried to push past him but Martin held him by the arm.

"Who the hell are you?" Max said, yanking free.

"A friend." He put out his hand to shake. Max reluctantly took it. "Believe me, Max, I'm not any happier about this than you are."

"You don't know shit."

"Oh, I know a lot more about it than you do." He made sure he had Max's full attention before saying any more. "I am a friend of the groom. The same way you're a friend of the bride." He gave Max a moment to get the point. "James Jr. and I live together. In Baltimore. Dear adorable Anna has it all figured out. She thinks her plan gives all of us time to get ourselves organized without throwing everyone into a tizzy. I think it's bullshit, but I didn't get a vote."

Max stood in silence, his expression growing ever more sinister. Martin tried to talk him down. "She said you'd need time to adjust, that you'd be feeling left out of things. And, yes, I'd say that would be understating it a bit."

"You and Jimmy."

"Ah, there you're getting it. And it's James, actually. Jimmy as a name is insufferable, don't you think?"

"I need a drink," Max said. "Join me?"

"If only I could. I'm the best man if you can believe it. Lots to do. Must make my presence felt. And wait till you see the lovely piece of arm candy I've invited. Magnificent creature."

"You're standing up with him. When he gets married. To Anna."

"Yes. Isn't it the most ridiculous thing ever? Life can be so entertaining, don't you think?"

"I am not entertained."

Martin patted his shoulder. "I have to go now. Are you going to be OK?"

"Honestly? I have no idea."

"Think of it as theatre!" Martin hollered, jogging down the road.

Max steadied himself on a tree. He suddenly felt old. Three young shits just turned his life into a farce. If he had the balls, he'd get Anna, take her off the island and convince her that honesty was the best approach. But he hadn't been honest with anyone since the first time he saw her at the foot of the stairs in Baldwin Cottage. He let her believe he could go on indefinitely seeing her on the side when all he really wanted to do was leave his family and marry her.

Their affair, the lying, the sneaking away, was hard enough for Max to live with. But this? Lie upon lie upon lie was not in his wheelhouse. Yet, there was a child coming. It would be a new start and he was already so in love with it he thought his chest might burst. He retreated to a bar in town, away from the wedding people, and drank. Heavily.

The next time Max saw Anna, she was dressed in an understated wedding gown, climbing down from a white fairy princess carriage drawn by a team of white horses, their heads adorned with huge white feathers. He watched from the park as she disappeared into a tiny stone church surrounded by six bridesmaids, all dressed in clouds of yellow taffeta. Max couldn't bear to watch the sham ceremony. What followed was a grand procession of wedding party and guests traipsing behind the bridal carriage, up a hill, dodging road apples.

The opulence of the flower-drenched tables occupying the expansive lawn of the Grand Hotel, the crystal and silver, the bandstand and bar, the black waiters in white jackets and white cotton gloves, the scores of people milling about in their formal wear, was all so absurd, Max had to laugh. Martin was right. It was pure theatre. He stood on the long porch of the Grand observing it all from the fringes. He threw back a double shot of bourbon as Anna threw her bouquet to a gaggle of arms dancing above a sea of fluffy dresses.

He noticed Carleton walking away from a table occupied by three sedate people, one of them a young man with stringy shoulder length hair. Drink in hand, Carleton looked somewhat sour for a father-of-the-bride. Max caught his eye and lifted his empty glass as if to toast. Carleton rolled his eyes, lifted his glass high, then guzzled it. He motioned to the stairs and the two men met half way.

"Some party you're throwing here, Carleton," Max muttered. "Who was that you were talking to?"

"My sister and her mortician husband. We see them, what, every seven or eight years? The one with the long hair?" Carleton said. "My nephew. Going to school on the six-year plan when he isn't protesting the war. His brother moved to Saskatchewan right after the lottery. His birthday pulled a four."

"Can't say I blame him. It's not the war we fought."

"Don't get me started. Over there," Carleton said, pointing, "that redhead twirling?"

Max looked around until he saw a woman spinning and falling into a man's arms.

"Jeanne's niece. She's only thirty and that's husband number three. Her sister is somewhere out around Seattle doing God knows what. That tall gentleman in the pale gray suit is Jeanne's older brother.

Widower. His kids aren't here. One's trying to break into the theatre in New York and the other is living in a commune somewhere in Oregon. Our country is going to hell if they're the next generation in charge."

A woman's cackle rose. "That would be Baldwin's sister. Inane woman. Enamored of her brother's success." Carleton grabbed two drinks off a passing tray, handing one to Max. "I had nothing to do with this shindig. It's all Baldwin. Personally? I've never seen anything so ludicrous in my life."

"Well, I'm relieved to hear you say that."

They each took a long draw from their drinks, wincing. "What was this?" Max asked, looking at the glass.

"Damned if I know."

Max looked around for somewhere to put it. Carleton took it and dropped both glasses into the bushes with a grin.

They perused the crowd of overdressed ladies who acted as if they were on a Hollywood sound stage with their exaggerated smiles and sweeping gestures.

"You'd think Baldwin was trying to prove a point or something," Carleton said.

Max took a breath to speak. It could have been the perfect opportunity to spill the whole ugly truth. But looking at Carleton who seemed overwhelmed, yet somehow coping with the day, Max kept quiet.

"Fanciest shotgun wedding I've ever been to," Carleton said.

Max was stunned.

"Yeah," Carleton said, his face deadpan. "She's pregnant. Jeanne's thrilled."

"And you?" Max asked.

"I don't know. Sort of always thought their relationship was platonic. More like siblings. Guess you just never know."

"Yeah. You never know," Max said. "Well, I'm out of here. Congrats, pal. Thanks for the invite."

"I'd leave if I could, believe me. Ah, but look down there," he said, waving to Jeanne. "Seems my presence is required. At least she's having fun. Thanks for coming, Max. Was good to have someone so grounded to help me through this thing." With that, Carleton went back into the fray.

The fraudulence of it all was more than Max could stomach. He left on the four o'clock ferry to Mackinaw City. Too late to make the drive home, he bought a bottle, got a room, and stared out the window to the island, overwhelmed with a sense of rage and possession. Anna was his. The baby was *his*. Who the hell were they, all those other people, coming between him and everything he loved? By the time he sobered up enough to kidnap her, the ferries stopped running for the night.

CHAPTER 13

Baltimore

While James and Martin had adjacent apartments, they lived in James's. By the time Anna moved in, Martin had moved all his clothes and treasures next door. Though James slept there with Martin, all his clothes and belongings stayed with Anna in case anyone came snooping unexpectedly. It only happened once. Baldwin knocked on her door midday, in town for a meeting or some lame excuse. She declined his offer of lunch, saying she was too tired, but invited him to wait for James to come home. Senior left nearly as soon as he arrived. He never showed up again.

Over the next few months, things settled down as routine filled in. Max told Betsy he was still mentoring at MSU, his excuse for being gone on weekends. Every Friday he lit out of work and boarded a puddle jumper to Detroit, then on to Baltimore. Betsy's lack of interaction made it easy on him. Had she confronted him, shouted, shown any sign of caring about their life together, he might have been roused to feel something. But she didn't. Betsy never questioned how he spent his time and he never asked how she spent hers. As Max's world expanded, he had no idea Betsy's was contracting into a self-imposed solitary confinement.

Max's time with Anna was sweeter than anything he thought possible. "Is it greedy of me to want more than this," he whispered as she slept, his hand cradling her rounding belly. In those moments, he knew she was right to hide what they had as long as they could. There was no room between them for anyone else.

In the dark, holding Anna, feeling new life rolling in her belly, Max was young again. They made love with such hunger they laughed afterward. He loved watching her walk naked through the apartment, her stride changing as the months went on, as her hips opened, her body making room for this new being she was creating. He was in awe of her.

Anna wrote a series of essays during her pregnancy, using Max as a sounding board for her more radical theories. He loved watching her work an idea, defend it, then tear it to shreds after talking it out. He only had to listen, and play devil's advocate. Two of her pieces were accepted for publication. A third was rejected with an invitation to send future work.

Max fed off her energy and ambition and came up with a redesign of the clothes dryer that was about to go into production, a change that would not only make it less expensive to produce, but offer two more settings for the consumer. Carleton and the team were so impressed, they reengineered to the new specs. Max got a huge bonus.

November came around. Leaving Anna was more difficult. She was due the end of December. Tensions were high. They argued. Anna began to doubt her plan.

Max took advantage of her lapse to insist they come clean. He would leave Betsy, move to Baltimore, and marry her. It would be rough on the families, but the new baby would smooth things over. "Babies do that, don't they?" he pleaded.

"My child will not be used as a tool," Anna shouted.

"Our child. Our child," Max reminded her. "How can you expect me to stay away from you? From the baby? How do you expect me to pretend around your father? Think about it, Anna." Max glared at her. "Let me play it out for you. Your dad comes into my office beaming with pictures of his grandchild, boasting about his grandchild. *MY* child. How do I do that? It's been rough enough just getting you through the pregnancy without saying something I shouldn't to him. You get to be here with James and Martin in your cozy, little hideout. I'm the one out in the real world, Anna. And I can't say anything to anyone. Not a single person! I'm the one having to carry this lie you insist on perpetuating!" He grabbed his overcoat and left the apartment.

"You can't leave now," Anna shouted down the hall after him.

He shouted back to her. "You should be used to watching me leave by now!"

After a brisk walk around the block, Max returned to find Martin comforting a sobbing Anna as James took her pulse.

"Please," she begged Max. "Don't do this now. Give it more time. I can't go into labor with all this hanging over me. I can't do it. I can't!"

Max panicked. "You're in labor?" He dropped his coat to the floor and knelt at her knees.

James assured everyone she was not in labor, but warned the quarreling couple to shut up and make up before her blood pressure blew up.

Tempers settled. Anna went to bed and slept the rest of the afternoon. Sunday was peaceful, with no mention of changing the plan. Max flew home in the evening as he always did. Arriving in Detroit for his puddle jumper to Edgewater around seven, he ran into Carleton catching the same flight. Max couldn't hide his shock.

"Don't sweat it, Max," Carleton said, apparently not at all surprised.

"What do you mean?" Max said.

"They're boarding," Carleton said. "Come on." He looked exhausted as they walked out into a gusty wind to the plane, their coats flying open. "It's going to be a bumpy ride," he said to a stewardess.

"Good evening, gentlemen," she said. "I'm afraid you're right, Mr. Post."

The two men took seats next to each other.

Carleton looked out the window. Lights of the terminal illuminated a flurry of snowflakes. "I know what you're doing," he said,

Max felt his throat constrict.

The stewardess made her pass down the aisle, telling Max to buckle up.

"You're having an affair, aren't you?" Carleton asked, turning to Max. "I know you go away every weekend."

Max could barely breathe. "What?"

"Friday nights. I've seen you catch the flight I come in on."

Max closed his eyes, searching for words, wondering how in the hell to explain himself.

"You never saw me. That's how I knew. One track mind. Blinders." He smiled a little, "Can't say I blame you. Honestly. Betsy is a handful."

If ever Max wanted to come clean with Carleton, that was the moment. Instead, he confessed to seeing someone.

"Good for you," Carleton said. "It's been evident these last few months."

Max did nothing to encourage the conversation.

The plane took off, its engines droning with the effort. Carleton said Betsy reminded him of an uncle he used to have. "Dementia took over his life. Interrupt his routine, and he lost it."

Max brushed it off without response. He had, to that point, tried to tell himself Betsy was immune to the family insanity. His certainty, however, was slipping.

"Whoever your woman is," Carleton said, "you deserve some happiness, my friend."

The rest of the thirty-minute flight was quiet until something crossed Max's mind. "You're not having . . ." he asked Carleton.

"Me? An affair? God, no. Jeanne is the best part of my life. It's that deal with Baker in Kansas City. I spent the weekend with him trying to hammer it out."

"Are we buying them out?"

"No. Too much debt. They came to us too late and want too much. They'll be under by Easter."

"And then?"

Carleton sighed and cocked his head. "We'll get the factory at liquidation."

"Poor bastard."

"Yup."

Anna was due on the 28th of December. Max couldn't manufacture a reason to be out of town over Christmas weekend. He was a wreck, talking to her twice a day, sometimes more. He flew out midweek, hoping to be there when the baby was born. He flew home on New Year's Eve. He called her every hour on Sunday, January first. And Monday. And Tuesday.

James called Max at six in the morning on Wednesday. Anna was in labor.

Max caught the early puddle jumper, barely made his connection in Detroit, and was at the hospital by half past eleven. He'd missed the birth by only a few minutes. James met him in the waiting room, all smiles. "It's a girl, Max." They embraced with all the love of a father and son. "You have a daughter," he whispered. Martin sat in a corner, tears streaming down his face. James said it would be a few minutes before Max could see Anna and the baby. He left the room, and Max went to Martin.

"It's a fucking miracle," Martin said, smiling at Max. "Just a fucking miracle."

"She was in a hurry," Anna said to Max. "I told you we'd make it work." She handed him the newborn. No joy was ever so powerful.

"Hello, Katherine," he whispered to the dozing infant. "Did we settle on that? On Katherine?"

Anna smiled and winced a bit.

"You OK?" he asked.

"I'm fine. She's a Katherine. Definitely."

Anna put off calling her parents as long as she could, giving Max another day with Katherine. She asked that they wait until she was discharged to arrive. They didn't listen.

As soon as the call came, Carleton loaded the four new grandparents into the company plane and showed up at the hospital, very nearly running into Max in the hallway. Max called James to hightail it to the hospital to play happy daddy as Martin arrived with a giant panda in his arms about to go into Anna's room. But when he saw Senior and Trixie, he went straight to the nurses' station.

In his most charming smile, Martin clued the nursing staff into the ruse. "That old man over there on the pay phone looking terrified," he said, "that's the real daddy. He's calling in the gorgeous young man they all think is the daddy. So, no slip-ups, Darlings. And I was never here." He flashed them a broad, well-dimpled smile.

"Not our first rodeo," one of them said. "The gorgeous young man's name?"

"James. I mean, Jimmy." He rolled his eyes. "They call him Jimmy."

One of the younger nurses perked up. "You mean the one with those beautiful blue eyes? He's delicious!"

Martin grinned and nodded.

"I've got this," she said and went directly to Anna's room. "Where's that handsome hubby of yours?" she said. Anna's eyes flew open wide.

"We all love his baby blues," she said to the grandparents. "We're all a little jealous. Jimmy's absolutely gorgeous." She winked at Anna and left. Martin caught Anna's eye from around the panda in the hall.

Max retreated to Martin's for the night, hoping to see Anna and Katherine again, but it was too risky. Once

Anna and the baby were settled in the apartment, Jeanne didn't leave. She was going to stay the week. It took everything he had to leave town. Martin was no happier. So long as the parents were in town, he had to stay in hiding. Nothing about the arrangement made anyone but unsuspecting grandparents happy.

As weeks passed, Anna did her best to keep her mother's visits to a minimum. Her dad was too swamped at work to make the trip. Jeanne spent three days midweek for the first six weeks, giving Anna much needed rest. It was a comfort for Martin as well. An infant in the mix took a lot of getting used to. While James agreed to Anna's plan, his schedule was exhausting enough without losing sleep to an infant demanding to be fed every two hours.

Max traveled to Baltimore every weekend. Babies, however, have a way of drawing other people in. Colleen, Anna's roommate from State, started showing up unannounced, eating into Max's private time. Once Anna suggested he think of her like a sister, he resigned himself to sharing.

About the time Katherine started walking, Colleen got a grant to study native culture in Alaska and disappeared from their lives.

As Katherine thrived, Anna and Max blossomed into the best possible versions of themselves. By the time Katherine was two, Anna was teaching a class in literary criticism at Johns Hopkins while she worked on a PhD. Max went into overdrive, and came up with a revolutionary re-design for a built-in icemaker, and Hamilton began manufacturing refrigerators. He was made executive vice president heading up the new division. James finished his residency and took a post at Johns Hopkins Children's Center as a General Pediatric Surgeon.

Martin thrived as Katherine's caretaker while the others were busy going about their successful lives. He cooked extraordinary meals for everyone and took pride in making sure their lives were as comfortable as possible, running both households, managing the cleaning and laundry services. They were a family of five happily reunited whenever Max could make it to town.

Though it was not a convenient arrangement, in many respects, it was perfection. Except for Max. Betsy was falling apart.

Betsy had taken to shouting at the television because the wrong program came on. Then she'd yell at Max like it was his fault. He tried to tell her she was confused about what day it was, but she insisted everyone else was wrong. He finally stopped arguing, telling her the network must have changed the schedule. It usually settled her. As months passed, she grew more subdued and more easily confused.

A few weeks after Katherine turned tree, Betsy called Max at work to say the car had been stolen. He found it in the parking lot at the grocery store. She'd just forgotten where she parked. When she couldn't tell him how it came to have a big dent in the fender, he took away her keys. Max arranged for groceries to be delivered. In April, she put laundry detergent in the dryer with a load of clothes. He flipped the breaker on both the washer and dryer and arranged for laundry service. He arranged for a cleaning lady to come in twice a week. Martin had taught him well. It was mid-July when Betsy almost set the house on fire, leaving an oven mitt on a hot burner. He began cooking dinner every night, flipping the stove breaker off when he wasn't using it. Every time he went to Baltimore, he double-checked the breakers and left a stack of sandwiches in the fridge for Betsy. Nothing was going to keep him from Katherine and Anna.

CHAPTER 14

Archie

The damp chill over Janet's first weeks on Mackinac was relentless, like the island testing her resolve to stay. Grandpa Max was heavy on her mind, a presence made stronger by rainy days. When she was a child, they used to walk for hours alone together, past the cemeteries, to a waterfall in the woods, to a lookout over the straits. Her favorite walks with him were on drizzly days when everyone else stayed inside, and it was like the whole island was theirs alone. Without intent, she often found herself on the same loop, guided by him still.

Her mother never did well on gray days. Michigan winters were hard on Ellen, when dreary weeks strung together, one after another. She often retreated to her bed to wait it out, a pall hanging over the house. Food was her only solace, devouring bags of cookies, salty chips, sugary drinks, anything to give comfort.

Opposite of her mother, Janet found rainy days a comfort, like a cozy blanket.

Moving to the shore of Lake Michigan after college showed Janet the beauty in gray days. She reveled in rivers of cool air flowing from water to shore, and marveled at subtle hues blurring water and sky. She liked how wet sand, like freshly poured concrete, left only slight indentions underfoot.

While most of the cottage had been thoroughly scrubbed, the stairs and landing upstairs needed attention. After taking each step one by one, scrubbing on her hands and knees, Janet went for a walk while they dried. She ended up on an unfamiliar trail through deep woods. A man on a big black horse approached from a distance at a canter. He slowed to a walk as he drew near and stopped in front of her. The animal was equestrian perfection. His rider, tall in the saddle, wearing shiny black riding boots, jeans, and a white broadcloth shirt under a sports jacket, was nearly as exquisite as the horse.

"This is a riding trail," he said as his horse dropped a load of road apples.

"I see," Janet responded. "I didn't realize." She stepped aside, and the horse walked by, breaking into a canter again, disappearing around a bend. But something about the man lingered with her, an uneasiness, a familiarity she didn't understand. She couldn't possibly know him from anywhere, yet she knew his face and voice. It stirred a yearning that didn't make sense. It was like a memory she couldn't possibly have had.

Upon returning to the cottage, she stoked the fire and started dinner, fragrant garlic imbuing the kitchen with aromas of home. She cut fresh tomatoes into the pan, covered it, and set it to simmer. Wrapping herself in a quilt, she looked out through wavy poured glass windows at the last of the crocus.

Walking up from town a week later with a tote of groceries over her shoulder, Janet peered into the yards of Annex houses, hoping for possible recognition. Of the three families she saw, no eyes rose to meet hers. Like her, they ignored road people presuming them to be tourists, invasive eyes peering in on personal spaces. She saw the man from the trail brushing a horse at the stable behind Pink House. He was tall, lean, broad-shouldered, and yet again, something about him struck a chord, and Janet felt the urge to talk to him, if only to figure out why. It wasn't attraction. It was deeper, unrecognizable. As he either did not notice her or chose to ignore her, she passed by without speaking.

Arriving home, she marveled at the blue wave of forget-me-nots surging from under bushes into her yard. As she checked out a new cluster of sunflower seedlings sprouting in a corner, she heard a clutch of people on the road, pausing at the hedge opening. She refused eye contact with them.

Sunshine woke her the next morning. On the stairway, she admired the clean gleam of their pale green paint, corners no longer packed with grit. An aroma of pine oil soap lingered. The cleaning that occupied the first few weeks was finally accomplished. Yet, in the middle of the hall downstairs stood a small table. She paused for a moment, viewing it with some curiosity before deciding that as tired as she'd been the night before, she'd just forgotten to put it wherever it belonged.

With coffee in hand, she stood in the living room, trying to remember where the table might have been. It didn't seem to fit anywhere. Shrugging it off, she went outside. The air was sweet, tinged with the crispness that sometimes slipped off the cold water of the straits. *Everything is as it should be,* she thought in a rare moment of contentment.

She heard a horse approaching slowly on the road with a lazy thudding, and she glanced toward the hedgerow. A black horse came into view. She recognized it as the horse from the trail and from Pink House. And the man, so tall in the saddle, in jeans and sports jacket.

"Good morning," he said.

"Yes, it is a good morning," Janet responded with an uncharacteristic smile.

"You must be Granger," he said, stopping near her hitching post.

"I am. Janet, actually."

"Ah. I hadn't caught that much. Just the Granger and the fact that no one knows who you are. Doesn't happen up here much. Used to be everyone knew everyone and that was that." It was an honest statement without condescension.

"Not anymore," she replied.

"Right. Not anymore."

"You're from Pink House."

"I am." He resituated himself on the sleek English saddle and looked out over her head toward the cottage. "Any more coffee in there?" he asked.

"If not, I'll make more," she said, her casual manner more appropriate to old friends.

He dismounted, led the horse into the yard, and let loose the reins.

"He won't wander off, untied like that?" she asked, concerned.

"No. He might eat some grass."

"Less to mow."

"Ha. Yes. Less to mow. I like you," he said with a little snort.

"You're the only one here who does then."

He followed her through the back door into the kitchen, the hinges squealing.

"I really need to fix that," she said.

The coffee was cold, so she made fresh, pouring oily black beans into a small electric grinder and handing it to him. "Have at it," she said. He did as instructed, its whine filling the room. She liked the look of his hands, strong, confident, graceful. She'd written off many men simply because their hands were too small, or fingers too fat, or they were just plain clumsy. Good hands invariably lead to good dexterity, a sign suggesting intelligence. If his hands were any indication, this man was brilliant.

"Archie Holly," he said. "That's my name. Archie Holly."

"Sorry for you," she said.

"For Archie or Holly?"

"Both?"

Archie shrugged.

"People think holly is such a festive plant, but actually it's deadly and prickly and a bitch to work with," Janet quipped, taking the grinder from him.

"I'm none of those things. Prickly or festive. Honest."

She tried not to appear to be sizing him up as she prepped the coffee maker and turned it on, but something about him was disconcertedly too familiar, and it bothered her. She looked more closely at him, something that would have bothered most people, but not Archie. He just smiled and let her eyes roam his face. Gold flecks in his gray-green eyes caught the light. He had a strong chin with high cheekbones, the kind that come from good breeding between beautiful people. His course hair, an interesting mix of blonde and gray, was captivatingly disheveled. She surmised he was about her age with maybe a couple of years on her. Suddenly she was overcome by a yearning verging on sorrow, and she almost started to cry. She turned away from him, but not before he caught her expression.

"Are you all right?" he asked. His voice had a gentleness she was unaccustomed to.

"I feel like I should know you, but that can't possibly be, can it?" she said.

"Hardly possible, I suppose." They stood in silence as the coffee began to sputter. "So, Granger --"

"Janet," she corrected him. "It's Janet."

"Ah. Right. So, Janet," he said, stepping into the hall. Dodging the errant table, he stopped at the edge of the living room. "How do you like it here so far?"

"It's fine."

Janet watched Archie wander about the room, looking at each thing as if taking inventory.

"Coffee's done," she said, and disappeared into the kitchen, returning with two fresh mugs. "How about if we just have a real conversation," she said. "Find out what we want to find out and do away with any bullshit." The look on her face was so delightfully straightforward he could hardly refuse.

"I like my coffee black," he said smirking.

"Good, cause that's how you got it."

"I'm fourth generation islander," he said. "You're not. That's about all you need to know." It sounded like boasting but was, yet again, simply a statement of fact. The game was on. "Your turn."

"I've been coming up here every year of my life, except two."

"Got me beat. I skipped five." He looked at the stairs, glanced at her for permission, and went up. Janet followed him as he meandered room to room. "My mother and her sister like to throw parties as if they were dowager countesses," he said, peering into one of the bedrooms. "Pray you never get invited. They'll eat you alive. Same people every time. Same topics of conversation, same worn-out stories, same tired drunks stumbling back to their cottages. She'll be here in July. My mother. Are you married?"

"I've never been married. You?"

"Widower."

"Oh, gosh. That must have been awful."

"Did you just say gosh?"

"I guess. Yes."

"Interesting. Yeah, it was pretty awful, especially for the kids. She was a good woman. Hated it up here at first. My mother didn't like her much."

"The five years you skipped?"

"Just after we got married. It changed once we had the kids. They gave her something to do with herself. She's been gone four years now. Cancer."

That word on top of widower could have taken the conversation down a dark alley. But Janet had endured enough crap in her own life to not feel the necessity to delve into any of his. She let it drop. "How old are the kids?" she asked.

"Tom is 29," he said, descending the stairs. "Tina is 30. Good kids, in spite of their dad."

"You started early. Grandkids?"

"Three. Two girls, one boy," he said. "I'm older than I look."

"Enough about me," he said. "Your turn. Again."

"There's really nothing to tell. Like I told Cecelia, I am nobody of note who has done nothing of interest . . ."

"Oh, yes," he interrupted. "We all heard about that. Then you shut the door in her face."

Janet thought about explaining her faux pas, but even she wasn't sure actually how it happened. She shrugged, and he put his empty cup on the table inhabiting the hall and walked out.

She followed and watched him climb into the saddle. "Do you ride?" he asked.

"No."

"If you'd like to try it, I have an old gentleman gelding that would be very nice to you. Early in the morning or late in the evening. Too many people in between."

"I'll think about it."

He nodded to her with a smile and disappeared around the hedgerow. She heard a little *tich-tich* and rapid footfalls trailing off into the woods.

It was easy for Janet to be casual with new people, almost to the point of being cavalier. There was never anything at stake, nothing to prove, nothing to lose. She never expected people to like her so she didn't try to impress. She'd read somewhere that one of the many gripes Europeans held toward Americans was their insincerity. They smiled too much. Janet did not suffer from this problem. Her smiles were tough to come by. While the rest of the world might appreciate that aspect of her personality, those who didn't know her well found her abrupt and alienating. Whether people didn't take to her right off because of this, or that she was like this because people didn't take to her was impossible to know.

She went inside, and pulled out the notepad, registering Archie's name with the date and time they met.

Janet was an anomaly to Archie. He was used to people treating him with a certain degree of deference. Wealth and beauty, both of which he had in abundance, had that effect on people. He carried himself with an air of confidence that comes from privilege and, to a certain extent, from security borne of success. He was rarely challenged and realized early on that people generally wanted something of him and said only what they thought he'd want to hear. It was annoying, and because of it, he wrote most people off with little more than a cursory observation. What appeared to be arrogance was basically a protection mechanism.

He found Janet's response to him unique. Her near indifference was a relief.

CHAPTER 15

Blooming

Janet returned home after a long walk to find Mr. Harris watching a young man unload a steamer trunk from a dray. "Right there," Mr. Harris said. "Just inside the doors." The young man dragged it into the stable and climbed back up onto the seat. Janet called out to him, asking where it came from. He dismissed her with a shrug and said he just drove the rig. With the sound of a simple *Hep*, the horses walked off. Mr. Harris stayed behind, stepping into the yard, looking up to the hayloft, its door open wide, sun spilling over a blue straight-back chair and the stray table from the hallway.

"Not the most obvious place for a table," he said.

"I think it's my new favorite spot here," Janet said. "Especially in the morning. I carried the chair up yesterday but had no place to set my wine glass. So I took the table up."

His expression, lost and distant, went unnoticed.

"Where was it," he asked, trying to be casual. "Where'd you find the table?"

"It was in the hallway this morning. Did you bring it over before I got up. I slept in and thought I heard something downstairs."

"Wasn't me," he said, turning to walk away.

"What's in the trunk?" she asked.

"Stuff," he grumbled over his shoulder, walking away. "Everybody's always leaving stuff behind."

"This place doesn't need more stuff," she said and asked him to move it into a corner out of the way, but he just kept walking. "Places to be," he said.

Janet went up to the hayloft and sat in the late afternoon shade looking out over the garden, past the hedge, to the straits. She didn't realize how tired she was until that moment of surrender when she let the quiet in. Her mind drifted into a lazy stream of consciousness, floating out over the water to Round Island, back to the lighthouse, over the vast expanse of the straits to Lake Huron. Underneath this little reverie came a muffled crunching noise from below, like a horse chewing grain, and the shuffling of hay or straw. It was a pleasant sound, comforting, until she realized there was no horse.

Too hungry and tired to delve into the trunk, she left it where it sat and went into the house to make supper. Taking a zucchini and onion from the basket, she opened a drawer for the knife. It wasn't there. It was always there. It's where she kept it. Opening every drawer in the kitchen, she found it in the last one, under the coffee pot on the other side of the room. After dinner, she washed it and consciously put it in the drawer with the cutting board.

Later that night, Janet awoke with a start, feeling as if someone was in the bedroom with her. She sat up and listened. Nothing. She poured a glass of water from the pitcher on the nightstand and noticed a light in the stable, its doors wide open. She was sure she'd closed them and didn't recall ever turning the light on. She went to the open window and listened for any sign of intruders, but the night was silent. Too awake to sleep, she slipped into her cotton robe and went downstairs.

Crossing the grass in bare feet, she was taken with the stillness of the night, her silent passage, air so still she wondered if she was awake or dreaming. Stepping into the stable, faint singing came again, *Slylark*. It stopped when she switched off the light. Waiting for her eyes to adjust to the darkness, she padded back in through the dark kitchen, sensing something she couldn't quite put her finger on, like she'd interrupted something. She headed up the steps, looking back down to the living room, seeing what seemed like faint shadows drifting about, edges blurred like looking through a fine gauze. "Yes," she said aloud. "I'm dreaming."

In the morning, remembering she left the stable doors open, she saw they were closed. She recorded the events as a dream.

Janet hadn't seen Archie again and thought about leaving a note at Pink House but decided against it. Her neighbors in the Annex had given her nothing but a cold shoulder. They didn't have time for new people, especially someone they didn't consider one of *them*. This was all conjecture on her part, but it sufficed to keep her living quietly within her hedgerow.

Without television, internet, or cell service at the cottage, what communication Janet had with her condo crew was through texts sent from the bluff and the occasional email sent from the island library computer. Proximity fueled her covey of friends, distance not so much. She missed laughing with them. She missed drinking with them. She desperately missed their presence in her life.

These privations added a layer of disconnect, one she took as a challenge. Desperate for diversion, she hit the library shelves and left with *The Great Gatsby*, *Moby Dick* and *To Kill a Mockingbird*. She flew through the first two like a student trying to finish an assignment early. She was halfway through *To Kill a Mockingbird* one night when it started to rain. One of her favorite things about the cottage was listening to rain on the roof. It was something about the pattering, and being tucked under covers. It was glorious. It was safe. Janet intended to read in bed but instead, fell asleep lulled by rolling thunder.

⌘

Janet sat at a high school desk, taking a test. All the questions were about the books she'd just read, but she didn't know the answers. She heard the teacher lecturing as she tried to write an essay about what the white whale represented to Captain Ahab. When she looked up to the front of the classroom, she was in the living room downstairs, and the teacher was behind her, speaking into her ear. *Books are not popcorn to be devoured thoughtlessly.*

⌘

The next morning, Janet recorded the dream in her notepad. She remembered it clearly. Still drizzling outside, she spent the morning on the porch reading with more care than before, sipping each word instead of taking whole gulps. Reading evolved from task to treat. She returned the first three books and picked up two. And so it was that days slipped by, her loneliness kept at bay by words and characters she came to know well.

June was colder than normal, allowing the Lilac blooms all over the island to linger. It was as if the flowers were held in suspended animation giving the illusion of time standing still. The stand of sunflowers, however, thinned by a hungry rabbit, grew taller and stronger each day.

Janet curled up with an afghan on the porch, coffee in hand, making her way through *Mrs. Dalloway*. Her frustration crawling through the first fifteen pages made her think Virginia Woolf had a mind almost as ragged as her own.

She went for more coffee, deciding to bring the whole pot out to avoid further excuses to give up on Virginia. Padding down the hallway, she heard someone speak and turned abruptly, splashing coffee from the carafe to the floor. There was no one there. From behind her, she heard more whispers and turned again, thinking it sounded like Mr. Harris.

"Mr. Harris," she called out. "Is that you? Come to fix the screen?" No one answered. Another voice startled her, sending the coffee carafe to the floor. It broke, sending glass shards and coffee to the wall.

"Oh, for chrissake," Janet grumbled. "I will not give in to this," she said out loud, grabbing the roll of paper towels from under the sink. "I am not giving in!" On the strength of that affirmation, she tried to conceive an array of rational explanations for the voices, but in the back of her mind, she was growing more certain of her future. She wrote in her notes: *The flowers are en route.*

When she went back to the porch, she couldn't concentrate enough to read. She closed the book and headed off island, hoping to find another carafe for her coffee maker.

Captain Leronge stood at the helm of the ferry doing the St. Ignace run. She knocked on the glass to his compartment, thinking he probably wouldn't remember her, but his smile said otherwise, and he motioned her in.

He asked her about her summer so far, and Janet did her best to make it sound like she was acclimating when she wasn't. "You'll get used to it," he told her, seeing through her words. He took a call from his wife just before they docked. Their conversation was simple, confirming dinner plans, their son's ball game, and his promise to get to the gutters before the next rain. The normalcy hit Janet hard. It made her miss her people. She wanted to be invited into his life and have instant acceptance into their circle of friends. But he didn't ask her to his house for dinner, or tell her where the ball field was.

He adhered to a social contract whereby he would acknowledge her by name when he saw her, give her a smile, and offer up some conversation to pass the time. She was obliged to do the same for him. It was a relationship that would appear to be genuine and meaningful without ever scratching the surface of their lives. She understood the rules and appreciated them. Sometimes, she thought as she disembarked, that's what everyone needs in order to get through, just a friendly face acknowledging their existence on the planet.

She went to a movie in St. Ignace, found a new carafe, bought groceries, and stopped at the fish market on the docks for fresh Whitefish and smoked trout.

On a chilly July morning, Janet put her breakfast bowl in the sink with all the dishes piled up from the week. Whether it was laziness or an ominous sense that this might be her last summer of relative sanity, she hadn't found motivation to clean it up until the ants arrived. There would be no more dirty dishes in the sink.
Reaching for a towel to dry her hands, she stopped short. She'd hung a yellow terry towel, but this one was white sackcloth with a blue stripe, one she'd never seen before. Anxious to find the yellow ones she yanked the towel drawer so hard it came all the way out and landed on the floor. It was packed with white and blue sackcloth towels. "God damn it!"
She charged out to the porch and curled up in the big wicker chair. Tears came on fast. Trembling wracked her core. Her mind raced to recall the last time she'd used the yellow towels, washed them, folded them, put them away in that drawer, and try as she might, there was no memory of blue and white towels. None.
Janet wondered how long she would remember who her friends were or even who she was. Her life was slipping away, and it was more than she could bear. She began to think the move to the island, breaking routine, cutting off from friends, had triggered the episodes. "What the fuck am I doing here?" she yelled.
Forcing a return to calm, she wondered if maybe there could be a coming to terms with losing her mind, a surrender to waning awareness. Is it only a need to control that keeps a person gripping at branches on the way over

the cliff? Is it really so important to maintain the count of time, how much coffee to put in the pot, how many rolls of toilet paper constitute a supply, when she ate last, or how old the eggs are, or where she lived or what year it is? Maybe sanity was overrated and relinquishing any need of it was like overcoming a craving. Her friends can just pack her off to a home when the time comes and bid farewell. Like the women before, she will lose all awareness of her life, and eventually not care.

She began to run through all the details she'd have to figure out before she was mentally incapacitated. She'd have to start visiting nursing homes to figure out where she'd have herself incarcerated.

"I am stronger than this!" she said over and over. It suddenly occurred to her that she'd pulled the wrong drawer, that the white and blue linen towels had always been there, and she'd just absent-mindedly pulled the wrong drawer. She rose from the chair and walked back into the kitchen, confident of a simple mistake. There on the floor lay the drawer. Full of yellow terrycloth towels. Shooting a look to the rack, the blue and white towel was gone. The yellow was back. She kicked the drawer across the room and ran back to the porch, curling her legs tight against her, rocking hard against the anger.

She wrote a text to Carmen: I think my flowers are beginning to bloom. Without service, it didn't go through. She deleted it.

Emotionally exhausted, she fell asleep and woke later with warm sun on her face and the sensation of being rocked in loving arms, something she had never known in her waking life.

CHAPTER 16

Leona

"Please tell me you've left the island at some point." Archie's voice sifted in through the kitchen screen door, catching Janet as she arranged peonies in a ceramic vase.

"Do you like them?" she asked, as if his presence was of no consequence.

"Yes. Very nice." He did not budge from the stoop. "Aren't you going to invite me in?"

She stepped back and waved him in with a smile.

He pulled on the door, surprised it no longer squeaked.

"I oiled it," she said.

"Well, making improvements then. So, you're keeping the place?"

She carried the vase into the living room. Archie followed, watching her every move. She had a gracefulness about her and a genuineness that drew him in. She put the flowers in the center of the dining table. It looked beautiful.

"Of course, I'm staying. Why wouldn't I?"

"It's just that you're all alone up here," he said. "Most people have a constant flow of visitors to entertain or be entertained by. I hear you haven't had any. Sounds lonely."

"People keeping tabs on me?"

"Of course."

She said she was about to have company and lots of it. In just a couple of weeks, all her friends from home would descend on the island and fill her house with wine and food. "You're invited," she said. "Whenever. Just show up."

He plopped into an easy chair, smiled, and said he'd take her up on it. Then he said he wanted to cook for her.

"At Pink House?"

"Hell no. Too many people there. I want to cook here. Later."

When she agreed, he jumped up and went to the back stoop to grab two fabric duffles of groceries.

"Are you ever going to invite me over to Pink House?"

Archie shook his head as he unpacked shrimp, wine, garlic, spices, butter, and a baguette. "They are my mother's people," he told her as he put the shrimp in her fridge. "The Thorns come from serious money. Eastern real estate, mostly. Half of them never had to work a day in their lives. Hell, more than half. I don't think you'd like them. They have a way of, well, they're snobs. My father never really fit in with them. He came from working stock."

"So, your mother was a rebel." He agreed. Janet asked if he felt like a walk, but he declined, saying he'd rather just sit. It was only noon, but she opened a bottle of cold Pino Grigio and poured some into two jelly jars. They settled into porch rockers.

"So, your mother," Janet asked. "She's a Thorn. You're a Holly. Prickly bunch, aren't you?"

"I knew you'd pick up on that. They're prickly. I'm not." He rolled his head over his shoulder and threw her a broad, sweet smile. Janet couldn't help but smile back.

"So," she said, "you were saying your mother was the rebel of the group."

"No matter how much money my dad made, it was never enough for her people because he actually got his hands dirty making it. He was a builder. I suppose, if he'd built skyscrapers or office buildings, they'd have appreciated him. But he built houses. Lots of them. Houses for the masses."

"Gawd, not *tract* houses?" Janet feigned revulsion.

"Exactly. One subdivision after another for all those families having all those babies in the '50s and '60s. Then, he built bigger ones when it was time for them to upgrade. He made a good living by anyone's standards but the uber-wealthy."

Halfway through the first bottle of wine, Janet learned that Archie was an architect. "Archie the architect," he'd said before she had the chance to tease him. His specialty was McMansions, a term he used freely, and he'd gotten rich at it. He sold the business to his partner in 2007, right before the bottom fell out of the economy. The partner tried to sue him when the company went under, but gave up when an attorney convinced him he didn't have a case. "Did I tell you that partner was my cousin?"

"You aren't the only one who works for a living then."

"Didn't mean to confuse. My generation has to work. There isn't enough to keep us all idle. I suppose when the oldies die off, there might be something left. The way they spend it? Doubtful."

When he said his cousin, the former partner, was visiting Pink House for the weekend, Janet reminded him she had several bedrooms. "You can hide out if you need to."

"Why do you think I'm cooking for you here?" He shot her a sly grin.

Finishing the wine, a breeze off the straits took away some of the humidity and heat, and it was time for a walk before dinner. Sauntering along a main path, Archie cut through the woods and led her to a lookout on a bluff. The remnants of what had once been a patio of sorts protruded from undergrowth like an ancient ruin.

"There was a house here," he told her. "A long time ago. I was a little kid when it was abandoned. I swore I'd come back and save it, but things happen. I went away to school, got married, had kids. But I remember the day I trekked back here to see how it was doing, and it was all caved in and overgrown. I still don't know why it hurt so much to see it that way. I felt like I'd betrayed something, some trust, a promise. Like it died, alone and forgotten." He got misty-eyed and then laughed at himself.

"Don't do that," Janet softly chided him.

"Don't do what?"

"Diminish the feeling. It was real, what you felt. It meant something. Don't laugh it off like it's nothing. It's dishonest."

Archie looked at her and sighed. "You're right," he admitted. "You are absolutely right."

Back at the cottage, he baked the shrimp in their shells bathed in Cajun seasoning and tons of butter. They peeled and ate them with their hands, sopping up the butter with baguettes. "Holy God," Janet moaned. "This is delicious."

A man hollered in from the porch. "Dad? You in there?"

Archie went to the door, wiping his hands with a dishtowel. His son stood on the porch with a sleepy toddler in his arms. "Hey, Tommy," Archie said quietly. "Looking for an escape?"

"Can't take it anymore," Tommy said with a soft Louisiana accent. He came in, laying the child on the couch. "When in the hell are they ever going to get over themselves. Damn, they're full of it."

Archie spread a throw over the child and kissed him on the head.

"This is Markus," he told Janet. "That's Tommy," he said, pointing the way to the liquor cabinet.

"The good stuff's in the back," Janet instructed.

Tommy eyed the shrimp and ate the last one. "Taste of home," he said.

"Beautiful little boy," Janet said.

Tommy grinned in agreement and went to wash his hands, taking the shrimp pan with him.

Archie watched their interaction. Tommy could make himself at home anywhere, and Janet accepted him with ease. But there was a distance in her graciousness, a vague tenuous hesitation Archie recognized.

A young woman appeared at the door, asking if there was room for one more. Archie waved her in. Jacqueline checked on her little boy.

"Not to worry," Tommy assured her. "He's out."

For the next couple of hours, Janet listened to Tommy and Jacqueline regale tales of their home in New Orleans. There was a melancholy in Jacqueline's voice. "We're in the Garden District. We were OK when Katrina hit, and the levees broke. We were OK, but so many of our friends lost everything. Some came back, but too many were cast to the winds, and life isn't the same anymore."

Tommy said they wondered if it ever would be. "My wife is Cajun," he boasted.

"So are you, love," Jacqueline said.

"Just a spit."

"A spit's better than nothin'," she countered. "Your mama was one-quarter Cajun."

"And her mama was half and her mama's mama full blood," Archie added.

That was plenty for Jacqueline's people to accept Tommy, but his people, all the Thorns, never quite accepted Jacqueline, just as they had barely tolerated Archie's Genevieve before her.

It was the first time Janet had heard anything about Archie's wife, Genevieve. She was from New Orleans, so that's where she and Archie settled. And from all accounts, she'd been a wonderful mother and probably a good wife, though Archie didn't say one way or another.

"We live in Dad's house," Tommy said.

"Half mine," Archie muttered.

"It's beautiful," Jacqueline said. "Festooned in wrought iron. Seven bedrooms. Four fireplaces. A high brick wall all 'round the yard ..."

"And the gardens are immaculate," Tommy chimed in. "They are Jacqueline's domain. I keep my hands out of 'em."

It thrilled Janet to see a man so in love with his wife.

"I have my little wing," Archie said. "But they have the run of the place."

Janet offered them a room for the night, but they headed back to Pink House. "Door's always open," she reiterated. "Lots of room here." She watched them walk across the yard into darkness with Marcus draped across Tommy's shoulder. She hoped they'd take her up on her offer some time, but Archie said they were going home the next day.

Back inside, Archie headed upstairs. "I'm taking the back room. See you in the morning." And with that, the evening was over.

A sadness fell over Archie. He sat on the edge of the bed, too weary to undress. It wasn't that he had too much to drink. That was a given. It was listening to Tommy talk about his mother. Genevieve was no saint, but through her son's eyes, she was perfect, and Archie had no argument. Opening windows wider, he undressed and crawled under the sheet. He tried to picture Genevieve in her courtyard by the trellis, or in their kitchen kneading dough on the marble counter, or in the shower with water running down her back. But her visage would not manifest – it never would – and he was left to his meager imagination. He tried to sleep, hoping to dream of her. Only in dreams could he see her again and, for a moment, believe she was still with him.

"I thought I heard you down here." Archie's soft voice startled Janet. She was lying on the chaise in the dark on the porch, listening to the night.

"Couldn't sleep?" she asked.

"Something like that. What about you?" He made his way to a rocker and melted into it.

"Keyed up, I guess," she said. She wanted to ask about his wife. She'd been curious since listening to Tommy, but she held back, asking instead about the house.

"In New Orleans?" his voice was hushed, intimate.

"Yeah. I've seen the Garden District. Some of those houses are magnificent."

"Theirs is one of the bigger ones. On a par with the West Bluff houses." Then came a silence that better suited the night than conversation. Something about Janet reminded him of Genevieve's people. Her mother and grandmother had survived hard times and though they were kind women, they carried with them a hesitancy, like some part of them expected inevitable betrayal. Seeing that in Janet, he knew she was worth the time it might take to get to know her.

"I can't believe my kids even speak to me," he said, having lost track of where the conversation had gone. "I was never there. Always gone for weeks at a time, meeting with clients, supervising some build."

"They must have understood because he clearly loves you," Janet reassured. "Kids have an instinct about adults, don't you think? They know the genuine article."

"I suppose," he admitted, accepting it as little consolation for time lost with his children.

"Lots of folks died in that house," he said, catching Janet off guard. "Four that I knew and probably many more before them. It's 160 years old."

Janet reached for a bottle of sherry on the floor and handed it to him. "Interesting transition," she said as he took a draw from it. "From kids to death."

It was peculiar, but he couldn't think about his kids without thinking about the home they were raised in. That house was as much family as any of them, and he sometimes wondered if it felt the burden of all that had transpired within its walls. "Leona used to say that everyone who lives in a house leaves something there. Some part of themselves," he explained.

"Leona?"

"Genevieve's grandmother. She said if they were bad people, some of that anger stayed behind. If they were good, all their joy and even their sorrows seeped into the bones of the house. She believed you could hear them, the dead, roaming about."

Janet chuckled, and Archie just shook his head. "Don't laugh, my friend. It's real. I lost Genevieve in that house, and her uncle Buddy, her mother, and her grandmother. Before them, four boarders died there. Before them, the owners who lost it in a card game were shot to death, and who knows who or how many others. I used to be in bed at night and jump at noises, and Genevieve would stroke my face and say it's just Leona, making sure the rest of them behave. So, yeah. It's real. It's just part of the natural world."

Janet didn't argue the point. If he believed, who was she to say he was wrong. She took her glass and went up to bed, leaving Archie alone with his thoughts.

When he reached for the sherry bottle, he noticed a small notepad. The cover was dog-eared, its pages fat with use. A pen was jammed into the spiral binding. He picked it up and leafed through it, the moonlight bright enough to make out the handwriting. At first, it didn't seem to be much more than random words, abbreviations, and numbers. Then he began reading, turning to the last entry first. *Son-Tommy, Jacqueline, Marcus-4. New Orleans Garden District house. Decayed house on bluff. Shrimp Cajun white wine. Thorns-Pink House. Archie-architect.*

He leafed backwards finding cryptic notes, some about weather, others just grocery lists. There were notes on wild flowers, how many squirrels or birds or tourists she'd seen on a section of trail. *ZERO PEOPLE!* was written after *high ridge path*. There were symbols next to some entries, a few solid circles, but mostly triangles. *Sunflower moved blue to white. Behind me - in my ear. Female? green glass to yellow AGAIN. Table in hall. More voices. More voices. Quilt moved. Light in stable, loft door open. Door slam. Brush to white. Thumping downstairs. Singing again, piano. Sunflower quilt AGAIN to white!*

As Archie read the entries, it seemed she'd used the bedroom colors to indicate things that seemed to move between them, a quilt being the most regular item, always returning to white. A violent shiver shot through him. While he'd been a casual believer in a spirit world, if what she was recording was real, it was beyond anything he'd experienced, and it definitely explained without question why the house had been empty for so long. Joking about a haunting was one thing. Suddenly, he was faced with a chronicle of what he presumed to be paranormal incidents, something else entirely. But if she was a believer, he wondered, why didn't she admit it? He carefully put the notepad back where he found it, feeling he'd violated her privacy by reading it. He went back up to his room.

In the morning, when he came down, the notepad was not on the floor, and there was no mention made of it.

CHAPTER 17

Katherine

Max, Anna, and Martin stood in their Baltimore kitchen watching James peel a grape with a scalpel, its skin falling in a little ribbon.

"Guess you really are a surgeon," Max joked.

Martin had already made Katherine's sandwich, carefully cutting the crusts off the bread, layering a slice of cheese and a slice of turkey breast without any condiment. Anna pulled a bottle of ranch dressing out of the fridge and poured a puddle on a Winnie the Pooh plate next to a couple of carrot sticks.

Martin leaned against the counter, watching, steeling himself. "Does anyone else think it's time to spill the beans? Get on with our true lives." He caught them off guard. They all looked at him like he'd just declared he was straight.

"What?" Anna said. "Why?"

"Why?" Martin repeated. "Because that three-year-old sleeping down the hall deserves to know who her daddy is. And Max deserves to hear her call him Daddy."

"Don't presume to know what I need," Max said. "Not sure even I know." He felt a pang of remorse. The life they had, the time they carved out to be a family, had been productive and happy. It was private and sweet and pure. Once the truth came out, everything would change.

"Don't you all feel like we're walking a tightrope?" Martin asked. "Without a net?"

"Doesn't this work?" Anna said, "Aren't we all happy? At least to a degree? Look at us. Four adults raising one little girl. How lucky is she!"

"They're all going to be pissed at us," James said. "No matter if we come clean on our own or they find us out. They can't do anything. We're still us. But," he added, looking to the ceiling for answers, "there will be consequences. My father will have a shit fit. Wouldn't surprise me if he jettisons both me and Katherine."

Max doubted he'd do that.

"Then you don't know the man," Martin countered.

Anna assured James that Baldwin would be angry. "But, your mother would never let him cast you out. And she adores Katherine."

James peeled another grape.

"So, what would this new true life look like?" Max asked. "Come on. Lay it out for me, Martin. I mean, as far as I can tell, you're the only one with nothing to lose."

Martin snapped back. "You don't have to be rude."

James said to settle down. "I'm a little curious, too, how you see this playing out."

"You and I declare ourselves," Martin said.

"You'll lose your lease," Max piped in without hesitation.

"No, we wouldn't," Martin insisted.

"They let you stay because you play their game." Max talked like a parent explaining life to a child. "Baltimore is a conservative town. Believe me when I say they'll kick you out."

James nodded. "He's not wrong."

"So we move," Martin said, spit-balling. "We buy a house and share it. A big one. With wings."

Max said he couldn't afford that, and the other three laughed.

"He can afford it," Anna said, glancing to Martin.

"Yes, Max, dear," Marten condescended. "I'm filthy rich. Thought you knew."

"Seriously?" Max asked.

"Seriously," Anna confirmed. "But putting that aside for the moment, I don't want to share a house with you guys. This works, but it isn't what I want her future to look like. I want her to have a mommy and daddy, and a yard and grandparents, and two fabulous uncles."

"Pipedream," James said.

Max laid it out. "We blow up our lives. First off, I'm not in a position to abandon my wife." He wanted to tell them how Betsy was entirely dependent on him, but held back. Nothing about Betsy belonged in this part of his life. "It would mean alienating my daughter, leaving Hamilton, losing my pension and insurance, with little hope of getting another at my age, and I'd lose my best friend in the mix. All so I can have my daughter call me daddy. And that's just me. You two want to announce yourselves? What parent is going to let a homosexual surgeon near their kid? I know your generation thinks the sixties were going to change the world, but it hasn't changed much yet. And Anna here. How does she recover from breaking her parents' hearts?" He looked at her eyes as they began to well up. "It's not in you. It isn't."

"What are you saying, old man," Martin said. Anna shot him a sneer. "Well he started it with his *your generation* slam."

"What he's saying," James said, "is we created this mess, and we're stuck with it until the world stops seeing us as freaks or everyone we love is too old or dead to know the difference."

"James!" Anna snapped.

"No," Max said. "He's right. By the time your parents pass, Katherine will be of age, or at least old enough to know the truth. Hell, I'll probably be dead by then, and it won't matter."

"Max!" Anna snapped. "Enough of this! Nothing has to be decided today."

"So, we decide not to decide," Martin said. Everyone nodded. "Well, that's a decision, isn't it." He grinned. "Lunch anyone?"

Little Katherine appeared in the doorway scowling, demanding everyone stop talking. "Sit down!" she told them.

"K! That is not appropriate language," Anna scolded. "You can't tell adults what to do. You may ask."

"Well, look who woke up," Max said with a big grin. "About time, lazy bones."

"Your lunch is ready, angel," James said quietly.

"Don't talk! Sit down!" the child demanded. When no one obeyed, she screamed at them and pushed James, trying to get him into a chair. "You have to sit!" she hollered. Anna scooped her up and carried her to her room, Katherine bawling all the way.

"I think we need a little attitude adjustment, young lady."

"What is she, three going on thirteen?" James joked.

When Anna came back out alone, the guys stood at the counter eating. "Remember, Max, we're heading up to the cottage for a month," she said. "We're meeting Daddy at the airport and flying in the Cessna. Do you think you can finagle a visit?"

"Sure he can," James said. "I think Carleton likes having a break from Baldwin now and again. And it's so much fun watching you two pretend you don't want to jump each other's bones."

"Welcome to our world," Martin said. "You know I'd love to be there, but I don't dare. She'd give me away in a heartbeat," he said, nodding toward the hallway.

Just then, Katherine slowly walked into the kitchen, her head hanging.

"Use your words, sweetie," Anna urged.

When Katherine spoke, all three of them stopped and stared at her as the words slowly slipped out: "I was so frustrated at you," she said with a perfect edge of exasperation.

Max picked her up. "So were we," he told her. "You don't want to be a Miss Bossy Pants, do you?" She looked at him as if to say yes, but didn't speak.

"I want you to sit down," she said politely.

"Katherine?" Anna warned.

"Please?" Katherine said. "Please sit down. I want to dance."

"You want to dance? OK, Kitty Kat," Martin said. "Now I understand. Next time, make that your lead."

"That's over her head," Anna said.

"I doubt it," Max argued.

"Lunch first," Anna insisted. "Then you can show us your dance."

"One, two, three!" James said, taking Katherine from Max, dropping her into her booster seat at the table. Katherine carefully took apart her sandwich lining her plate with all the parts. Then, one by one, she dipped each item into the salad dressing and ate them. Bread first, then cheese, then meat, finishing up with carrot sticks. "Fruit, please," she asked and Martin put the peeled grapes on her plate. She ate only one, pushed the plate away, and reached toward Max with a huge smile. "Time to dance!"

Max helped her down, and she pulled him by the hand into the living room and pushed him onto the couch. The others followed and sat next to him. Loud and almost in tune, Katherine sang the ABC song. She swayed back and forth, arms over her head. As everyone clapped and laughed, she finished, bowed, and looked to James. "Daddy, I need a cookie."

"How do I say no after that show?" he laughed, but Anna insisted Katherine ask nicely.

"Cookie, please, Daddy?"

"That was wonderful!" Max said, holding his arms out wide to her.

"Thank you, Max," Katherine said, diving into his embrace. "I love you, Max! I love you!" He wasn't daddy to her, but there was no doubt there was love.

CHAPTER 18

Hawk & Owl

"Jeanne's been on the island almost three weeks already," Carleton hollered loud enough to be heard over the engine. The Cessna soared over farmland and woods. "Ever since Anna and Katherine arrived. James came in a day ago. So glad you could get away this weekend. Boy, that little girl is a spitfire! Wait 'till you see her."

Max had become practiced at listening to Carleton talk about Katherine, bragging as any good grandpa would. Max had volumes to add to the conversation but fought the urge.

Landing on the island, Carleton took a taxi with the baggage and Max went off for a walk. "Hey, Max," Carleton said. "I know this eats into your time with your lady friend. But it's going to be good to spend some time with you."

Max was confused until he put it together. "Yeah," he said. "No worries."

"Maybe you could invite her here sometime. I'd love to meet her."

Max stifled a laugh. "I'll think about it."

Max made his way to the other side of the island to a hidden waterfall in the woods. As he approached, he saw Anna sitting on a log, her hair glowing in a ray of sunlight. The vision took his breath. He stepped on a twig, its snapping alerting her to his presence. She turned, smiled, and ran to him, intoxicated by the thrill of the furtive rendezvous. "I brought a blanket," she whispered in his ear.

He lifted her sundress off over her head, revealing nothing but bikini panties. Her breasts were pale triangles against otherwise tan skin. "She darted away, waving her dress high over her head like a banner. He stood like a tree, rooted in place, watching this wood sprite dance in the dappled shade. She fell to the blanket, sprawled on her back, and laughed. "What the hell are you waiting for?" she laughed. He went to her slowly, savoring every moment, and made love to her like a young man, energetic, anxious, hungry.

They lay on their backs afterward, looking up through the branches, seagulls crying overhead. "I have to get back," she sighed. "But I'd rather stay here all day."

"How's our girl today?" Max asked.

"Delightful. She's busy charming everyone."

"Just like her mother."

When Max finally made it to the cottage, Anna was on the porch with Baldwin and her father watching Katherine chase butterflies in the yard. When Katherine saw Max, she surprised everyone by calling out to him. "Max! Max! Max!" Anna quickly said she'd been going over everyone's names and photos so Katherine would be comfortable, and she'd latched onto the name Max.

Carleton patted his daughter on the hand saying how thoughtful that was of her.

Katherine ran to Max, dragging him by the finger to show him her world. "These are my flowers," she told him. "And these are my horses," she said in the stable. She pointed out the hay and the swallowtail's mud nest in the rafters. She dragged him into the house and upstairs, where she showed him her bed and her quilt. Trixie appeared and scooped her up, apologizing for the child as if she'd been a nuisance.

"She does this to everyone," Trixie said. "A bit overwhelming, I'm afraid."

Max was enraged. Who was she to yank his daughter away from him? He watched Katherine carried away, her sunflower quilt clenched in her little fist.

Trixie accosted Anna on the stairs. "She's rearranged things again, Dear. Put them right, please." Trixie tugged the quilt free. "Here," she said.

Anna took it and went into one of the bedrooms to retrieve several perfume atomizers, returning them to Trixie's dressing table.

Going to Max, she dropped Katherine's quilt on the bed and took the silver hairbrush from the dresser. "This belongs in Trixie's room, too. Katherine leaves Grandma Baldwin's stuff all over the house," Anna quipped. "We really need to work on that with her."

Max stood up and closed the door, turning to face Anna. "We're telling them," he said. "Today. Right now. They're all here. Quick and clean."

"Are you crazy?" Anna argued. "No."

He cupped his hands to her face and pleaded. "Nothing could be worse than this. Your parents will get over it. Come on, Anna. Be mine. Let Katherine be mine. Let's be brave."

His eyes held such confidence she could hardly resist. "You're right," she said. "You're absolutely right."

He kissed her and held her tight, feeling released from captivity.

"Just not today," she said. Max pulled back. "We'll go home, make a plan, and do it together. All four of us. James and Martin need to be part of it."

"This is about us. The three of us. No one needs to know about Martin and James. We'll just say you married your best friend to get out of an awkward situation. It doesn't have to be a total reckoning."

"But Martin and James have been raising her. It will be a total life change for them if Katherine is suddenly taken away to live with you and me. It won't be fair to them to decide this on our own."

"Not fair to them? She's my daughter," he said, looking more stern than loving. "I need to raise her."

"Yes, I know and you may be right," she said, but Max could see the wheels turning behind her eyes.

"So, we'll do it," he insisted. "No more waiting."

"Yes. It's time to stop this charade," Anna said, her voice certain. "Before Katherine gets any older."

Anna spread the small sunflower quilt neatly on the bed, feeling as if her life was about to implode. "But, we need to include James. And Martin. This is so much bigger than the three of us. You know that. It will turn Katherine's world inside out."

Katherine called from the yard to James up in the hayloft. "Come play with me, Daddy" she beckoned. "Pretty please?"

Max watched from the window as James slipped out of the stable and darted through the sunflowers, peaking from between giant leaves, Katherine laughing and squealing when he disappeared again. Max marveled at her little legs, so strong and confident, arms rosy with sun, auburn curls bouncing with every step. And James, so delighted, like a child himself. Anna was right. It wasn't about the three of them. It was only about Katherine.

When James retreated back to his sanctuary, he signaled Max to follow him up. "Here," he said, handing over his journal. "I think you might like this one."

The book was open to a poem scrawled in the middle of a page by itself:

Nothing is quite so intimate

as a furtive glance

a momentary union of souls

transmitting volumes

decipherable only by two.

Until witnessed

"You're not being careful, Max. Back off, or they'll figure you out."

"It's just so impossible sometimes."

"Tell me about it," James agreed.

"Did Anna tell you yet? This is over. We're coming out."

"Now? Anna finally agreed?"

"Waiting on Martin. She wants to get her ducks in a row, I guess."

"About time. I'd have done it in the beginning. But Anna doesn't know how to break hearts. And this is going to break a number of them."
Max flipped pages in the journal. "Ah, here it is. My favorite," he said, reading it aloud.

it rings in my ears

joy

like water from a teapot

she tinkles

Saturday evening, Katherine crawled up onto Max's lap, and Trixie snatched her up, apologizing again. Anna stepped in, suggesting if Max didn't mind, it would be all right, at which point Trixie reluctantly returned the child to his arms.

"I understand you're quite a poet, Jimmy," Max said, emphasizing the use of Jimmy instead of James. Doubtful eyes looked up. Anna said she'd mentioned it in passing.

Baldwin assured everyone poetry was not necessary in the practice of medicine.

"Well, darling," Trixie said to her son. "Why don't you recite one for us?" Her tone, sounding more like a teacher in front of a classroom, made Max sorry he'd said anything.

"Katherine has a favorite," Anna said with a big smile. "Kitty Kat, want to do the birdie poem with Daddy?"

James scooted to the floor in front of Katherine and began slowly. She caught a few words, trying her hardest to keep up. It was all Max could do not to say it with them.

> *nuthatch, bluebird, chickadee, finch*
>
> *the downy caches a seed*
>
> *blue jay, sparrow, woodpecker, crow*

Katherine stopped. "Where's Uncle Martin?" she asked. "I want Uncle Martin to read with me." James flushed, and Anna spoke up, chirping out reasons why her toddler would be asking for a man she could hardly know.

"He's stopped by a couple of times. You know Martin, so flamboyant, she just adores him." Anna flashed a glance to Max. Baldwin caught it, got up, and left the room.

"Let's start again, shall we, Pumpkin?" James pleaded.

> *nuthatch, bluebird, chickadee, finch*
>
> *the downy caches a seed*
>
> *blue jay, sparrow, woodpecker, crow*
>
> *the redhead steals it away*
>
> *titmouse, robin, hummingbird, wren*
>
> *all feast upon the flowers*
>
> *groundhog, raccoon, fox and bunny*
>
> *eat shoots and grass for hours*

while hawk and owl are on the prowl

to eat any and all not watchful

When they finished, Katherine clapped and opened her arms to James, who hoisted her up and twirled her around, both of them reveling in pure delight.

"But that didn't rhyme, dear," Trixie complained. "Isn't a poem supposed to rhyme?"

Sunday afternoon came too quickly. Carleton decided to stay the week and flew Max to Pellston, a small airport on the mainland, to take a commercial puddle jumper back to Edgewater. "See you in a few days," Carleton said. "Coming back on Wednesday. Baldwins are leaving. Jeanne wants some alone time with the kids. I think she gets tired of sharing them all the time."

"I imagine she does. So, see you back in the office Thursday then?"

"Yup. Thursday."

Carleton didn't even cut the engines, stopping only long enough for Max to climb out.

Thursday morning, Max was about to head into a production meeting when he noticed some sort of commotion in the hall outside his office. His secretary, Mrs. Wood, was huddled with other office staff. She appeared to be consoling Carleton's secretary.

It wasn't in Max's nature to jump to the worst scenario, but recognized it in others. "What's all this," he asked, presuming it wasn't the crisis they made it out to be. Mrs. Wood ushered the women away and returned to

Max. She was fighting back tears, and he attempted to console her. "Hey, now," Max said. "Can't be all that bad."

He suspected nothing. Had no inkling. His day had begun like any other. He woke. Showered. Shaved. Went to work. There had been no seismic shift in the universe.

Mrs. Wood could hardly get the words out, and when she did, they were barely audible.

"Come now," Max said. "Something about an accident?"

"It's Carleton," she said. "They were on their way home yesterday. Their car was . . ."

"Car," he said, confident of crossed wires. "No, no, they flew in yesterday."

"They had to put down in Pellston," she said. "Bad weather. They were driving home."

Max went directly into containment mode. He accepted they were driving. There had been an accident. Carleton was injured or worse. He'd manage the situation. It's what he did. He managed things. He'd see how badly Carleton was injured, collect the others, and bring them home. If it was serious, he wanted to be with Anna and Katherine, to help them any way he could. More than anything, he wanted them both in his arms, safe and sound. "Where are they? I'll go and . . ."

Mrs. Wood fought to not break down. "Max," she pleaded. "Listen to me. It was bad. They're all . . ." She couldn't finish the thought.

"What are you saying?" He could feel panic rising and had to keep control. Control was everything. "I'll make some calls and get to the bottom of it."

He looked down the hall at women and men, all looking back at him. When the look in their eyes registered as something between fear and pity, he looked back to Mrs. Wood, a woman trying her hardest to break the worst news of her life.

"I'm sure they made a mistake," Max said, his expression registering the truth before his mind caught up. "Has anyone called the house?"

"Max," she sighed. "Carleton is gone. The whole family. They're all gone."

CHAPTER 19

Prepping

Janet went to St. Ignace on Wednesday as had become her routine. July's tourist crowds were in annoyingly full bloom, packing the ferries. Making her way through them all, she silently ran her grocery list, recalling items against the list in her notepad.

She knew this grocery store now and could go aisle by aisle with intention, but this time, the pasta wasn't where it was supposed to be, and other things stopped looking familiar. Assuming a failure of memory, her heart began to race, and her breath came up short. It never crossed her mind stock had been rearranged.

A northwesterly wind sweeping across the northern expanse of Lake Michigan turned the hot muggy morning into a cold abysmal afternoon. The horizon grew darker as she waited for the 2:30 ferry. Gulls screeched overhead.

It was a rough ride back across the straits. A little boy ran down the aisle, stopping short of Janet, leaning over abruptly, and throwing up at her feet. His father whisked him away leaving the putrid puddle to ooze into the indentations of the steel floorplate.

Wind whipped Janet's hair as she carried three tote bags of groceries to the lower deck and disembarked. Carrying her load through town, one of the tour carriages stopped and gave her a ride up the hill to the annex. "Baldwin Cottage, right?" the driver asked. Janet laughed, climbing up next to him.

The young man was a good tour guide, reciting all the details she had once recited by heart. Pulling into the Annex, he dropped her at her hedgerow. "Baldwin Cottage," he announced as she stepped off. "Built in 1886 by the Baldwin family, their wealth derived from timber used to rebuild Chicago after the great fire." He tipped his hat to Janet as he pulled forward beyond the open hedge and got down off the rig. "Everyone see those red straps up overhead? If some of you would be so kind as to pull them loose, I think we're about to require shelter from the rain." One by one, the plastic walls unrolled, and he quickly secured them to the side of the rig.

As Janet opened the screen door, a gust caught it, snapping it away and back, knocking a tote out of her arms, spilling apples, toilet paper, carrots, and a box of crackers down the steps. Rain came on suddenly, pummeling her as she gathered it all.

She ran through the house closing windows, pushing away angry curtains whipped inward by the wind, rain splattering the floor. She saw the tour guide, in a rain slicker now, climb back up and continue with the tour. Something crashed upstairs, and she flew up to find two lamps on the floor in one room, a vase shattered in another. She slammed down window after window, one of which stuck. As she struggled with it, the rain drenched her jeans, the rug and the arm of the big chair. Outside, trees bent beyond all imagining, branches creaked and cracked, small bits of leaves and twigs flew about. She ducked as a small branch took aim at her and ricocheted off the screen. The wind, roaring outside, whistled inside all throughout the house. Thunder broke. The house shook. A blinding flash of lightning crackled as the window finally gave way and slammed to the sill.

Heart pounding, Janet ducked to the floor. Through her back she could feel waves of wind and rain pound the wall, one after another. The house seemed to whine as if it was frightened and Janet heard herself comfort it, involuntary words spilling out. *Embrace the wind. Sway like a tree. Embrace the wind.*

The brunt of the storm passed, rain turning into a steady peaceful shower. Janet stood up, stunned to be clenching the sunflower quilt she was certain she'd put in the hall drawer that morning. She slid back down the wall and sat for what could have been a few seconds or minutes. Moments besieged by doubt could be elastic like that.

The weather had been unpredictable the week before the condo crew was due to arrive. Hot then cool, windy then dead calm. Janet had every intention of doing a grocery run to the mainland before they all arrived but never made it. It wasn't in her to have another kid throw up at her feet on a ferry.

The day they were due in she went down to the post office finding a postcard from Mattie with two words on it: RICE PUDDING.

On task, Janet stood in line in the little market in town with a quart of milk, whipping cream, rice, and raisins in a hand basket. She didn't like shopping on the island in high season, the store always overrun with tourists.

Next in line, she pulled out her cell and called Mattie. As it rang, the cashier slapped down her CLOSED sign without so much as a glance to Janet and walked away.

"Really?" Janet snapped.

"Really what?" asked Mattie on the phone.

"Crap. Nothing," Janet muttered taking her place behind two families in another lane. "I need you guys to hit the market on the mainland before you come over."

"What's she need?" Sam hollered in the background.

"Everything. Tell him everything," Janet said. "Booze, beef, two chickens. Anything fresh – veggies, salad stuff, fruit. You want it, you bring it. I got nothin'."

The checkout lady, probably fourth-generation islander, scowled. Janet shrugged her off.

"Got it," Mattie said. "We're a good five hours out."

"Maybe six," Debbie hollered. "Just got to Traverse."

"Doing wineries," came another voice from the car.

"Who was that? Sam?" Janet spoke loud enough to be heard by everyone in the car and the store. The man in line behind her threw back his head and heaved a vocal sigh.

"No. It was Mike," Mattie said.

"Take as long as you like, just don't miss the 8:15 ferry."

The family in line in front of Janet, a woman with a baby in the cart, two young boys, and a grandmother, pulled forward and started to load groceries to the conveyer. The family in front of them was gathering up their bags when one of their kids, a toddler, squatted down and peed on the floor.

"Christ, lady!" hollered a clerk.

"I gotta go" Janet told Mattie. "It's getting interesting here. Oh! Stop at the stand by the dock and get some fresh whitefish. And smoked salmon and trout." She tossed her cell in her purse and watched the parents of the peeing toddler, without hint of apology, leave without so much as offering to clean up.

It was then that Janet caught a whiff of something not altogether pleasant and looked to the youngster in the cart in front of her. It seemed to be happy enough and the smell didn't quite smell of diaper. It was a waftier aroma, airborne. Then she noticed the grandmother's hip rise ever so slightly, followed by a quietly rippling fart. The small boys standing in close proximity to the source both yelled, "Grandma farted!" and pushed their way clear, laughing as they bolted out of the store. Undaunted, the grandmother lifted her purse, pulled out her wallet, and paid for the groceries.

In preparation for their stay, Janet spent the rest of the day making all the beds and rearranging furniture in the bedrooms. Up to that time, she'd left things as they'd been when she got there, but Mike liked waking with the morning sun full in his face, and Mattie loathed it. She put the bed in the blue room to the west wall for Mike and Debbie, imagining morning sun streaming into their eyes. The shady green room had a good view of the straits, perfect for Mattie and Sam. She moved their bed to an opposite wall between two windows and took an overstuffed chair from another room for Mattie, knowing she would likely take an afternoon nap in it. In Carmen's room she shifted the twin beds away from the windows because she didn't like air directly on her. All this moving of beds meant moving tables and dressers, rugs, and lamps. By late afternoon, after having moved nearly every stick of furniture in three rooms, she was exhausted.

The crew was due in at 8:30. Janet arranged a carriage to meet them at the dock. She made the rice pudding and put it in the oven to bake at seven, then placed bath towels on all the beds. She collected an array of flowers from the garden, making little bouquets for each dresser.

The last thing she did was place a framed photo of her and her parents on the storage bench in the upstairs hallway. She'd meant to put it out weeks earlier to honor her dad for insisting on annual island visits and for getting her the summer job there. She didn't have a picture of her dad alone. A group shot had to suffice. It was taken just after Max died. It was the only photo she had of anybody.

Finally, off task, she slumped onto the chaise on the porch with a wine goblet in hand and promptly fell asleep. A loud bang woke her. She jumped up only to cut her foot on a shard of broken glass. She'd dropped the wine. Cussing out loud, she gimped into the kitchen to clean her foot leaving spots of blood in her wake. The timer went off and she pulled the pudding out of the oven. She was testing it with a toothpick when she heard a door slam upstairs. She presumed it was the wind through an open window but there wasn't even a breeze. The air was eerily still.

Wrapping her foot in paper towel secured with scotch tape, she went upstairs. Two steps from the top she saw glass on the floor.

The family photo had fallen.

The bedroom doors were closed.

When she opened the door to the green room, her legs gave way beneath her. All the furniture she rearranged hours earlier was back as it had been originally. The bed, chairs, dresser, and tables had all moved back. Even the pink rug she put in there for Mattie was gone, the original orange one taking its place. She forced herself to her feet and opened the blue room door. It, too, had reverted, every last thing back as it was.

"I'm OK," she told herself out loud. "I'm fine!" She leaned on the wall trying to breathe when she glanced to her room and saw the sunflower quilt spread across her bed. It should have been in the drawer. It should always be in the drawer. Every time it showed up, she put it in the drawer. "Stop it!" she shouted. "Just fucking stop it!"

As if daring the situation to deteriorate, she opened the door to the yellow bedroom next to hers. Nothing was as she'd left it for Carmen. Gasping for breath, a sudden wave of cold air wafted over her, and all four doors slammed shut.

Bolting downstairs, out the door, across the porch, she imagined her mother doing the same thing, running from her house through the ravine to the river, stripping down, afraid of everything around her, running until she hit the water. Janet was only a couple years younger than Ellen was when she was committed to the memory unit.

,

CHAPTER 20

Confab

When the taxi pulled up with the condo crew that evening, Janet was asleep in a chair in the yard. Mattie actually had to nudge her awake. Janet jumped, frightened, and was relieved to see friends. She looked to the house to find the front door wide open.

"This is fantastic," Sam hollered, lifting bags to the road.

Mattie urged Janet inside. "You're freezing out here." The sun was setting, and the air had turned chilly. Janet stood up, dazed, and followed everyone into the house. She looked at the floor, thinking she needed to clean up the blood spots from her foot, but there weren't any. She looked at the blazing fire in the potbelly stove and figured Mr. Harris had stopped by, cleaned up for her, and built the fire. Or had she done it all. She was sure of nothing anymore.

Debbie asked what she did to her foot and took it upon herself to search out some band aides. Mike saw the broken wine glass on the porch and cleaned it up. Carmen pulled a bottle out of a case of wine and opened it. Sam took bags upstairs.

"We'll take this room," Sam announced. "No morning sun!"

"Oh, watch out for the broken glass up there," Janet said, but he hollered back that there was no glass. She went upstairs to find the photo back on the dresser in the hall, intact, and all the bedroom doors were wide open, everything back as she had arranged it earlier in the day. The sunflower quilt, however, was still draped over her bed. Janet said nothing, her mood unusually sullen.

While she would normally have stayed up with all of them drinking and talking, she went to bed early, leaving them to fend for themselves. She awoke in the middle of the night to a quiet house, save the snoring coming from Mike and Debbie's room. She went to the porch. Curling up with a down throw, she listened to the silence of the night, overwhelmed by earlier occurrences. When she heard a voice behind her she spoke up, assuming it was Carmen, the insomniac of the group. She looked inside, but no one was there. Giving in to her new reality, she stepped inside, tripping on a side table in the middle of the hall. Sleep finally came to her, but it was shallow and restless.

The next morning, Mattie and Janet were busy making breakfast when Carmen shuffled in.

"Good morning, Honey Bunny," Janet said and pointed to the percolator on the counter.

"Was it just me, or was somebody moving shit around down here last night?" Carmen asked, taking her first sip of coffee.

"I didn't hear a thing," Mattie said. "Out like a light." She poured a mug full and dropped in four sugar cubes.

"It was me," Janet said. "Stubbed the hell out of my toe."

"That's what you get for crapping out on us so early," Mattie said.

Janet finished cutting bananas into a large bowl of fruit. Carmen cracked eggs into a bowl. Their movements were like a well-practiced ballet.

"And what's with the light in the stable," Sam asked from the hallway. "I could swear we turned it off after I went exploring last night." Mattie gave him the coffee she'd just fixed and went to stir potatoes.

A voice came from the back porch. "The house is haunted, didn't she tell you? Always has been." Archie stepped in and went straight for the coffee. "Smells good. What's for breakfast?"

Janet handed him the fruit and pointed to the dining table. "Not haunted. Loose wire or somebody left the light on. Everybody, this is Archie, my neighbor. He comes from serious money." She grabbed some potholders and pulled a pan of sweet rolls out of the oven. Just then, Mike called out from the front room to say there was a horse in her front yard.

"I know," Janet hollered back.

"How serious?" Carmen asked Archie.

"But he's loose," Mike hollered.

"Very serious," Archie answered.

"I know the horse is loose, don't worry about it," Janet hollered back.

"If you're so rich, why are you scrounging around here for breakfast?" Sam asked.

Archie graciously replied, mocking himself. "All the wealthiest are freeloaders. How do you think we stay wealthy?"

Mike made his way into the kitchen and eyed Archie like a jealous lover. "Down, boy," Debbie said from the back steps. "I need a shower before breakfast."

"You'll have to settle for a bath," Janet quipped.

Debbie kicked off her running shoes to the grass and charged through the kitchen. "Don't say anything important until I come back out. Hey, Archie."

Archie smiled, handing her a glass of orange juice. "Hey, Deb."

Mike was speechless, watching this perfect stranger treat his wife like an old friend. Debbie flew past him into the bathroom. "It's a small island," she said.

"What do you mean by haunted?" Carmen asked.

From the bathroom Debbie's voice rang out. "Nothing important until I'm back out. I mean it!"

Everybody threw the table together for breakfast, scrounging around in cupboards and drawers for plates, , glasses, and silverware. Carmen went out into the garden and picked daisies and the last of the iris for the table. Sam dragged a couple chairs across the floor and plopped them into place at the table. As they were about to sit down to eat, Mr. Harris appeared at the front screen door, and Janet went to invite him in.

"There's plenty for one more in here," she told him.

"No, no," he grinned. "Just nice to see the place come to life again. Maybe some other time. Got things to do today, but I appreciate the invitation." He walked away.

She went back inside and filled a plate. Debbie came through wrapped in a towel with wet hair and rosy cheeks. "Be right down," she said, bolting up the steps.

Archie hoisted his glass of champagne. "To Baldwin Cottage. Long may she live." Though glasses were raised and the toast heralded, no one was entirely sure what he meant, and Mattie finally asked.

"Yeah," Mike said. "We want to hear this."

"Nope."

"What do you mean, no?"

"Not till Deb comes down," Archie said, at which time Debbie appeared and grabbed a glass of champagne.

"To Baldwin Cottage," she said.

As they ate, Archie told them no one had stayed in Baldwin Cottage a whole week in decades. Whatever family was left always cut visits short, then stopped coming altogether."

"Hell, I think I could be up here all summer and be perfectly happy," Mattie said.

"Why didn't they like it here?" Mike asked.

"It's not for everybody," Archie said. "Some people just don't appreciate it here. Baldwin blood was running mighty thin, and it was all they could do to pay the taxes on it, much less keep it up. The association had to cover it for the last few years just to maintain it. They paid for the paint and the new roof on the stable."

"Yeah," Janet said. "That ended up falling to me, as I recall."

"That's not fair," Mike insisted.

"It is what it is," Janet muttered, reminding them the asking price had dropped four times.

"Why do you suppose it didn't sell?" Sam asked. "Seems like a great place. I'd have thought one of the other families in the Annex would have picked it up."

Mike asked Janet what she was doing downstairs overnight. "Sounded like you were moving furniture."

"You were dreaming," Debbie said in a dismissive spousal tone.

Carmen hollered from the kitchen, happy to have someone corroborate her observation.

Archie grinned. "Ask her about it," he said, nodding to Janet.

"What do you mean?" Janet countered.

"Your notepad. Things moving from place to place, never where you left them, lights on when you left them off."

The room fell to an awkward silence. Janet's expression turned icy as she walked out of the room.

"What did I say?" Archie asked, confused.

The crew exchanged glances until all eyes fell to Mike.

"We don't talk about the notepads," Mike said.

"I don't understand. . ."

"Let it go, Archie," Mike instructed.

Carmen walked in with a big pitcher of orange juice in one hand and a bottle of Prosecco in the other. "Mimosas, anyone?" The climate immediately warmed, and chatter resumed. Sam placed his hand on Archie's shoulder without speaking. His glance alone suggested there was much more to say.

"This is bull shit," Archie said, and went to Janet on the back porch.

"I'm not sure what I said, but I'm sorry," he told her. "We good?" Even in asking it, he felt a chill between them.

"It's all good," she said with an insincere grin.

"Do you want me to leave?"

"What? No. No, don't go. I want you to stay."

To Archie's way of thinking, what should have followed in any other exchange of that sort would have been a hug or some physical reassurance, but Janet brushed right by him, turning at the kitchen to wave him in. He didn't understand what had happened, what he'd done, but he knew something was different. He decided to stick around until he figured it out or until she told him to get lost.

"Well," Debbie said as she took the last sausage from the platter. "This is all very interesting, but it is a gorgeous day."

"Agreed!" Janet announced. "Away with you! Spend your day in the delights of the island. Hike. Bike. Explore. Sit in the garden and read for all I care." Within a few minutes, all sign of the meal was gone, leftovers put away and the dishes washed and dried. "Debbie, Mike, Archie, tee time is 12:12," Janet said on her way to take a bath.

Mid-afternoon found Mike standing in the fairway on the back nine, watching his wife slice a seven iron into the woods. Archie hit next, and though his stroke was a thing of beauty, his ball landed in a deep sand trap not far from where Debbie's ball disappeared. Mike and Janet hit, both landing on the opposite side of the fairway. Debbie and Archie took a cart in one direction, Mike and Janet took the other.

"So, what's up?" Mike asked.

"What's up with what?"

"I don't know. You were freaked out last night. When we got here. You tried to cover, but something was definitely wrong."

"I don't know what you mean. I've missed you guys, and it was good to finally have you here. That's all."

"Right. So then, what's up with Archie? You sleeping with him?" All the condo crew hoped she was.

"Jesus, Mike. Give it a rest." She pulled a seven-iron and hit, reaching the far edge of the green. "Not bad for someone who golfs three times a year, eh?" The path to the green took them up a rise, the top of which offered a view of the Mackinac Bridge. Mike didn't even notice. He chipped to the edge of the green, not where he wanted, but at least within putting distance of the pin.

"Well?" he said.

"Well, what? Look at that view, would you?"

"Are you sleeping with him?"

"We both know I'm not sleeping with him. Not doing anything else either."

They stood on the far side of the green, waiting for Debbie and Archie to emerge from the woods. "I heard you last night, Babe. You're dreaming again, aren't you?"

"Please don't call me Babe."

"Yeah, all right, but I'm right, aren't I? The dreams are back."

"And how would you know that?"

Mike hesitated.

"Well?"

"I heard you. You make this weird sound, like a whimper."

"You never told me that."

Mike shrugged.

Janet took a deep breath and fought back the angst. "Yes," she admitted. "They're back."

"Why do you suppose now?"

"I don't know." She stepped out of the cart and pulled her putter from her bag. "My arm hurts again, too."

"Christ, Janet."

"Yeah."

A ball dropped to within inches of the pin.

"Is it the same dream? Where you wake up feeling smothered?"

"Yeah. Only this time, there's more to it. I smell something. Like sour vanilla, and it's overwhelming. I can't breathe. I wake up feeling crushed."

He looked at her, then looked away. "Sucks to be you."

She hesitated before confessing to him. "There's been other stuff. All summer. Ellen kind of stuff. I think it's beginning."

"The notepads."

"Yeah."

"Look. We got your postcard about blooming flowers or whatever. You are not your mother." He gave her a shoulder bump as another ball dropped at their feet.

"Fore!" Debbie hollered a bit late.

"What if it is the FTD?"

He waved to Archie and Debbie as they approached. "Let's not go there till we have to."

Carmen and Debbie had gone shopping in town, coming back with a lovely silk sweater, a scarf, floppy hat, and three new books. "What, no fudge," Janet scoffed. Mattie took up the task and went back down.

"She's only going so she can call the shop," Carmen said. "You wait and see."

Upon returning with caramel corn, five pounds of fudge, and a hoodie, Sam asked Mattie what took her so long. As expected, Mattie started to run through a litany of issues at the shop. "Well, it's not like I can call from here, is it?"

Debbie asked how Mattie expected her new manager to manage if she insisted on micromanaging her every decision."

"That's easy for you," Mattie harped. "Your marina can run itself."

Debbie took a breath to retaliate, but Mike intervened, hoisting a bottle of wine. "This was one of our favorites from the Leelanau peninsula." Tempers settled.

The next afternoon, Mattie, Carmen, and Janet walked down to a stony beach with a big thermos of vodka lemonade and paper cups. After prowling the shoreline, they perched on a couple of warm rocks, their feet dipped in icy waters of the straits, sun warm on their skin. Tourists bicycled behind them along the rim road, chattering as they passed.

Mattie nudged Carmen, who shrugged.

"OK, what?" Janet asked.

"The notepad."

"Ah. That's what this is?"

"What?"

"You two got the assignment to gauge just how much I've lost it up here?"

They both scoffed it off and suggested it was time to pour some lemonade.

"Has anyone told Archie . . . does he know about . . ." Janet asked.

"The FTD? Fuck no," Mattie assured her. "Not our story to tell."

"We do have some boundaries," Carmen said. "Really. I like him."

Mattie agreed everyone liked Archie so far but she wanted to know more about stuff moving and lights going on and off. "That never happened at home, did it? So why all of a sudden would it start now, up here? It doesn't make sense."

"Dementia doesn't exactly make sense," Janet said, refilling her cup.

"But," Carmen said, "what if it's something else? What is it exactly that's moving around? What lights?"

Mattie said to look at it clear-eyed, detail by detail.

"OK," Janet said. "There are these beautiful perfume bottles I found. The ones on the table in your room, Mattie."

"You mean my room, don't you?" Carmen asked. "There are two on the dresser in my room."

Janet's dead-eyed stare gave them all a chill. "You see?" she said. "That is what's been happening. I'm certain I put them in your room, Mattie."

"What if it isn't the flowers," Mattie said. "I mean, let's just contemplate another scenario." She refilled her cup and Carmen's. "What if Archie has it right? The place is haunted."

"Don't be ridiculous," Janet scoffed.

Their attention was drawn to a freighter making its way toward the bridge. "Damn, they're big," Carmen said.

"I've been having these dreams," Janet finally said, breaking a long, sun-soaked silence. "They aren't dreams exactly. There's a little girl. I get the sense sometimes of a little girl running around. She's very happy, so it isn't scary, but . . . I feel . . . connected to her somehow." She stopped talking when she saw Mattie and Carmen staring at her, mouths hanging open.

They looked at each other and started talking over each other until Janet hollered for one at a time.

"We went to the cemetery yesterday to look at old gravestones," Carmen said.

"I never understood your fascination with cemeteries. Everywhere we go, you two . . ."

"Shut up and listen," Mattie said. "We found the Baldwin family plot." She looked at Carmen.

"And . . ." Janet urged.

"There's a little girl buried there," Carmen said. "Died in 1970."

"What if . . ." Mattie said with hesitation, "what if it's her? What if it's the little girl? Maybe she died in Baldwin Cottage."

"Don't be ridiculous," Janet said, putting the thermos out of reach. "I'm cutting you both off."

"Janet, there's more," Mattie said, eyes wide. "It's no big surprise you feel a connection . . ."

Carmen interrupted. "You and that little Baldwin girl have the same birthday!"

CHAPTER 21

Losing

The summer of 1970 found Max as hopeful as he'd ever been. He was about to declare Katherine as his own and lay claim to a life with Anna.

He was in his office about to go into a meeting when news broke about the accident, that it took Carleton and the whole family, but it didn't sink in. It couldn't be true. He refused to believe.

He saw the chairman of the board and bolted to him, desperate for any information. The man said he heard Carleton and Jeanne died instantly. "Anna and her husband died en route to the hospital."

"The child!" Max asked, not even trying to hide his panic. "Their daughter?"

"I don't know. It didn't sound like there were any survivors."

Max charged back to his desk, slamming his door behind him. He called Pellston police. The woman answering the phone told him the child was injured, but not seriously, then Max heard someone interrupting her, telling her to hang up. She did. He called every hospital within sixty miles of the accident. When he finally found where she was, they couldn't tell him anything. He wasn't family.

He couldn't face losing Anna, not yet, not while Katherine was unaccounted for. He couldn't reach Martin. He tried calling Baldwins at home but a housekeeper said they were up on the island.

The drive up from Edgewater was the most difficult six hours of Max's life, fear and grief swirling until nothing made sense. The loss hadn't taken a firm grasp yet when he shot off the ferry, heading straight up to Baldwin Cottage, presuming Katherine would be there. He was going to confront Baldwin. He would take the child.

There was a small crowd milling about the yard and on the porch when he appeared at the hedgerow. He scanned for Katherine but didn't see her. Then he heard some women on the road. "She was so sweet," one cried. "Such a beautiful child," another said.

Max grabbed one of them.

"Who? Who are you talking about?"

The woman ripped her arm away.

"The little Baldwin child. She . . ."

Another finished the sentence. "She died in the crash that killed the . . ."

Max charged across the yard, his heart pounding. Baldwin didn't see him at first, but someone nudged him, causing him to turn. With a subtle nod, he motioned Max around to the stable. When the men were alone, face-to-face, Max was still winded from the walk, his shirt soaked in sweat. "Is it true? Katherine?" he demanded.

Baldwin stood calm, resolute, tapping a large manila envelope against his leg. His dead eyes held little but contempt. "Care to tell me why my son and daughter-in-law would assign you legal guardianship over my granddaughter?"

"So she's alive? Goddamnit, tell me!"

"It's not that I don't appreciate your distance in all this," Baldwin admitted.

"Tell. Me."

"Yes. She's fine."

"But those ladies said . . ."

"Yes. They said she's dead. And it's going to stay that way."

Max leaned on the stable wall, trying to find equilibrium.

Baldwin looked at him. "It's been three years that you've played along. Can't say I'd have been so gracious if it were my child."

"When did you know?"

"Know?" Baldwin raised his voice, but being aware of others nearby, headed down the lane. Max followed. "I knew my boy wasn't the father. He was queer as shit. But I never guessed it was you!"

"So, you knew about your son," Max said.

"I'm not an idiot. Of course, I knew. And he had mumps when he was nearly eighteen," Baldwin said. "Nads swelled up to the size of tennis balls. He was sterile! I always thought it was a blessing the boy shot blanks. Kept his mother's expectations in check."

Max could have said something consoling but was too fearful at that moment to say anything. If he'd wanted to, Baldwin could fight for custody of Katherine.

"I loved my boy," Baldwin said. He turned to face Max. "But I'm not raising that little bastard."

Max stopped cold. He'd imagined several versions of this conversation, but this one, this man expressing such hostility toward the child, had not been one of them. James had been right. Baldwin was jettisoning Katherine. "She's not a bastard."

"You defiled Anna, that beautiful girl. I wish Carleton were here to beat you to a bloody pulp. I'm not well enough to even try. Anna used my son. She stole my name. She tried to pass that little bastard off as my blood, and I won't have it. No money. No name. Gone. You're her guardian. So you manage that. And I swear if I ever lay eyes on her again after this..."

"Fine. I'll get her right now, and we'll be out of your life."

"No."

"I need to see her."

"Impossible." He handed Max the envelope. "Everything you need to know is in there. Pick her up Sunday. Eleven o'clock at the airport in Pellston." He turned to walk away, then stopped. "Some part of me wants to thank you for your part in all this." The words seemed difficult for him to eke out. "Even though I knew it wasn't real, for a short time, Trixie and I had a real family. Her dreams came true."

"I'm sorry for your loss," Max said, almost meaning it.

"You have no idea what we've lost."

"What about Carleton's people? Won't they..."

"It's all been taken care of," Baldwin said, pointing to the envelope. "You sign those papers, you get the girl. It's that simple."

"I need to know where she is. Now."

"Just shut up and get off my island. This is a family affair." With that, Baldwin headed back to the cottage.

Max didn't leave the island. He took a room in town and opened the envelope. A legal document dictated the terms of an agreement whereby Baldwin would set aside money from Carleton and Jeanne's estate for Katherine, with the stipulation Max could not reveal her identity. If Max didn't sign, Baldwin would make sure he'd never see Katherine again, and she would never see her inheritance. Attached to another envelope was a Polaroid of Katherine sitting on a hospital bed with her arm in a cast. Inside was a death certificate for Katherine Lorraine Post Baldwin and a note indicating a new birth certificate for Katherine Smith, the daughter of Carl and Harriet Smith of Iron Mountain, Michigan. Medical records would follow. Baldwin had indeed handled the situation. Money, it seems, could buy anything.

Max couldn't fathom the depth of Baldwin's animosity. How could the man throw away an innocent child? How could he watch his wife grieve? A man capable of such heartlessness was capable of anything. Max signed the papers and asked a woman at the hotel desk to deliver them.

He walked the woods and sat by their waterfall imagining Anna, imagining her face in the dappled sunshine, picturing her bare skin, her eyes, her touch, until the pain became too much, and he broke down.

Max tried to attend the funeral Saturday morning but was turned away by big men in black suits. Once again, he found himself standing against the wrought iron fence across from the stone church, this time watching a procession of shiny black funeral carriages convey three caskets, one of them so small, up the hill toward the cemetery. Even the horses seemed to mourn, walking heads down, large black plumes on their bridles bobbing slowly with each step. Like a stalker, Max followed at a distance, clutching the Polaroid if only to assure himself his baby girl was alive and not in that box.

He stood in the far corner of the cemetery behind a monument, watching the graveside service, too far away to hear what was said. He watched as mourners disbursed afterward, some climbing into carriages, others walking away. So many people. So much sorrow. He watched the crew fill in the holes by hand, each shovel of dirt weighing heavier on his heart. Only when they were finished, when they had placed all the flowers so carefully around the mounds and left, did Max visit the graves and collapse.

Someone knelt down, resting his hand on Max's back. "How do we go on without them?" Martin asked. "How do we go on without our little Katherine? Our precious little Katherine."

Max handed Martin the Polaroid. "She's alive." He watched Martin struggle with disbelief. "Look at it, Martin. This was taken Thursday. She's alive. Baldwin did this. She isn't in that hole. She's fine. She's fine, Martin. She's fine."

Martin took the photograph and pressed it to his heart, sobbing. "For three days, I thought she was dead!" he shouted. "Three days! Of hell! Fucking Senior," Martin shouted, pulling himself to his feet. "I feel like burning his house down."

"I'll light the match," Max said. "He knew about you and James."

"Of course he did," Martin said. "It was his ugly little secret."

"But I thought . . ."

Martin cut him short. "Everyone has their secrets. Some are just easier to live with if you pretend otherwise."

"Why do the big wedding? Why go through all that? If he knew, he could have – should have – stopped this whole charade. Everything might have . . ."

"Max, boy. Settle down. Senior put on the huge wedding because if you're going to tell a lie, make it a big one. People see right through the little ones."

A slight wind kicked up, branches swaying, leaves sounding like waves to shore. Something in the suddenness of it, the way it brushed by the men and just as suddenly quieted again, brought a sense of presence, as if they weren't alone.

"Doesn't mean he didn't love his son."

"I guess it's all in how you define love," Martin said, more subdued. "You know what he said when I showed up at the cottage?"

"Let me guess," Max said. "Shut up and leave my island. This is a family affair. I know. You're not the only unwelcome asshole around here."

"As if his family has been here longer than mine," Martin sniped.

The men stood in silence for a moment, grieving.

"Look, Martin," Max said. "Remember what you told me at the wedding? There's a plan. It's all going to be all right."

Martin shook his head. "You know you sound just like Anna right now, don't you?"

"I mean it," Max insisted. "Meet me in Pellston tomorrow morning. At the hanger."

CHAPTER 22

A Plan

Sunday, Max held Katherine on his lap in a small waiting room at Pellston airport, staring out wide picture windows facing one lone runway. She leaned on him, her arm in a sling, fiddling with the edge of plaster around her thumb.

He kept looking behind him, waiting for Martin to walk through the door. If he didn't get there soon, he'd miss the puddle jumper to Detroit and their connection to Baltimore. When the flight was announced, and Martin still hadn't arrived, Max started spiraling. Had Martin changed his mind? Was the whole plan a mistake?

The commuter boarded and waited for a private jet to land. Max watched the jet taxi and the commuter take off, trying to calculate his next move.

"Martin," Katherine said.

"Yes, I know, we miss him, don't we."

Katherine called out. "Martin, Martin!"

And there he was, walking away from the Lear jet.

Martin was all smiles taking Katherine from Max, both men with tears in their eyes. For a moment, Katherine leaned into Martin but held Max's shirt in her good hand.

Max looked at the plane. "Yours?"

Martin shrugged.

"I knew you had money, but . . . hell, we don't even have a company jet. Carleton thought it was an extravagance.

"The whole family uses it," Martin said. "We share it."

With Katherine secured in one of eight seats, Max had to say goodbye. He thought it would be difficult for her, but she showed no emotion. She didn't even look out the window.

"I hope to hell you know what you're doing, Max," Martin said. "I could just disappear with her, you know."

"I'm sure you could. But you won't. Call me when you land."

The pilot motioned to Martin.

"Max."

"Yes?"

"You need to deplane. So we can take off. So I can get this angel into her own bed."

Max kissed Katherine and left her. Of all the times he'd had to leave her, this was the most difficult.

Katherine was asleep when Martin carried her into Anna's apartment. Though he was accustomed to being alone with her there, there had always been the expectation of James or Anna coming home. Without them, the emptiness was unbearable. He was about to put Katherine to bed but felt his legs weaken and barely made it to the couch before they gave out. She stirred a bit with the jolt, then settled. The quaking of his chest as he sobbed did not wake her.

The next morning, Max attended Carleton and Jeanne's funeral alone. Betsy wasn't up to it. When the family complained they didn't know anyone, Max took on greeting duties. A stream of locals filled the standing-room-only parlor, making their way up front to the two closed caskets bathed in flowers. There were tears and stories and laughs.
Carleton's long-haired nephew arrived in an army surplus camo jacket. His parents, Carleton's sister and husband, stood in the hall arguing with the funeral director about something they'd have done differently in their mortuary. Max watched Jeanne's niece flirt with some towny while her latest husband glared on. The niece from Seattle didn't make the trip. Jeanne's older brother appeared to be the only one of them grieving, sitting on a sofa, head in hands. His kids, who didn't make it to the wedding, didn't make it to the funeral either.
Max thought it odd that James and Trixie Baldwin weren't there. He had no way of knowing that up on the island, Trixie Baldwin lay dead in her bed. She'd been given a bottle of pills to help overcome her grief. She used them to overcome life.

Max returned to the office to find nothing short of chaos in the wake of Carleton's passing. Though he'd been CEO for three years, there was no succession plan in place. Max was told to pick up the slack and take on one of the acquisition projects. It meant traveling, and he refused. "I'm an engineer. Not a negotiator," he argued.

Then he said he was about to turn in his resignation. "I have family issues to contend with. I'm moving." He was met with an abrupt response: Impossible.

Leaving Katherine in Martin's care, Max flew to Georgia to assess a competitor's facility while two others looked over their books. His mind and heart weren't in it, but he muddled through out of respect for Carleton's legacy. He'd had big expansion plans for Hamilton.

When Max came home two days later, the kitchen was torn apart. Betsy had run out of sandwiches and went looking for food in the cupboards. He found her huddled in a corner of the living room, crying. He sat next to her and held her until she calmed.

She tried to speak, but couldn't find any words and her tears came again. She looked at Max with such yearning he couldn't bear it. Then she found a word: Hungry.

Max took her to the kitchen and wiped her eyes. He called the Sandbox for a take-out order, put Betsy in the car, and drove around town until it was time to get the food. Betsy's glance never seemed to land on anything. It just drifted over everything they passed. She sat slump-shouldered and silent. His guilt could not be assuaged.

"You can't seriously take Katherine away from here," Martin yelled to the phone that evening. "I hate your plan. It's horrible! This is her home, Max! Let me raise her, Max."

"What? Not a chance. You. A homosexual man. Raise my daughter. Not a chance." Until that moment, Max had not had to face his feeling toward James and Martin. He'd tried to see them through Anna's eyes, but without her, and without James to temper Martin's more theatrical mannerisms, his discomfort revealed itself.

The silence on the other end of the line was achingly painful, then Martin spit out his response. "Then you need to come here and be her daddy."

"Martin, I'm fifty-six. I have no business raising a little girl on my own. Wouldn't be fair to her."

"You're a fucking coward, Max. Your plan is the worst." The line went silent again. "She shouldn't have to lose everything she knows." Martin's voice cracked as he fought back tears. "I'll miss her."

"You think I haven't gone over this thing a hundred times?" Max spoke as gently as he could. "Martin, I know that pain you're talking about. Every time I had to leave. Every minute I'm away from her. And from Anna."

The line went silent again.

"I don't know how you did it, old man. I really don't know how."

Max's silence said more than words could have.

"Martin. It's all arranged. Almost. A few details to iron out is all."

"She's different, you know," Martin said. "Not the same angel. She doesn't want to eat. She cries. She calls out, demanding Mommy tuck her in. She doesn't understand any of it. And taking her away is only going to make it worse."

"Maybe it will make it better."

"You're insanely wrong about that."

"Look, Martin. It will be a change for all of us. Ann Arbor is. . ."

"So, you've settled it already? It's a done deal?"

"Not quite, but it's the best option. Ann Arbor is a wonderful place to raise a child. I'm moving there to be close by. You can, too. I'll make her bedroom there as much like her old room as I can. Bring her things with you when you come. The lamb, donkey, the cloud pillow . . ." Max had to stop before he broke down.

"I've got it covered," Martin said. "I'm having the girl across the hall watch her in my apartment while I pack it all up. Won't upset her so much."

"Have you gone in yet, to your apartment?" Martin did not answer. "You haven't, have you?"

"He's not there. He never will be. How . . ."

"Think about moving to Michigan, Martin."

"Me? In Michigan? I don't think so."

"You can be closer to us. To Katherine. You don't have a life in Baltimore without James. That was his life."

"Now you're going to tell me to go find a life of my own? Is that it? James was my life. All my life!"

"We both need to find new lives without them. But we have Katherine. And I need you here for her. So do what you need to do to close the place up there, and come to Ann Arbor with us. You can teach or whatever it is you do."

"I take care of Katherine. That's what I do."

"So come here and keep on doing that. We'll figure it out."

Martin's voice turned wistful. "It was splendid for a while, wasn't it, Max?"

"Yes. It was a beautiful dream." Max paused. "And now, we wake up."

"Dear Max. I'll see you next week."

"Hug her for me."

"I try to hug her for all of us. All the time. She won't let me." Martin hung up.

CHAPTER 23

Sacrifice

Max sat in a corner booth in a small dark bar in Ann Arbor, hoping Howard wouldn't show up. Given time to reflect, Max got caught up in the things he could have done differently. Martin was right. He'd been a coward. He never should have let Anna keep the truth from her parents. He should have been brave enough to face Carleton from the very beginning. But all the soul searching was worthless in the thick of loss. His only job now was to keep from losing anything more. Doing what was right, something he'd always instinctually known, was suddenly unclear.

He didn't notice Howard standing at the table.

"Max, I'm sorry about your friends," he said, sitting down. "How you holding up?"

He ordered a beer and another Scotch for Max from a nearby waitress. "Sorry, I'm late. This new job is gunna kill me. You can't believe the stuff that comes out of the mayor's mouth. I have my hands full. I may be the assistant to the city manager, but I spend all day brokering peace between him and the mayor . . ."

"I thought you were an accountant or assessor or something." Max said.

As Howard explained himself, Max paid little attention to the words, waiting for an opening, until he interrupted Howard mid-stream. "How's the house coming? About ready to move in?"

"Carpet goes down today. Ellen's packing up at home. Movers come day after tomorrow."

"Is she looking forward to living in Ann Arbor?"

Howard shrugged.

The drinks came.

"Howard, do you ever think about having a family?"

"What? Where did that come from?"

"It's a simple question. You're over thirty, and Ellen is, what? Pushing thirty? You two ever talk about having kids?"

Howard shook his head and took a long draw from the beer just placed before him.

Max couldn't recall ever having a real conversation with Howard. They'd engaged in small talk, griped about work, but nothing substantial. He wasn't even sure he knew who the man was in regards to much of anything. He downed the drink and dove right in. "Ever thought about adoption?"

"Adoption? No. Not really. I don't understand where all this is . . ."

Max pulled a photograph from his pocket and slid it across the table. Howard looked at it casually and slid it back.

"Cute kid."

"She just became an orphan. Lost her parents the same night . . ." Max stumbled over the lie and stopped talking, for how long, he had no idea. "She's Anna Post's daughter."

"I don't understand. Wasn't she k . . ."

"No." Max wouldn't let Howard wouldn't finish the word. "She's fine."

Howard shook his head. "Ahh. Poor kid. Wait. I read she died in the accident with her parents and Posts. I don't understand."

"She's my daughter."

Somebody burst out laughing on the other side of the room. Howard said nothing. His expression said nothing. His eyes locked on Max.

"Howard, she's my daughter. She survived the crash." He took a deep breath and delivered the words he would regret as soon as he said them. "I want you to adopt her." Max started to explain in a slow, deliberate cadence. "Her name is Katherine. She's three. Her mother and I . . ."

"Anna Post," Howard interjected with an accusatory tone. "Your best friend's daughter. A woman young enough to be your own daughter." He drank some beer and shook his head. "Hell, she was younger than Ellen! Christ almighty, Max."

"Look, I ran into her on campus. One thing led to another. It wasn't intentional. We fell in love."

"Then why'd she marry somebody else?"

There was only so much Max was willing to share. He held back the rest of the story, saying it was only a way to make the best of a difficult situation. "All that time I was supposed to be at State? They were trips to

Baltimore. All to see them. To be with my daughter. Katherine. And Anna."

Howard sat quietly, pushing the rest of his beer aside. Max waited, his throat tightening.

"You have to tell them," Howard urged. "Ellen and Betsy. You have to tell them."

Max slammed his fist on the table. "This was a mistake." He got up to leave, but Howard grabbed his arm, and Max slumped back into the booth.

"I am so sorry for you, Max. Really. I'm in no position to make any judgments. I get that you need, well, somebody. Believe me. I get it. We're both married to a version of the same woman. Like mother like daughter. They are not easy women to love."

"I need you to adopt her. I'll make it worth your while."

Howard shot him a cutting glance. "Worth my while? You're talking about raising a kid!"

Max sighed, embarrassed. "What I mean is, I'll help support her. We'll do it in a way Ellen won't figure out."

"Oh, you don't have to worry about that." Howard rolled his eyes with an annoyance Max hadn't expected. "All she does is spend it. Never thinks about how the money shows up so long as it does."

Max ordered another round and asked Howard if he was as miserable as he sounded.

Howard shrugged. "You know exactly how miserable I am. We have our good days. And maybe a kid would give Ellen something to do with her time. Maybe it would give her something, someone, to love. She sure as hell doesn't love me." He winced as if he'd gone too far, said too much. "It's just that . . ."

"I know, Howard. I get it."

"Don't you just see through them sometimes? And I can't help but think somewhere in her is a really good person. I see it, get a glimpse every so often and I just think I have to take care of her. I mean what would happen to her if I didn't? If I just walked away? Who'd ever take her in? You know? For all her bluster, she's fragile in a way I can't even comprehend."

He'd nailed it, something Max had never been able to do. He'd always thought himself weak for staying with Betsy, but Howard made it sound noble. Whether it was noble or not, he smiled, realizing the two of them were bound by a common malady. "We're moving here," Max said. "I found a small house not far from your place."

"You're too young to retire. What are you going to do?"

"We're situated pretty well. Portfolio is strong. I'll sell the house, my club membership. Maybe U of M will find a place for me. Don't worry. I'll figure it out."

New drinks arrived. Max gripped his glass, waiting for the hurricane of emotions to let up. "Will you do it? Will you raise my daughter as your own?"

Howard hesitated, refusing to take his glass or even look up.

"Howard. I'll beg if I have to. If you don't do this, I'll be forced to leave Betsy and do it on my own." His eyes filled with tears. "That's not exactly an option. She can't be on her own."

"What are you saying, Max?"

"Nothing," Max lied. "She's just . . . forgetful. Let's leave it at that. Do this, Howard. Take her on. She's a beautiful child. You'll love her. I know it."

Howard lifted his beer, took a swallow, put it down, and stood up. He scanned the bar, shook his head, and looked to his feet. "I'll do it," he said before walking away.

Max watched Ellen reach over his dining room table, the fullness of her body lying on the polished walnut, trying to reach the centerpiece bouquet of silk flowers. She pulled out a rose and stuck it back in on the other side. Betsy stood from her chair and repositioned it back where it had been. She sat down without speaking, without making eye contact.

Max studied his daughter. Her puffy face resembled the toddler she'd once been. He tried to find something warm and inviting in her eyes, but saw only boredom.

"No idea what this is about," Ellen complained.

Max began his lie, explaining there had been more to the accident the night Carleton and Jeanne died. "There was a young couple with a small child." He glanced at Howard, who looked away and crossed his arms tight against his chest.

"We know, Dad," Ellen said, exasperated. "The Baldwins."

"No."

"Yes," Ellen said, rolling her eyes.

"No, I mean yes, the Baldwin couple died. There was another car involved. Another family."

"So?"

Howard's knee began bouncing.

Max thought Anna would have known how to better spin the tale. He even entertained the idea that she was orchestrating it all from the grave because he would never have been capable of such deceit before knowing her. "Both parents died," he said. "Very tragic. The police told me about them when I went up to see about Carleton.

About the accident." Howard cracked his neck. Max cut the story short. "They had no family and I heard there's no one to take the child. She'll go into the system if someone doesn't come forward and adopt her. Of course, I thought of you."

"I'm too old," Betsy said.

"No, mother," Ellen groaned. "He wants me and Howard to take her, not you. Imagine Dad at his age being a father again. Absurd."

Max rubbed his head slowly, fuming. "With your move to Ann Arbor and Howard's new job, it would be like a brand new start for you," he urged. "And you'd finally have a little family."

"Boy or girl," she Ellen asked. "Because I don't want a boy."

Max did all he could to control his revulsion. "It's a girl. Almost three years old."

"We need to get a bigger house," Ellen grumbled.

"The house we found will be just fine, Darling," Howard said. "It has three bedrooms, doesn't it?"

"One's a guest room and the other one was going to be my hobby room, Howard. You know that."

Max suddenly calmed. It was over. No more games or lies. It was time to tell them the truth. He would raise Katherine on his own, someplace where no one knew the Posts or Baldwins. Martin would continue to be in her life. Except, Baldwin made it all impossible when he destroyed the guardianship papers and forged the death certificate. Her future was in the hands of a Baldwin attorney who would facilitate her private adoption with falsified documents. And the Posts, if the truth came out, all of them would come for her. He started to spiral.

Howard took Ellen's hand. "Max and I have talked it over, dear. I think . . ."

Ellen snapped back. "You talked about this behind my back?"

"He just wanted to run it by me before he talked to you. We didn't make any decisions. He was just, you know, testing the waters."

"What's she look like?" Ellen asked as if the adoption depended on how cute the girl might be.

Max showed her the same photo he showed Howard, one taken at a park that spring.

"Does she look like that all the time?" Ellen asked. "She's grinning so hard."

Howard said she's grinning because she's happy. That's a good thing.

"And what's her name?"

Before Max could answer, Ellen proclaimed that no matter what it was, she'd change it. "What do you think about Paula, Mom? Or Peggy? Karen's a good name."

"Look," Max said. "She won't be ready to travel for another few days."

"With all that extra laundry, I'm going to need a bigger washer," Ellen stated, starting a list. "And a bigger refrigerator. And she'll need clothes, lots of clothes. I can't possibly be expected to get everything settled in the new house and do all this extra work at the same time. I mean we're only just moving in. Everything takes so much time."

"I know it's a lot of work," Max interrupted. He explained he'd have a decorator make the room as close to what the child was used to as possible. "You won't have to lift a finger. And I'll buy the appliances."

Ellen asked if she came with any money. "Surely her parents had some money."

"No. No money." Max could feel his face turning red. "I'll help out. Just as I would for any grandchild you had."

Complicit in the ruse, Howard assured his wife adding a child to the family would not be a financial hardship. "I think it would be nice," he said. "To have a little girl running about? Doesn't that sound nice, Dear?"

Ellen relented.

"Yes," Ellen said, "but adoption carries the stigma of failure."

Max suggested they claim her as their own. "Nobody in Ann Arbor knows you. Who's to be the wiser?"

The decision was made. Howard and Ellen would adopt Katherine. There were, however, no smiles to indicate impending joy. Ellen appeared as if all she anticipated was added responsibility. Max recognized that look of imposition, the one she wore as a child every time she was told to make her bed, or clean her room, or do anything else she didn't want to do. He felt the room closing in. He and Howard walked outside, neither of them speaking anything of what they were thinking.

Howard finally broke the silence. "She'll come around. I'll see to it. We'll make it work, Max. It's for the best. She'll come around." He couldn't convince himself, let alone Max.

Martin met Max at a park in Ann Arbor and handed Katherine over to him. He'd flown her from Baltimore. Both men had reservations about the arrangement, but there was nothing left to say. The situation was difficult enough without hashing it out yet again.

Max hung a new car seat over the passenger seatback and transferred the boxes from Martin's rental car. The three played hide and seek, Katherine running off her pent-up energy, her little cast flinging from side to side. There were, however, no giggles, and it seemed she was playing the game just to placate them, until she sat down and started crying. She wanted Daddy.

Martin suddenly hoisted her high and spun her around before kissing her goodbye. She did not see him cry as he walked away.

Max spent the afternoon with her in the park, quietly reading to her on a blanket in the grass. She napped. Max watched her every breath.

Max didn't notice Martin on the other side of the park, watching. And he didn't see Martin follow and park down the street from Ellen and Howard's house.

Like a raging flood, the plan was in motion, lies washing away everything beautiful in his daughter's life. Max carefully lifted Katherine from her car seat, about to deposit her like debris on Ellen's doorstep.

The first thing Ellen said upon laying eyes on the little girl with her arm in a cast nearly gave Max the courage to tell the truth. "Why, look at the poor little thing," Ellen said. "She's broken."

Katherine cried and kicked when Ellen tried to take her from Max. It made no sense that Katherine kept crying for *Max Max Max*. Howard insisted the child had lost everyone she knew and was just clinging to him because he was now familiar. "You've been spending time with her over the last couple of weeks, haven't you, Max,"

Howard said, putting forth one more lie in a long string of them to placate his wife.

"Well," Ellen said to Howard. "Janet lives here now, and I'm her new mommy, and you're her new daddy."

"Her name is Katherine," Max said.

"She'll have to get used to Janet and the sooner the better. You can leave, Dad. We'll figure it out from here."

Ellen succeeded in extricating the child from Max's arms and turned her back to him, walking through the living room out of sight. Katherine screamed all the way.

Howard's expression held no pity for Max. "This is all on you," he said.

Martin watched the exchange from a distance, his heart breaking beyond all repair. Gripping a small stuffed giraffe, he watched Max collect a box from the car, the last of her things from the apartment, and take them inside, closing the door behind him. The deed was done, joy extinguished.

In Katherine's bedroom, Max began to unpack the box, but Ellen insisted she didn't need any of it. "We'll buy all new. Throw that all away. They're old."

Katherine reached out to Max, crying hysterically, almost falling out of Ellen's arms. He hoisted her into his arms and sat in an overstuffed rocking chair in the corner, the one from the apartment, the one Anna used to nestle in when she nursed her. He began to see the error in trying to recreate Katherine's bedroom. All the elements were there, but they felt like shreds of the past reconstituted into some cruel imitation. As he swayed gently, Katherine began to calm. Without making eye contact with Ellen, Max told her to keep all the toys. He said it in a manner reminiscent of her childhood: *Do what I say or else.*

And so it was that the exceptional Katherine Lorraine Post Baldwin became common Janet Marie Granger, her previous life erased; the accident forgotten, her doting parents deceased, her original grandparents eliminated, abandoned by her Uncle Martin. She was displaced from Baltimore and situated in Ann Arbor with a new mother the polar opposite of Anna. This was the only life she would know. She was only three. What could she possibly remember at that age? She would soon learn to call Max Grandpa Max.

CHAPTER 24

Transition

Ellen's first full day alone with little Janet did not get off to a good start. Janet was still in her pajamas at lunchtime. Ellen tried to change her into a new outfit but got caught up on the cast, and Janet screamed, the endless scream, the one that conveyed rage. When Ellen stopped trying, Janet stopped screaming. They were both quick learners. Ellen hung the little checkered dress with matching tights back in the closet.

Having no idea what to do to entertain the child, Ellen sat on the bed next to her and tried reading to her, but Janet kept kicking the book away. Ellen picked her up but Janet wiggled, and kicked and whined until Ellen almost dropped her. Ellen tried singing to her, a song she'd heard on the radio that morning. *She wore blue velvet, ooh ooh, bluer than velvet were her eyes, woo woo woo, softer than something was her sigh ...* When she couldn't remember the words, she hummed, but Janet told her to stop singing, her words clear, crisp and defiant:

STOP SINGING. Ellen stopped singing. Janet stopped whining.

"Fine then," Ellen said.

Ellen went to the kitchen to make breakfast. Janet followed as far as the family room, climbing onto the couch where she fiddled with the fringe on a throw pillow and stared out the window into the empty backyard.

Ellen looked at her once, and only long enough to surmise she was safe before returning to her task. She made toast with butter and jelly and poured milk on a bowl of cheerios. She collected Janet and tried to lift her into her booster seat at the kitchen table, but Janet kicked and hollered "One, two, three!" and she started screaming in a pitch so high it tested the boundaries of human tolerance. Ellen put her down. Janet stopped screaming.

Ellen put a placemat on the floor, and put Janet's plate and bowl down on it. Janet wouldn't eat the toast. She picked cheerios out of the bowl but would only eat the dry ones. Ellen finally poured a pile of them on the plate. Janet ate them all.

Lunch was an equal clash of wills. Ellen made two sandwiches of white bread, mayonnaise, cheese, lettuce and bologna. She cut them both in half, into triangles, and put them on plates. Opting for the floor again, she put down the placemat and the plate.

Janet sat down and started taking her sandwich apart, eating only the cheese, putting everything else on the placemat. Ellen put it back together. Janet dismantled it. Ellen put it back together. Janet got up and walked away. Ellen threw away both sandwiches.

Max left work early to go to Ann Arbor to check on Katherine. Ellen turned him away. "She has enough to contend with getting used to me. You can play happy grandpa later. Not now."

"Is she eating?"

"Of course."

"Is she sleeping through the night?"

"So far."

"No crying?"

"Of course, she cries. All the time. Children do that."

Max felt another fissure in his heart crack open.

"She settles down eventually. Last night, it was only fifteen minutes. You're not supposed to give in to . . ."

"I want to see her," he insisted.

"She's sleeping. Come back tomorrow."

"I'm coming in."

"Not now. Or do you think I'm a bad mother?"

Howard pulled into the drive and told Ellen to let Max in. Ellen relented.

Max saw his sad little girl was indeed sleeping. He sat watching her for the longest time, shrouded in a melancholy he feared might never lift.

On his way out the door, Howard asked Max when he and Betsy were going to move to the Ann Arbor house. "The house is ready, isn't it?"

"Loose ends to tie up at work," he lied. The move was contingent on Betsy's instability. "It may be a while yet." Max drove the two hours back to Edgewater, learning on his arrival that James Baldwin Sr. had crashed his vintage Timm M-150 Collegiate airplane into a field and died in a ball of fire.

His death negated the contract Max signed.

Events, however, had already unfolded in a way not conducive to truth-telling. Katherine had already been deposited in her new forever home and renamed like a shelter dog,

Janet's refusal to eat anything Ellen prepared continued. She wouldn't eat a peanut butter sandwich for lunch, mashed potatoes, or roast beef or peas at dinner. She wouldn't eat fried chicken or meatloaf or oatmeal. All she wanted was applesauce. After three days of not getting Janet to eat anything substantial, Ellen took her to a doctor. Surely, he could fix whatever was wrong with her.

Janet kicked and cried in Ellen's arms as the receptionist took a large envelope from her.

Pulling an X-ray out, she said she needed records from her previous physician.

"I don't have them. That's what you need to know."

"But, ma'am, we need . . ."

Ellen put Janet down, telling the woman behind the counter to make do.

In the exam room, Janet quietly sat on the high table protected by a nurse, a large woman who reassured her continuously that she was a pretty little girl, a sweetie, such a good girl to sit so still. Ellen was about to comment on the rarity of good behavior when the doctor entered.

Opening the child's file, he put the X-ray of her arm up to the light. "We'll need official records from her previous physician," he said.

"I don't have them."

"Where did you move here from?"

Ellen glared at him and finally said, "We adopted her. From Up North. We don't want her to know."

"I see," he said. "I wouldn't have guessed. She looks just like you." He gently touched Janet's knee. She did not look at him. "We'll want her adoption papers for her file. When you get around to it. No hurry." He touched her clothing, caked with dried applesauce.

"What brings you here today, Mrs. Granger?" he asked.

"She won't eat. She screams when I change her clothes. She hardly talks."

"Is there anything that triggered the behavior? Has it been going on for long?"

Ellen hesitated. "All week."

"I see. How long has she been in your home with you?"

"What does that mean?"

"When did you get her?"

"Four days ago. Five. I'm not sure."

"I see." His inflection was not judgmental. He spoke to Janet in a soft voice. His touch was reassuring, a whole flat hand supporting her back, cupping her face. He gently did a thorough exam. She did not resist. He asked her to count for him and say her ABCs. Janet remained silent. He showed her pictures of animals on flashcards to see if she would identify them. She refused. He tested her hearing by whispering her name from across the room. She did not respond. When he was finished, he wrote notes. Lots of notes.

"What? What are you writing?" Ellen insisted.

The nurse carefully dressed Janet, powering through the squirming and whining. Ellen said nothing.

The doctor closed the file and spoke to Ellen in a direct manner. "Janet has deficits, Mrs. Granger. Cognitive deficits. It may be a result of the trauma, the accident that broke her arm, or going from her home and family to a strange one. Or it could be congenital. It's hard to say. She's behind in language skills. She should be able to at least count to ten by now and have some knowledge of the alphabet. It could be that her natural parents didn't teach her. Without knowing anything about her background, I don't have much to go on. I suggest you keep trying different foods until you find something she likes. If all else fails, give her baby food. At least she'll get some nourishment. And practice patience. You both have an adjustment here, so my advice is to let her know you love her and she'll come around. If the deficits I mentioned seem permanent, I can recommend some early learning programs for her."

"You're saying she's retarded?" Ellen asked, horrified.

"That's not what I'm saying at all. Let's give her time to acclimate. Be kind to her. Be gentle with her. Be consistent. And I want to see you both back here in two weeks."

"Dad!" Ellen yelled over the phone. "The doctor said this child has cognitive deficits! She's retarded! He didn't come right out and say it but he was thinking it. What did you get us into, Dad? For all we know she came from ignorant trailer trash, and now I'm left to deal with her for the rest of my life?"

Max tried to calmly assure Ellen that Janet was not retarded. "I'm sure it's the result of all she's been through. Her whole life is turned upside down. She doesn't know you. It will take some time. Be patient with her. Love her. Let her know you love her."

"Like you loved me, Daddy?"

Ellen hung up.

Max went into a board meeting. The company was in a tailspin of infighting without Carleton to wrangle opposing sides. By the time it let out, it was too late to go to Ann Arbor.

After spending years in Dearborn as a tax assessor, Howard had taken the job in Ann Arbor expecting it not only to be a pay upgrade, but work he might like. It wasn't. Instead of dealing with disgruntled property owners, he found himself brokering peace between the city manager and the mayor's office. He came home exhausted to a new house, a grumpy wife, and an emotionally fragile child. By the time Ellen unloaded on him about the horrible day she'd had with Janet, he was depleted.

Accepting Janet into his life seemed like an act of contrition or penitence. He couldn't decide which and sometimes imagined her to be his second chance to get something in his life right, to make up for his inadequacies. He felt the child was too young to be so unhappy. It became his mission to help her.

On Janet's fifth night, she woke up screaming. Howard got up, but Ellen grabbed his arm. "Don't go in there. She has to learn."

Howard ripped his arm away and went to Janet, but every effort to comfort her made her more manic, her arms flailing, her sobs sounding more horrific than anything he'd ever heard. Then she suddenly stopped moving. Her eyes glazed over in a dull stare, and she went limp. Terrified, Howard took her to the emergency room, thinking there was something horribly wrong with her.

The ER doc called it surrender syndrome. "Like a wild animal, young children sometimes shut down when confronted with too much stimuli. If it was a night terror that brought it on, she'll probably grow out of it."

"What do you mean, if it was a night terror. That's what it was. She woke up screaming." As Howard was about to collect Janet to leave, a social worker intervened asking about the broken arm. At first, he didn't grasp the nature of her request. When he saw a police officer loitering nearby, it struck him. "You think I did this?"

"Surrender syndrome generally means she's responding to a trauma," the social worker said. "Can you tell us what that might be?"

When he explained the accident and adoption, she said he needed to supply the paperwork. He didn't have any. For a moment, it seemed they weren't going to let him take Janet home. He pushed past the nurse standing between him and the child. Janet reached for him as he picked her up, his shirt tight in her fist, hiding her face in his shoulder. "I'm taking her home. I'll get your paperwork. It's only been days since she lost her family. And you think you're taking her away from me? No way in hell!"

"That's a bad word," Janet said.

Howard's eyes welled up. She had hardly spoken a word since she arrived. "Yes, it is. I'm sorry."

They let him leave with instructions to provide adoption papers and medical records.

A currier delivered a packet to Max at work the next day. It held a collection of stock certificates in Janet Marie Granger's name, a forged birth certificate and medical records for the fictitious Katherine Smith from Iron Mountain, Michigan, and adoption papers. At least

Baldwin had followed through on his commitment to Katherine before committing suicide.

Max gave the stocks to his lawyer, a rather disorganized but reputable Edgewater attorney who placed the big blank envelope on his desk with every intention of writing a corresponding letter of intent to release the stocks to the child on her 21st birthday. The attorney's secretary, in an effort to maintain a modicum of order, tucked the envelope into Max's folder. The attorney's procrastination, however, was out of her control.

Howard didn't tell Max about the emergency room visit or surrender syndrome but seemed overtly relieved when Max delivered all her paperwork. Janet's medical records were assimilated into the system with only her adoptive name, erasing the false trail forever.

On Janet's sixth day, Howard came home to an unusually quiet house. Ellen was busy in the kitchen making dinner. She said that Janet was sleeping or playing or whatever. Her point was that she wasn't screaming and that made Ellen happy.

Howard found Janet in her bed, perfectly still. Her little undershirt was stuck halfway over her head. Her good arm was tangled and pinned behind her back. Her cast arm was pinched in the twisted shirt. He broke down and sobbed as he carefully took a pair of sheers and cut the shirt off of her. Whether she recognized his pain or was just too far gone to fight, she let him pick her up. He tenderly spread a soft blanket on the floor and put her on it. He laid down next to her without touching her. She scooted over to him, leaned against him, her back on his chest. She closed her eyes, slumped into a ball, and slept. He curled around her, laying a blanket over her like a tent to keep her warm. He stayed there all night and in doing so, committed himself to the child.

Max took the morning off and took Betsy to Ann Arbor. She wouldn't get out of the car. He went in without her to find Janet sitting on the floor next to a plate with a puddle of applesauce and a graham cracker on it.

"What's this?" Max picked her up and asked where her booster seat was. "She's a little girl, not a dog!" When he felt the diaper, he swore out loud.

"Bad word, Max," Janet said.

"Yes. Sorry." He took her to the bathroom to put her on her little potty seat. It wasn't there. He found it in the cupboard under the sink. As soon as she sat down, she pooped. The expression on her face spoke volumes. "Good job holding it, Pumpkin. We'll just throw this icky diaper away, shall we?" They went back to the kitchen, where Ellen was still stewing about Janet's eating habits.

"If you think it's so easy, you try to feed her!"

Max never wanted to strike a woman as much as he wanted to slap Ellen. "I'm going to the market."

He coaxed Betsy into the house and took Janet to the car. "Big red," she said, and Max put her red car seat in place up front next to him. Riding high enough she could see out the windows, she watched houses go by as he drove toward a grocery store he'd seen on the way. He passed right by it. He drove a block further, and another block, and saw a sign for the highway. He looked at Janet, her head leaning back, bored, silent, and he saw before him a life with her and her alone. He'd leave Betsy with Ellen and leave them all behind. It would be beautiful. She would be Katherine again. He saw her blossoming in kindergarten, doing a school play, doing homework in a bedroom full of books, graduating high school with honors and going off to college. It was the happiest he'd felt in months. He stopped at a red light. There was a Kroger on the corner.

He pulled in and together he and Janet went shopping.

Max and Janet walked into the house to Ellen hollering at Betsy. He handed over a sack of groceries, telling Ellen be kinder to her mother.

"She's ignoring me, Dad. How do you live with this? I asked her to fold some laundry, and she just sat there. Won't lift a finger."

Max ignored her complaints and unpacked groceries. "Make the mac & cheese with a little extra milk and make sure it's mixed thoroughly. Boil a hot dog, and cut it up into quarter-inch pieces, and put it on the plate next to the macaroni. Don't let it touch. Peel the apple and cut it in thin slices. Put them on the same plate. Three piles. That don't touch. Do you understand? Because the way you're looking at me, it looks like you don't understand."

"Yes, Dad," Ellen whined. "I understand."

He took Janet to her bedroom and pulled a book from the shelf to read to her.

"Not that one," she said in her quietest voice.

"Well, there you are," Max said, thrilled to hear her speak. "Which one would you like?"

She got off the bed and tried to reach the books, but the shelf was too high. He moved all her books to the bottom shelf, and she picked one out. "This one."

They sat on the floor against the bed, Janet on his lap, leaning on his chest. He'd just begun reading when he heard Howard come home and the ensuing argument. Ellen's shrill voice carried throughout the house.

Before he left, Max told Ellen to give Janet orange juice without pulp, mild cheese slices, bite-sized plain white meat chicken pieces with ranch dressing for dipping, and sweet seedless grapes cut in half."

"And how would you know what she wants?" Ellen barked.

Max lied as best he could. "It's what you wanted at that age."

"Like you would know anything about what I wanted at any age!"

Max nearly exploded but somehow kept his voice in check. "And no more diapers. She's potty trained."

"No. She isn't," Ellen barked.

"Yes. She is. You need to be consistent with it. Her little potty chair is . . ."

Walking away, Ellen said Janet was too retarded to know how to use the potty.

Howard could see Max was about to lose it and told him to leave. Collecting Betsy from the couch, Howard walked her to the car and called for Max to drive her home. He had to call out twice, but Max finally came out.

"I'll see to it Janet uses the potty chair. I will. I'm making headway with her. With Janet. She lets me dress her. And she'll sit with me. I read a book to her last night, and she almost snuggled. Almost. It's just, well, I thought Ellen would come around. But she's so . . ."

"Cold. She got that from her mother."

Max got in his car, gripped the wheel, and looked up at Howard. "What the fuck was I thinking?"

Howard said he'd make it work. "That little girl has been through hell. I won't let her down, Max. I won't."

As soon as Max got home, he called Martin.

CHAPTER 25

Reinforcements

While Max was in Ann Arbor telling his daughter how to feed Janet, Mrs. Osterman, his cleaning lady in Edgewater, was changing bed linens when she heard Betsy shouting. She got downstairs in time to see Betsy throw a kitchen soup can at the grocery delivery boy. Mrs. Osterman intervened, taking the sacks and apologizing to the young man. She put the food away. Betsy went to the living room and stared at the television. It was turned off.

Mrs. Osterman, no stranger to caring for the infirmed, stayed the afternoon. When Max was not home at dinner time, she fried some hamburger patties and baked two potatoes. Betsy ate a few bites and left the table. When Max came home, Mrs. Osterman offered to spend afternoons with Betsy.

"They have more difficulty in the afternoon," she said. "People with dementia. She's had a rough day. Been sittin' in her chair all day except when she yelled at the delivery boy. Let's arrange deliveries when I can be here from now on."

To that moment, Max had no concept of how closely he'd held the secret of Betsy's condition. In that simple act of someone acknowledging the dementia, he found a sense of relief.

"It won't be for that much longer," he told Mrs. Osterman. "We're moving to Ann Arbor soon."

"Oh, my, my, my, Mr. Crawford. You can't do that," she said with alarm. "She can't make that kind of change in her condition. She can't." She gathered her cleaning supplies and headed to the door. "I'll be back tomorrow. We'll figure out payment later. She needs me now. You enjoy your dinner and try to get her to eat some more. She's too thin."

Max made two plates of food, but Betsy wouldn't eat.

Max picked Martin up at the airport in Ann Arbor, admitting the whole arrangement, the adoption, was a mistake.

"I knew it," Martin said. "What have we done to our little Katherine?"

"Janet," Max corrected him. "Must get used to Janet."

"I will NEVER get used to that insipid name."

Max introduced Martin as a friend from work. "He's had experience with little kids, I thought maybe he could help." Ellen was smitten with Martin the instant she saw him. Her flirting was hysterical, and it was all Martin could do not to laugh in her face. "I understand you have a daughter," he said with well-practiced charm.

"You're lucky," she said. "She's sleeping. You don't want to be here when she's awake."

This sent a chill across Martin's face, something Ellen was too blind to notice. Max took him to see Janet, and Ellen followed, begging them not to wake her up.

"She won't let any of us touch her," Ellen sniped.

When they stepped into the bedroom, Janet stirred and opened her eyes. The first person she saw was Max. She waved at him but did not smile. Then she saw Martin and put her good arm out to him. He was about to pick her up when Ellen yelled *stop!* He ignored her. The child did not cry, or scream, or kick, or flail as he drew her into his arms.

"Well don't you have the magic touch," Ellen shrugged, more annoyed than pleased. "Do what you want. I've got soup on the stove." She left them on their own.

Janet rested her head on Martin's shoulder, gripping his shirt tight in her fist, staring at Max. Martin tapped on her cast and cooed at her with a silly expression. She giggled, something she had not done since her arrival. He stroked her head and did tickle fingers on her belly and gently squeezed her toes. She giggled again.

Max kept Janet occupied while Martin went to the kitchen to fix her something to eat.

"My sister's kids are little," he told Ellen, who sat at the kitchen table leafing through a magazine. "I learned a few tricks you might employ." Digging through the fridge, he pulled out a carton of eggs and a bottle of ketchup. "You have a special plate for her, don't you?" he said knowing full well she did, because it was in the box he packed.

"I suppose so, I haven't dug it out yet."

"Well," he urged. "Go find it. Silverware, too. It should all be in there."

Ellen did not have the presence of mind to question how he would know what might be *in there* and went to find the box in a closet.

Martin heaved a sigh audible even in the next room. She did not notice that either. He was scrambling an egg when Ellen returned with the full complement of little girl tableware, including the Winnie the Pooh plate. "Remember," he instructed, "children don't like crusts. So when you make toast or sandwiches, you always cut them off." The toast popped up, and he cut the crusts, making sure she watched.

With a fair amount of cajoling, Martin taught Ellen about dipping. "Everything is more fun if she has something to dip it in. Kids like sweet things, so ketchup makes eggs taste better. They even like to dip toast in it."

"In ketchup? That's disgusting," Ellen said.

"Let's just accept that her palate isn't as refined as ours, shall we?" He described Katherine's favorite foods, from crustless sandwiches without condiments to peeled fruit of all kinds. "Tomato rice soup made with milk. She loves that."

"How do you know that."

"All kids love that. And their mouths are small so they like to eat things one at a time. She may want to take things apart, like sandwiches, and eat everything separately. It's OK."

"But it's a sandwich," Ellen protested.

"Let's try a little flexibility, shall we? She's only three." He scooped the eggs from the pan to the plate, poured a puddle of ketchup, cut the toast into strips, and set the plate on the table. "No butter. Just plain. There. Now, let it cool a bit. Kids don't like hot food. Let's call her into lunch."

Ellen threw her head back and hollered to Janet, demanding her presence.

Martin cringed. "Maybe sound as if it might be fun instead of like you're about to chop her head off."

"That was uncalled for," Ellen sniped.

"Oh, darling Ellen. You just aren't used to children. You have to pander to them to get them to do what you want. Think of it as a game," he cooed, pandering to her with a hugely fake smile.

"Janet, honey?" Ellen tried again, sounding almost evil. "I have some yummy lunch for you here. Time to eat."

Janet still didn't come. "Oh, for fuck sake," Martin snapped, and he went in to retrieve the child. Ellen couldn't believe she actually heard a giggle from the other room. Martin reappeared, Janet running in front of him. He counted one, two, three before lifting her to the booster chair.

"She won't let me do that," Ellen complained.

"Did you count? Children love to count."

"She doesn't know how!"

Martin glared at Max.

As Janet dipped her toast into the ketchup and ate it, Martin wrote down the list of her favorite foods. "Grilled cheese with soft white bread and a single American slice, then cut in strips like the toast and always without the crust. She will love Spaghetti-Os, smooth peanut butter and grape jelly, a very thin coating of each, and no butter. Cut carrots sticks skinny. Cook green beans until they're soft, peeled strawberries, and wash blueberries . . ."

"I'm supposed to peel the strawberries? I'm not doing that."

Martin continued as if she hadn't spoken. "… sliced bananas, butterscotch pudding, chicken cut up in strips, and Ranch salad dressing for dipping anything and everything. Corn cut from the cob. No butter. No meatloaf or complicated stuff. Keep it simple. Recognizable food." The list covered breakfast, lunch, and dinner. "There. See?" Janet's plate was empty. She'd eaten her first full meal since arriving.

"Did we forget anything?" he asked Ellen. "Possibly a beverage with which to wash it all down? Maybe something wholesome like a glass of milk?" He handed Ellen a double-handed sippy cup. "She's not ready for an open cup. Ruins their self-confidence if it spills."

He stirred the soup Ellen had simmering on the stove. "These pieces are too big for her," he said, taking a taste. "And it's too peppery, and these pieces of beef are too tough. She'll choke. Stick to canned soup. All the bits are sufficiently mushy from a can." When Ellen glared at him, he said to think of it as making her own life easier by making Janet's life happier. "Win, win." He flashed her a broad, insincere smile and winked. Ellen melted.

"Here," he said. "I've written out a grocery list for you and made a few notes. I guarantee you won't have any trouble feeding her if you follow it."

And so it was that this magical man ingratiated himself into their lives. It took only a handful of visits to get Janet singing her ABCs again, but there was no dancing, no joy. She was counting again and identifying trees and birds, smiles and frowns. By her next doctor visit, she was declared healthy and normal. No sign of cognitive deficits.

Uncle Martin became part of the family, spending some part of every week with Janet. His charm and enthusiasm had Ellen looking forward to his visits. He brought an air of sophistication to her monotonous little life. She even entertained the illusion that his attentions were in part because of an attraction to her. She dyed her hair blond. She wore makeup. She tried to diet, though losing five or ten pounds wouldn't touch the nearly one hundred she'd put on.

Two months into Janet's new life, Max was still trying to extricate himself from Hamilton. They asked him to go to Georgia again. He said it was his last. He'd sold his house and needed to move.
Mrs. Osterman agreed to spend nights with Betsy while Max was gone. When the movers arrived to pack up the house, she tried to keep Betsy isolated in the bedroom. But once they left, the boxes and upheaval confused Betsy, and she was agitated, pacing and muttering. By the next morning, she seemed fine, and Mrs. Osterman left her, saying she'd be back by 2:00. She had no idea one of the movers found a set of keys hanging on a nail and put them on the kitchen counter before he left.

"Where the hell have you been?" Ellen was livid.
Max arrived home to find Ellen and Howard waiting for him. "The police picked up Mom!" she hollered. "They put her on a psych hold at the hospital! Where the hell were you?"
Max put down his duffel and heaved a sigh. "Calm down. Where's Janet?"
Howard said she was upstairs sleeping. Max went to check on her. She was asleep on a mattress on the floor,

surrounded by a barricade of boxes. He kissed her and went back downstairs.

"Dad, they arrested Mom."

"You're not making any sense. Howard, what's this all about?"

"What, you think he's going to tell you something different?" she sniped.

"No," Max said quietly, "but maybe he won't yell it to me."

"I give up," Ellen shouted and stormed out of the kitchen.

It was an unseasonably hot evening in October. A bit of muggy air stirred through the kitchen window as the men sat at the kitchen table.

"Betsy went into the wrong house today," Howard began.

"What do you mean the wrong house?"

"She drove to the wrong house and . . ."

"What was she doing driving?"

"What do you mean?"

"I took away the keys. She hasn't driven in, damn, over a year."

"Really. Well, she drove today."

As Howard explained, Max stepped down to the landing and reached around the corner, feeling for a nail on a wall stud where the keys should have been.

"She went to the wrong house," Howard continued, "and accosted two little kids, told them to get out of her house, and then got into a fight with their mother."

"A fight?"

"Uh, yeah. Betsy punched her."

"Holy fuckin' shit." Max hung his head.

"She thought it was your house. When the police got there, she was raving. Couldn't tell them who she was or where she lived. Her car was parked in the middle of the street, still running. They figured out who she was, and called your office, and your secretary called Ellen." Howard shook his head. "When did she get this bad? We knew she was starting to lose it, but . . ."

"Seriously. You two noticed she was losing it."

Howard shrugged. "We haven't seen much of her."

"Yeah. I know."

"Look, it's not like she's our responsibility," Ellen said from the doorway. I see her every week, twice a week for half an hour. She seemed fine." Howard raised his eyebrows. "Well, OK," Ellen said. "Not every week. It's hard to make the drive all the way to Edgewater, and you know how impossible it is to find a sitter for Janet?"

Max glared at Ellen know full well she hadn't seen her mother in months.

"Why didn't you tell us she was bat shit crazy, Dad?"

"I've had enough," Max said. "Go home."

"Fine!" Ellen headed upstairs.

"Leave her here," Max told her. "She's sleeping. I'll drive her home tomorrow." Ellen did not argue. As Howard and Ellen closed the door behind them, Max did some calculations in his head. Betsy was about the same age as her mother when she was institutionalized.

He went up and lay down beside Janet. His life had imploded so entirely, he was at a loss. His whole world now came down to the two of them, he and Janet, on that mattress. He stroked her arm, happy the cast was gone. She stirred and nestled closer to him without fully waking.

Betsy was diagnosed with advanced dementia and remained in the psych ward until Max found a bed for her in an Ann Arbor nursing home capable of taking her. Ellen had a fit, demanding her mother be allowed to go home. She was even angrier when the nursing home placed her mother on a special wing with locked doors so she and the other patients couldn't wander off, not that Betsy was likely to. She never got out of her chair.

Max sat Ellen and Howard down to explain the family history of institutionalized women.

Howard looked wide-eyed. "What are you telling us, Max?"

"It appears to run in families."

"But she's fine," Ellen cried. "She just got confused and . . ."

"She hasn't driven in over a year," Max said, explaining what the last year had been like in his house.

Ellen began ranting. "So, this is just to make your life easier, then? You just cart her off to some warehouse and . . ."

Howard pounded his fist and told Ellen to shut up. Whether he saw his own future in his wife's eyes or not, he was done with the conversation. "We're leaving. And you're not going to say one more word. Your mother is where she needs to be."

"And I bet you can't wait until the day you stick me in one of these places!"

She was right. It was something Howard looked forward to. But, with his luck, the dementia would skip right over Ellen.

Max finally left Hamilton with his pension and investments intact. He sold the house and his club membership and moved alone into the little house in Ann

Arbor, a few blocks from Janet. He visited Betsy several times a week until she died less than a year later, having just turned fifty-six.

It didn't take long for Ellen to grow annoyed by the inequities of her father's affections. While she felt ignored all her life, Max became a doting grandfather to this little adopted girl, taking Janet everywhere with him. Max flew them all out to Disneyland in California to celebrate Janet's fifth birthday. While Ellen and Howard were busy complaining about the crowds and the heat, Max and Janet disappeared for hours at a time, the only ones having fun. After that trip, Max took Janet away two or three times a year. Uncle Martin met them every time. Howard and Ellen were not invited except for the annual Mackinac Island trip each August, the one Martin steered clear of.

CHAPTER 26

Implosion

As Max parked the car, Janet, her parents, and Betsy were being seated for lunch at an outdoor café downtown Ann Arbor. Ellen tried to squeeze into a space too small for her girth. Howard offered her a different chair, but she insisted the waiter move the people at the next table to make room. Her request was ignored. Nine-year-old Janet tried to pretend she didn't know her parents.

Walking back from parking the car, Max was about to join this little drama when a woman stepped up to him, wrapped her arms around him, and kissed him on the cheek, catching him quite off guard. Ellen watched, mouth agape.

Max quickly motioned to his family, certain the woman had not noticed them, and upon seeing them, would certainly alter her behavior. She did not. She clung to his arm.

"This is Colleen Jennings," he told them, trying to recover the moment. "We know each other from Michigan State." He introduced his family.

"Funny," Ellen said with overt skepticism. "You don't look like an engineer. Dad taught engineering."

"No," Colleen said. "Anthropology."

Max tried to pull from her grasp.

"I'm confused," Ellen said. "So how is it you know my father so well?"

Howard froze and looked hard at Max, then at Ellen.

Swept up in the excitement of seeing Max, Colleen suddenly realized her familiarity with him was inappropriate, and she stepped back.

Janet, who had been more interested in the menu at the time, looked up.

Colleen gasped seeing the girl's face. "Oh my god," she said. "She looks just like, but it couldn't be. She's . . ."

Max cut her off. "What brings you to Ann Arbor, Colleen?" he asked.

"She looks just like who?" Ellen insisted. "Because everyone says she looks just like me."

"It's nothing," Colleen said, but her intense stare said otherwise. "She's just the spitting image of my best friend." She looked at Max, her eyes asking the one question he could not answer. "She was beautiful at that age, too. She died a few years ago."

Ellen pressed on with tight eyes and a false smile. "What was her name, this friend of yours?"

Max tried to interrupt, but Colleen spoke too quickly. "Anna Post."

Ellen had not yet observed the terror in her husband's eyes.

Colleen grew nervous. "Max?" she asked, her eyes filling with tears. His expression was unyielding. She began stammering that she was running late.

Ellen spoke loud enough to draw attention from nearby tables. "So, Dad, this friend, Anna Post. Carleton's daughter? Died in that car crash in 1970?"

Colleen turned away to leave. Her parting glance to Janet, heartbreakingly sad, did not go unnoticed.

Max sat down to a momentary silence before Ellen, in a somewhat lurid tone, began the inquisition. "Dad, Anna went to state, didn't she? How is it that Colleen woman, such a close friend of Anna, knows you so … personally?"

Max looked at his menu.

"Daddy?" Ellen dug deeper. "How is it my daughter looks like Anna Post?"

"I don't know that she does," he said.

"Really," she said, recognizing a familiar contempt in her father's eyes.

Howard glared at Ellen and told her to calm down. "It's nothing," he said.

"You're telling me to calm down?" she asked Howard.

Howard looked to Max.

Max looked to Janet.

Ellen saw the fear on both their faces. "What the hell?" she muttered.

"Who is Anna Post?" Janet asked.

"Nobody," Max said with a sad smile.

Howard quickly knocked a glass of water onto Janet's lap to distract her and took her from the table before she heard any more.

"Did you pawn Anna's kid off on me?" Her loud protestations drew the attention of patrons, some rolling their eyes, others chuckling, several grimacing.

Max told Ellen to settle down without bothering to deny her assertions.

"Does Howard know what I think he knows? Is he in on it?" Ellen began to shake. "I knew this thing was fishy from the beginning! Taking in some stray orphan. Who does that, Daddy? Who does that?" She would not settle.

"She's Anna's kid, isn't she? So why didn't any of the Posts take her? Or the Baldwins? She married a Baldwin. The stinking rich Baldwins."

Max remained still, speaking with a condescension Ellen knew well. "You need to settle down and stop letting your imagination run rampant."

A momentary détente settled over the table, but only because Ellen was putting the puzzle together in her head. "Holy shit," she muttered and glared at her father. "Oh my god. No. You didn't. Daddy, you didn't! Is that why she took to you so easily when we got her, when she wouldn't let any of us touch her? Because she already knew you?" She saw her father's disgust. "And," she stopped short at another thought. "Holy shit, Dad. Is that why she looks like *ME?* What did you do, Daddy?"

Max glared at her.

"So, how'd it happen, Daddy? When you were *teaching* at Michigan State? Spending all those *nights* at Michigan State? With your best friend's *daughter*?"

Max stood up.

"I knew it," Ellen said. "I knew you were screwing around. I knew it! But Anna Post? Seriously?"

"You're making a scene," Max said, his voice annoyingly quiet.

"Damn right, I am!" Ellen shouted.

Max walked away.

"Are you going to deny it?" Ellen yelled.

Max did not answer, just kept walking.

"So, I'm right? I've been raising my goddamned sister!" As she stood, she knocked over a chair and bumped into another patron.

The café manager approached and told Ellen to leave.

Janet and Howard were far enough away to have missed the explosion of truth.

The Granger family frayed entirely. Janet didn't know what happened, only that her mother could not be mollified on any given day for the rest of her life. Once Ellen discovered Janet was her half-sister, her estrangement deepened. She'd never managed to like Janet, let alone love her in the nearly six years since her arrival, but suddenly Ellen found it difficult to even be civil to her. Presuming Martin had been in on the lie in one way or another, he was ostracized. The only time Janet saw him was when Max took her on vacation, something Howard insisted be continued.

As far as Howard was concerned, Ellen took every opportunity to remind him he was a traitor, a lying, cheating traitor. He never confessed as to how long he'd been in on the ruse or how much he actually knew. None of that mattered. She never let him forget.

A year later, Max lay in the hospital. His heart was failing. He had so much more to teach Katherine. He wanted more time to show her there was life beyond Ellen and Howard. He wanted her to experience freedom, to explore strange places, and discover life and love in ways he never had. He wanted more time, and he wasn't going to get it. There was a gnawing regret that his selfishness had placed her in the bosom of boredom and resentment. Had he been willing to let her go, maybe she'd have been placed better, with brilliant parents, lively people, people who had some sense of joy and adventure. If he'd only insisted Anna marry him, they'd have raised her together. He was drowning in failures, the greatest of them being Katherine's happiness. He wanted for her all the things he never thought of giving Ellen. Ellen was born of Betsy, negating any possibility of *specialness*. But Janet was born Katherine, daughter of Anna. Beautiful, charismatic, Anna. So many possibilities for her would be wasted if he were not there to guide her, protect her, if she were to remain *just Janet*.

As Max drifted in and out of consciousness, he recalled all the wonderful things he and Katherine had done together. He could only guess how much of it she would remember. He begged to see her, but the rules prohibited children from visiting the Intensive Care Unit. He wouldn't get to say goodbye to her. She would never know the truth. And in that failing, he envisioned for her a life only half lived. The only hope he held for her was the assurance of money when she came of age. With the stocks Baldwin set aside for her, she'd be able to be independent. That thought, being his last, brought some comfort as he drifted from life, unaware of Martin sitting bedside, holding his hand.

Upon hearing of Max's death, the attorney in Edgewater began organizing his estate and discovered the unmarked envelope of stocks. He'd never gotten around to writing the letter of intent. Deciding to tend to it after lunch, he left Max's bulging folder on his desk on top of a stack of other folders before venturing across the street to the diner. He heard a woman holler that her dog had gotten loose and the attorney saw the disheveled little critter dart down the sidewalk, yapping, dragging a leash behind it and he stepped off the curb to catch hold of it. He didn't see the cat it was chasing, the cat that streaked out in front of a beer truck, causing the driver to swerve, missing the cat and dog entirely but plowing straight into the attorney.

His secretary and sole employee, overcome with grief and enraged at the thought of having to organize the residual disarray, in one sweep of her arm, sent all the files and folders to the floor, everything careening into a mass of intermingling papers. The blank envelope full of stock certificates slipped into an open box marked dormant files. The phone began to ring. Taking several deep breaths, she went back to her desk, collected her purse, coffee cup, a potted cactus, and walked out, leaving the attorney's wife to sift, sort and pack it all up. The wife, overwhelmed with the task, attempted to organize it all, moving dormant files to the basement for later disposal after disseminating client files through phone calls and letters. She gave up after a week, walked out, and never looked back.

When the new owner, a dentist, bought the building, he was dismayed to find little had been done to clear out the remnants of the law practice. Box after box went to the curb for trash collection, all but one, forgotten on a high shelf in the basement.

CHAPTER 27

Cowardice

The last time Janet saw Martin was at Max's funeral. Soon after, Ellen told her he'd died in a horrific car accident, his body mangled to death. Ellen's cruelty knew no limit.

At ten, Janet felt she'd lost the only two people who loved her. She withdrew to her room, refusing to speak.

Howard was certain she sensed the betrayal and deceit in the house, though she had no concept of its root cause. He accepted she had every right to shut him out. He was guilty by association and, in large part, by participation. She refused his attempts to reach out until all he could do was watch his beautiful girl withdraw deeper and deeper into her seclusion.

When it was time for the annual trip to the island, the first without Max, Janet locked herself in her room. Ellen also had no intention of going, but Howard stood his ground. "We're going," he declared and started to pack his bag. Ellen sat on the bed, arms folded tight against his insurrection. "Come, don't come, I don't care," he told her, his voice charged. "But I'm taking Janet Up North."

"You are not," Ellen proclaimed as if it would be the last word. "She's never setting foot on that island again if I have anything to say about it."

"Good thing it's not up to you then." Howard slammed a drawer so hard, a figurine on the dresser fell to the floor and shattered.

"Now look what you've done!" Ellen yelled, collecting the pieces and shards. "I was sick of that place the first time we went. Year after year. I'm not going! He probably met his little whore up there! I bet that's what started those annual . . ."

"You shut your mouth." Howard shot a glance down the hall to Janet's bedroom. Without realizing it, his hands were clenched in fists. He glared at Ellen and, for the first time ever, saw her back down.

"She doesn't want to go," Ellen said as if it mattered.

"What? You've never given a shit about what she thinks or wants."

"You can't talk to me that way!"

"I'll talk to you any goddamn way I want to. Now get yourself packed! We're leaving in an hour."

"No!"

"Fine! I'll take her by myself."

"Like hell, you will!"

Janet came out of her room, suitcase in hand. She didn't look at either of them as she walked past them down the stairs. She waited in the car until Ellen and Howard came out and got in.

On their first evening on the island, Howard leaned on a post outside a fudge shop smoking a cigarette, trying to ignore Ellen and Janet arguing inside. He watched the crowds begin to thin out, leaving only those few who would spend the night. Howard liked that moment when the last ferry pulled away from the docks, and the whole town seemed to let their guard down and relax.

When the girls came out, Howard sent them on ahead to the room. He wanted to take a walk. As they disappeared down the street toward the Windward, he headed to the park below the fort.

A team of Belgians pulled the last of the empty tourist wagons up the hill to the stables. Hundreds of rental bicycles stood crammed together, all leaning to varying degrees on kickstands. Weary owners of gift shops, clothing stores, and souvenir shops closed their doors and filtered up side streets to their homes on the interior. Summer help made their way to big houses turned into dormitories.

Then came the summer locals, emerging from their refuge for a late supper, the elegance of their polished antique carriages matched only by the extraordinary horses pulling them, Morgans, Warmbloods, and Friesans prancing under snappy black harness. A line of private buggies formed along the massive lawn, where a few remaining tourists gathered to admire them. Howard wandered by, imagining a life where such extravagances were routine.

Something was so familiar about a man stepping from a smart single-seat buggy, Howard did a double take. It was Martin.

"What the hell are you doing here?" they both said almost simultaneously.

"You can't be here!" Howard blurted.

"Well, old friend, that's going to be a bit difficult," Martin quipped. "This is my summer home."

"What do you mean? Your summer home? You can't be here. I swear, if Ellen sees you ..." but he was cut off.

"What can she do?" Martin asked, already weary of the drama.

"Martin ..." Howard began but couldn't put the words together.

"Ye-e-e-s?" Martin teased.

"Martin. You're dead." It popped out of Howard's mouth a bit too carelessly, but there it was, splat between them like a fetid road apple. "Ellen told Janet you died."

"What the fuck?"

"It was an accident," Howard said, trying to explain.

"I died in an accident?" Martin shouted, drawing surprised looks from a few people.

"No, well, yes. I mean, it just happened before I could stop it."

"When? When did she kill me off?" Martin pushed for an answer. "When?"

Howard hung his head. "Just after Max died."

"That fucking bitter bitch. No wonder Ellen kept telling me to stay away. I called. Repeatedly. But she always made excuses."

"Janet kept asking about you, and Ellen got fed up."

"So, she killed me, and you said nothing," Martin sneered.

Both men stood silent. Martin had never seen anyone wear their failures as openly as Howard Granger.

"The damage was done, Martin. What could I do? Tell Janet her mother was a liar?"

"Yes."

Howard was too humiliated to respond.

"And Katherine?" Martin asked.

"Janet? She's a wreck."

"And?"

"Please. She's been through enough. She's just now coming around. Look, it took all winter to get her to talk to us."

"She shut down."

"Yeah. You showing up now would only confuse her and she's on such shaky ground already. If Ellen sees you, well, I'll never get her up here again. She'll take the island away from her."

Martin looked everywhere but at Howard. "Well," he finally said. "We can't have that, can we? Keep bringing her. Perhaps if you gave me a little heads up I could remain sequestered during your visit. And maybe you could let me catch a glimpse from time to time."

Howard looked almost apologetic. "Too risky. You know it would be too risky."

Martin looked hard at Howard. "Where are you staying?"

"The Windward, but you can't go there!"

Martin took a step toward town, but Howard grabbed his arm and stopped him.

"You can't see her, Martin! I'm begging you!"

Martin stood in Howard's grip with no choice but to surrender to the new reality. "I never come up before July," he said quietly. "Bring her up in the spring. The lilacs are spectacular in June. She'll love it."

"Thank you," Howard said. "You don't know what this means."

"Oh, be assured. I know exactly what it means." Martin always knew Howard had no backbone, but he'd only just realized he didn't either.

Howard could see the pain in Martin's eyes. While he sympathized, there was an element of pragmatism at play, a stark reality better faced head-on. "Martin," Howard began, faltering. "I think you have to accept that the Katherine you knew, the little girl you helped raise, well . . . you lost her in the accident. The little girl I took home is not her and likely never will be. I'm doing what I can to help repair the damage, or at least help her live with her history, but she isn't the joyful, exuberant child you knew before the accident. You know that. In your heart, you know it." Martin did not speak. "You and Max tried your best, but . . ."

Martin interrupted. "Enough." It was true, and nothing could change it. Katherine always had to come first, and as it stood, he no longer had a place in her life but as a loving memory. He climbed back into his buggy and drove off.

No one enjoyed the trip north, yet they powered through. Subsequent trips would be made in June for the annual Lilac Festival. The tradition of constant squabbling, however, was not abandoned.

Janet hit puberty drenched in Ellen's unrelenting alienation. She came right out one day and asked her mother why she hated her so much. Ellen almost told her but remained silent, her angry eyes offering no answers. In response, Janet disappeared for days on end, stole from their house, ditched school, and came home reeking of marijuana. When she was home, she locked herself in her room, which was preferable to interaction with Howard and Ellen, as she began to call them.

Howard generally tried to stay above the fray, but Ellen could not keep from prodding the girl, chiding her for her sloppy clothes, ratty hair, and horrible disposition. "How could anyone love you?" she said as if words had no consequence. But they did have consequence and sometimes Janet turned silent, dead-eyed. Ellen saw it as a sign of conquest, but Howard knew otherwise. It broke his heart every time he saw it, yet not knowing what to do or say, he sat passively by.

One night in the fall of Janet's junior year, Ellen was on a rant. Janet matched her insult for insult. It was ramping up when Ellen hit her peak. "I wish you'd never been born!" This time Janet did not back down, or shut down, or give up. "That makes two of us!" she yelled back and put a dent in the drywall with her fist.

Howard stormed into the room and slapped his wife hard across the face. She fell back against a chair in utter shock. "You are a horrible human being," he shouted at her so loud his voice cracked. "And if you ever say one more discouraging, slimy, disgusting thing to our daughter, I promise I will beat the shit out of you! Do I make myself clear?"

For the second time, at Ellen's provocation, his hands were clenched in fists. It was all he could do to keep from slugging her, but he fought against the adrenalin pumping through his body. Janet ran out the back door. A few hours later, Howard was called by the hospital to retrieve her. He brought her home, her arm again in a cast, having broken her hand when she punched the wall.

After that, Ellen backed off and Janet's junior and senior years turned out to be as good as they could be. Howard kept the peace by threatening Ellen and encouraging Janet. He said he would pay for college if she could keep her act together. Every Sunday, he and Janet counted down the days left until she graduated to freedom. It seemed to motivate her. "Get as far away from here as you can," he told her, promising to help any way he could. She turned her grades around, stayed out of trouble, and a week after graduation, she was on a ferry to the island to work for the summer before heading off to college.

Howard struggled over whether to tell her the truth, that she was adopted, that Max was her father. He worked it over and over in his head for years, wondering if telling her would help her or only make things worse. Never coming to a conclusion, he chose to maintain silence. Like his mother before him, he lived in a constant state of waiting in the futile belief that fate would step in and save Janet from all his failings.

He hoped against hope that she and Martin would cross paths that summer. It was a passive attempt at rectification. It failed. Martin was in Italy that whole year.

CHAPTER 28

A Visitor

The condo crew stayed the week. Days slipped by with ease, without need, or expectation of being entertained. They were a comfortable lot. No one griped when it rained. They played cards or read or napped. There was laughter, food, and alcohol. They packed lunches, rented bikes, and circumnavigated the island, stopping along the way to wade in the cold waters, daring each other to take the plunge. None did. Archie showed up for dinner each evening, lingering deep into the night. He arranged a private carriage tour for them all, joining in and treating them to lunch at one of the big hotels downtown. Janet took her hikes every day, with one or more tagging along. She wanted them to stay for the rest of summer, fearful she would be lonely when they left. But leave, they did, as did Archie. He had business to tend to.

It took Janet a few days to regain her rhythm, but soon found herself content, filling her days again with reading, long walks and mindless chores. She missed Archie and looked forward to his return any day.

Weeding the garden on a lovely sunny afternoon, she looked up from the flowerbed to see Archie's horse. She could tell by the one white sock. But it wasn't Archie. It was a man like him, only much older, with stunning white hair and deep leathery dimples.

"I know," the rider said. "We're the spitting image of each other, don't you think?"

Janet scowled a little and stood up, brushing dirt from her bare knees.

"Yes," she said. "You are." Something about him made her want to laugh and cry at the same time, much as she did when she first met Archie.

Another horse approached and Archie made introductions. "Janet, this is my uncle. I've brought him by for a visit. He just arrived and wanted to meet you straight away."

"Oh, well," his uncle sighed. "This one and I are old, dear friends." He slowly climbed down from the horse and reached for her. Janet backed away, avoiding even eye contact. "Well," he said with a bittersweet tone. "I suppose that's to be expected. Why would you remember me anyway?"

Archie watched, wondering how his uncle could possibly know Janet.

"You used to ride with me," the man told Janet. "Do you remember? I used to meet you and your mother on the trail. I'd hoist you up. You liked being taller than everybody. And walking never suited you. You wanted to fly through the woods. You were fearless."

"You cantered holding a child?" Archie was incensed.

Martin rolled his eyes. "Yes, and children played on monkey bars and rode bicycles without helmets and lived untethered lives. We weren't as paranoid about protecting them from every little scrape and scratch as you people are these days."

Archie shook his head and let it go.

Janet told the old man he was mistaken. I am not who you think I am.

"We'll give it some time," he said. "Not to worry. We have lots of time."

Archie walked the horses into the yard and went in after a bottle of wine. He stopped just inside the door and hollered out. "He says he has answers, Janet. To all those questions you have. To all those photographs in the trunk."

Janet called back, "I didn't know I had questions! And what photographs?"

Archie's uncle carefully took Janet by the hand and led her toward the porch. He glanced up to the hayloft. The doors were closed. "I was a good friend of Max's," he said. "Max and I went way back. And I knew you when you were just a kid. I can't believe you don't remember me. Honestly, I thought I made a stronger impression than that." His smile was infectious, and Janet responded with a quizzical grin.

Archie called out from inside. "Uncle Martin! You want red or white?" And suddenly, something clicked in Janet's psyche. "Uncle Martin?" She looked at him hard, trying to remember something long forgotten. "You're not the Uncle Martin they said was dead?"

"Not dead! Ostracized, my dear. Banished to the hinterlands. Waiting. Waiting for you to surface again, and here you are. At Baldwin Cottage. I should have known." He put his arms out and Janet stepped hesitantly into them. For a moment, she was a child again, overwhelmed with a sense of being safe and loved, and she felt Max everywhere all around her. Then some dark pain overtook her, and she pushed away.

Martin looked at her with deep disappointment. "You haven't changed, my dear. I'd hoped . . . but I suppose . . ."

Archie watched the exchange from inside, growing ever more curious.

"You really do look fabulous!" Janet said, trying to shake off the pain. ". . . for someone I haven't seen in forty years."

All Martin could do was stare at her and try to breathe. He recognized the stubborn child behind that beautiful face. "And you look old," Martin replied. "Not enough joy in your life. So obvious."

"It is what it is," she said.

"You poor girl. I should have been there. I should have carried on for old Max. But I couldn't contend with the Ellen. Christ almighty, she was hideous. There. We're past the awkward part."

"The awkward part?" Janet sniped. "Losing both of you at the same time was more than awkward! You left me all alone with Ellen. You died!"

"Dead. Living. Who's to say? That was none of my doing, my sweet child." He cupped her face in his hands. "All in good time, love." He wiped tears from her cheek. His loving smile made her respond in kind, and she took his arm to climb the steps.

Martin was happier than he had been in years. "The boy," he said, nodding to Archie, "will never look as good as I do when he's my age. Doesn't believe in moisturizer. Or sunscreen."

"How old *are* you?" Janet asked.

"Really? You're really asking me that? That's the girl I knew! I'm over seventy, and that's all I'll say. And I'm only saying that because I look damn good for a gentleman over seventy."

Archie opened the wine. "Don't let him fool you. He's pushing eighty."

Martin took a glass and sat down, but he couldn't take his eyes off Janet. "That's not your name, you know. You were christened Katherine."

"What did you say?"

"Your name is Katherine. Doesn't she look like a Katherine, Archie? Certainly isn't a Janet."

As soon as she heard it, she realized it was the whisper she'd been hearing in the house, the name that came from the corner of an empty room, from the foot of her bed, from just over her shoulder when she sat on the chair in the hay loft. Always in a woman's voice, soft, insistent. It wasn't *gathering*. It was *Katherine*.

"There are a lot of lies in your life," Martin said. "And it's about time they got sorted out." He took a sip of wine, then put it down. "We're going to need something a bit stronger. Got any bourbon in there?"

Janet went inside to retrieve a bottle of the good stuff. When she came back out, Martin stood up. "Come with me," he said, taking her hand. "I changed my mind. We're going for a walk." He told Archie to hang back and tend the horses.

Martin thought he'd take her to the cemetery, go straight for the jugular of the thing, and get it over with.

Quick and clean. But as they walked, he couldn't find the words.

"The only happy memories I carried forward," she told him, "all these years, were of you and Max and our trips. Disneyland, Weeki Wachee, a dude ranch out west, New York City when you took me to *Godspell*."

"Don't forget *Pippin*," Martin said.

"That was a different trip when I finally got you to take me to the Statue of Liberty. You refused the first trip."

"Ah," he said. "True. All those tourists. Do you remember the food in New York?"

"No. I remember getting dressed up for everything and being the only child in the restaurants you took me to."

"Well, I don't suppose one can hope to have an impression on a child's palate when all she got at home was slop."

"I asked Ellen to cook some fish for me like we had in Charleston, and she bought a box of fish sticks. She got really mad at me when I refused to eat them."

"Good girl."

"Do you remember when you refused to ride horses to the edge of the Grand Canyon? Max and I did that one without you. It was really fun. And we went to a wax museum in San Francisco."

"I remember all of it and can't believe you do, too. That would have made Max so happy."

"When he died, and then you died? I took every photograph I had of us and put it in an album. It was jammed. And, I took one of my school notebooks and filled it with everything I could remember about what we did together. And I read it over and over and looked at the pictures over and over. Did you know I seriously thought everyone flew in small planes?"

"You mean the private jet," he said.

"Yes!"

"Shocker, eh?" Martin asked if he could see the photo album.

"Ellen took it. One day, the album and my journal just disappeared."

"Bitch."

"Evil bitch," Janet corrected him.

"That works, too."

They walked a bit without talking, letting ideas and memories settle.

"Why did you go away? Really," Janet asked. It was an innocent question. She'd lived long enough to know that people drift in and out of each other's lives.

"The last time I saw you," Martin started to say, "The last time ..." He repeated himself and stopped talking, walking silently down the path. The cicadas buzzed overhead. Janet padded along next to him, waiting.

"It was Ellen. I came for your ..." He stopped again. "I came for Max's funeral and she told me to leave. I was no longer welcome. I was to have no more contact with you. Ever. She broke my heart, that fucking whore."

"I don't understand," Janet insisted.

"You will."

They walked in silence for a while, until Martin stopped and stared off into the woods. Something that had been so bright in his face when he arrived faded. It had been decades since he disappeared from Katherine's life and only now, after Ellen was gone, did he feel he had permission to re-appear. He felt every bit the coward Howard had been.

"I tried calling the house after I saw your dad's obituary," he said. "The line was disconnected. I kept waiting for Ellen to show up in the obits, hoping I'd find you then . . ."

"I didn't post one."

"That would explain it. I had no idea where you'd gone off to. Or if you'd even want to see me again." Even saying the words it felt like a litany of excuses. "And to think I might have missed you now if I hadn't found Mrs. Cecelia Coventry's little gossip column from last fall lying about. Did you really slam the door on her? Not that I blame you." He laughed a little, then sighed and stopped walking. "We shall resume tomorrow. I'd like to walk alone for a while. To clear my head. We'll talk tomorrow." He reached out, and Janet took his hand for a moment. He held it tightly as if letting go would mean losing her all over again. Without another word, they stepped away from each other and turned in separate directions.

Janet headed back to the cottage, and Martin hollered out one more thought. "Your mama nursed you in that yellow rocker right out there in broad daylight under that wisteria. Brazen woman, your mother!"

"Couldn't have been me," Janet corrected him. "My mom and dad have never been here."

Martin walked away, overwhelmed by all the lies.

Janet stood in her bedroom window staring into the night. Through the trees, she could see the lights of Pink House. There was no way to know how many times her path and Martin's had crossed over the years, missing each other by a breath, passing on a lane, or in town. Whether he'd have recognized her then, or she him, was impossible to say. Every year brought a new opportunity to run into each other. And every year, fate kept them apart.

She thought about everything he'd said, and it only led to more questions. A voice, muted in the heavy night air, came from the lane below. "Can't sleep?"

"That you, Mr. Harris?" She looked down but only saw the dim edge of someone standing below, hands in his pockets.

"Yes. It's me. Just taking in some of this beautiful summer night." He sauntered away, his footfalls too muted to hear.

After an hour of tossing, Janet slept, waking up gasping, pain shooting down her arm. She finally pushed the sheet off, got rid of the pillow, and laid spread eagle. A door slammed. "Stop it!" she shouted and ran downstairs to the porch.

CHAPTER 29

Revelation

Archie showed up in the morning to find Janet asleep on the chaise in her underwear and a tank top. He gently woke her and went in to make coffee. "Rough night?" he asked. When she did not speak, he did not pursue.

Janet had always heard that crazy people don't know they're crazy. But having total awareness that she was losing her faculties was cruel, and she wondered how long before others would notice. Archie hollered for her to get dressed, that Martin was waiting for her.

"I don't feel like it today," she called back.

"What's that got to do with it?" he hollered again as he looked for a thermos. "Get dressed."

Archie waited on the porch with a thermos of coffee in one hand and an old photo album in the other. When Janet came back out, he handed her a mug and told her the album was from the trunk in the stable. "Martin wants to see it," he said. "Come on."

Janet took a gulp of coffee as Archie held the screen door for her. "That trunk from the stable? Seriously?" she whined. Archie waved her forward with a move straight out of Martin's playbook, and she obeyed.

It was every bit a summer day, nine o'clock, and already hot. "Turning a corner, she recognized where Archie was headed and asked what he was up to. He wouldn't answer except to say Uncle Martin would explain everything.

Deep in the woods, they arrived at the island cemetery where a handful of tourists were already on the prowl, meandering among tilting gravestones, stopping at the larger monuments surrounded by wrought iron fences. Janet thought the huge trees throughout the cemetery must surely have fed off those buried among their roots, coffins shifting with their intrusion, stones and bones heaving.

Martin sat in a folding chair at a gravestone in the far corner. He hollered as Archie and Janet approached. "Did you bring it?" Archie held up the album. Janet offered coffee, but Martin pulled a flask out of his jacket pocket. "Too early for coffee," he said.

He began leafing through the album, finding a picture of James, himself, and Anna when they were teenagers. "That's me," he said, pointing. "And that's James Baldwin the second, AKA Jimmy. Damn, he hated that name. Tried to get people to call him by his middle name for a while."

"What was it," Archie asked.

"Carson. Never caught on. The Carson he'd been named after was a son of a bitch no one liked, probably some in-law. It never took. And to me, he just wasn't a Carson."

Janet read the gravestone. James Carson Baldwin II 1939-1970 and his loving wife Anna Eileen Post Baldwin 1940-1970. "They died together?" she asked.

"Car accident," Martin began. "They were on their way home. Anna and James, their daughter, and Anna's parents." He was reciting the facts as if he'd rehearsed them, but the words stuck in his throat. Archie took over, trying to keep the facts straight.

"Anna's father was flying them off the island when the weather turned. He put down in Pelston and they rented a car. They were driving when somebody T-boned them and plowed them into the pines." He stopped and reached out to Martin's shoulder. "It was a drunk driver. Killed everyone." Archie pointed to a third, more diminutive gravestone. Katherine Lorraine Post Baldwin January 4, 1967 – August 14, 1970.

"Their daughter," Archie explained. "She was only three years old."

It registered to Janet it must be the gravestone the condo crew had seen.

Martin spoke quietly, but pain being what it is, sometimes converts itself into spite, and his words were sharp. "There's only one thing buried in that coffin," he said, pointing to the small gravestone. "A lie." He glared at Janet. "That's your grave, Ms. Janet Marie Granger. That's where Baldwin buried you so no one would find out all his dirty little secrets."

Janet and Archie stood mute, caught off guard by Martin's vehemence.

"In all these years, didn't anyone ever tell you that you were adopted?" he blurted. "Because you sure as hell were. You were in that car when it crashed. You were pinned between Anna and Carleton. They pulled you out, half dead, barely breathing." Martin lowered his voice and fought back tears. He looked at Janet and spoke as if she were still that three-year-old little girl. "And your tiny arm was so broken."

Janet's legs failed her, and she dropped straight to the earth. The dream from the night before came flooding back, the one she could never remember. The screaming, flying, crushing, all made sense. It had never been a dream. It was a memory, and finally she understood why her arm hurt and why she always woke feeling smothered.

Archie knelt down next to her as Martin pushed the album at her, open to a picture of when she was three with Anna, James, and Martin, a couple weeks before the accident.

Janet looked at Anna and shivered. "I know her," she whispered. "I know her," she said again, uncomfortable in the new reality. "I've had dreams about her. In the cottage." she gasped. "It was her."

"This picture was taken in Baltimore. Where we all lived."

"I've never lived in Baltimore," Janet insisted.

"Damn it! You're not listening!" Martin grew deeply melancholy and took another draw from his flask. "She was your mother," he said quietly, "and James there? That handsome devil? He was the love of my life. Telling everyone you were dead was Baldwin's way of cleaning up our mess."

Janet snapped at Martin. "I don't understand. How can she be my mother? I wasn't adopted. No one ever said I was adopted. I don't understand!"

"Calm yourself, woman. You're getting it all wrong." Martin's face went sallow, and Archie could see he was struggling. "What I need you to understand is that we loved you so much," Martin sighed. "Anna married James, and we all lived in Baltimore. With you. For three years. James was in residency at Johns Hopkins, and I helped out, watched you when Anna needed to get some rest. I fed you and burped you and changed your diapers and I was the one who was there for your first step. That was me. You trusted me with that treasure."

It was a lot for Janet to take in, and she sat motionless on the cool ground waiting for something as if such tectonic shifting of history changed the physical world. Nothing but Martin's hushed voice filled the void between past lies and present confusion.

"You and James?" Archie asked carefully. "All these years?"

"Yes. James was the love of my life. And he was taken away from me by that stupid ass drunk. I lost everything that day."

Janet touched his arm, and Martin smiled. She turned the page and saw the first photo that rang true to her. The childhood memory her parents had always said never happened was right in front of her. There she was, on the chaise, on the Baldwin Cottage porch, holding a mayfly. It had happened. They had all lied to her. Her entire life.

"Why," she blurted out, the anger welling. "Why not tell me? I'm a Baldwin? I live in the family cottage, for Christ sake. I don't understand!"

"Well," Martin groaned, "there's a little more to it than that." He took back the album and smacked it closed.

Though it hadn't dawned on Janet yet, Archie realized that James was probably not her father, but he could see Martin was tiring and suggested they get some breakfast. Martin waved an arm, and a waiting carriage appeared at the stone wall behind them.

The ride into town was silent. The horses' slow cadence along the dirt road fit the mood. Janet tried to wrap her mind and heart around Martin's revelations, reaching back for memories, anything that might help to tie all the threads together. As she processed, Martin dozed, and Archie began coming to his own conclusions.

The jerk of halting horses in front of the crowded restaurant woke Martin. Janet stepped out of the carriage, and Archie asked her to get them a table. Martin started to get out when Archie stopped him. "Who's her father, Martin?" Martin ignored him and got out. "Who?" Archie exploded. Martin pushed past him to get inside.

The restaurant was packed and noisy, and when breakfast arrived, Janet, Archie, and Martin did little more than toy with their food.

"Tomorrow is the anniversary," Martin said. "The 50th anniversary of the accident." By his second Bloody Mary, Martin was newly committed to telling her the whole story, but how in the hell does one deliver that kind of news? *Well, dear, your grandfather was an adulterer humping some girl less than half his age and oh by the way he isn't your grandfather he's your father and the woman you thought was your mother was really your half-sister.*

"Tell her, Martin," Archie said. "You may as well tell her the rest of it."

"What are you talking about?" Martin tried to dodge, but he knew Archie was right. His third Bloody Mary arrived, he drank it down, gathered his courage, and told her. "My dear child, Max was your father, not your grandfather." The news was received in silence. "Max and Anna were in love . . ."

"Stop talking," Janet said. Martin looked at her and saw a familiar three-year-old behind her eyes.

"Max was your father," he repeated.

"Stop. Talking."

"Anna was your mother."

Janet almost threw up. Her chair fell away behind her as she stood and bolted through the restaurant and out the door wanting nothing more than to get the hell out of there, away from Archie and Martin and Baldwin Cottage and back to the condo where life made sense.

Archie apologized to nearby families as they left. Martin flagged down his carriage and caught up to her a few blocks away. She refused to get in. The carriage followed her step by step all the way to Hubbard's Annex.

Upon stepping through the hedgerow, Archie was the first to notice the porcelain nameplate over the door was missing. It had fallen to the ground, the Baldwin name broken into pieces. Janet asked who'd left the front door open but neither Archie nor Martin could come up with an answer.

Martin noticed the hayloft door wide open, the chair and table ablaze in late morning sun. He felt his knees quake and he planted his feet, hoping not to fall. It didn't take much imagination for him to see James sitting up there, writing in his book, a cup of tea, or a beer on the table next to him. Martin slipped back to a time when he would lay on the hay up there on lazy mornings when Baldwin was not around. He'd watch James write, then listen when he spoke a phrase or stanza to see how it felt, if it rang true off the page.

"I can't take any more," Martin said. "My darling, it's all too sad." He began to tremble. "Some days," he muttered, "I feel like a very old man."

"But you don't look a day over sixty," Janet said in a failed attempt to lighten the mood.

Archie decided it was time to get Martin back to Pink House. "Are you going to be all right?" he asked Janet. But she didn't know how to answer. She felt like her heart had been put through a shredder, and there was no gluing it back together.

"I'm exhausted," she said. "I need to be alone." And with that, the two men took their leave and Janet collapsed on the chaise.

"We'll be by tomorrow to collect you," Martin said through the screen door. "Around three o'clock. That's when it happened. Three in the afternoon." They disappeared around the side of the house.

Something rattled around in her head, trying to break free. When it finally materialized, she yelled out. "Hey! If Ellen's not my mother, I'm not losing my mind!"

"Let me tell you, my sweet," assured Martin from the carriage. "That you aren't a raving lunatic is a testament to good genes because that woman who ended up raising you was out of her fucking gourd."

Though this one element had risen to awareness, the depth of her transformation had not yet registered. Sifting through the debris of past and present, Janet felt the weight of the day's news to the point she could barely lift herself off the chaise. She wanted so desperately to have Max back and to have known her mother and James.

Later in the day, forgetting she'd been drinking bourbon, straight, all afternoon, she stood up to go find Martin, feeling an urgent need to console him and for him to console her but, she tripped down the steps and did a faceplant into the grass.

CHAPTER 30

Love

Some time during the night, Janet woke in bed, her head throbbing. She'd had the dream again, this time revealing itself for the memory it was.

⌘

She felt very small in the back seat of a car, playing with a silk scarf embroidered with sunflowers. Her mother was right there next to her, looking out the window at the pouring rain. It was Anna, and every detail of her face was familiar. Janet touched her hand, feeling her smooth skin. She smelled Arpege. There was a crack of lightning and thunder, and an old man she didn't recognize but felt she loved, smiled, and squeezed her hand. Anna turned to look at her with a reassuring smile when suddenly a woman screamed from the front seat, and the car jolted, glass shattered, and a sensation of flying and the old man was thrown on top of her, and the car came to a crunching halt. The stillness was sudden and silent. A horrible piercing pain tore through her arm. She could barely breathe under the weight of the old man's motionless body, her face buried in his chest, pungent vanilla tobacco mixing with Anna's perfume. A warm liquid ran down her neck and pooled under her chin. Anna's breathing underneath her was jerky, then slowed, ceasing in a sorrowful whimper.

⌘

Waking from other dreams, she only recalled a dark, indecipherable vacancy. All her life, she felt a bone-deep loss the way she imagined an amputee felt about a missing limb. Yet what she yearned for could never be identified.

Waking from the dream this time, she remembered not only the accident but a life filled with love and comfort and hugs and grandparents who laughed a lot and a mother who twirled and three fathers, two young and one old, who sang to her and read to her. The memories swept over her, bathing her in love as if all that had been stripped away was returned. Her heart, so unaccustomed to such emotion, felt it might burst, and Janet sobbed and grieved for who she was and what she lost, and who she might have become had she not been held captive within the lie. And for the first time, she recognized what had been amputated from her life. It was her heart.

She cried for much of the night until, on the edge of sleep, she heard a comforting voice. *You'll be all right, Katherine.* After hearing it, she slept through to morning.

Waking with a headache, she sat up and pulled a notepad from the bedside table to record the dream and the voice. Opening it up, she stopped and tossed it into the wastebasket. The reason for keeping track of everything was gone. But, rethinking, she pulled it out and looked at all the entries with the triangles. *Heard bedroom door slam closed but is still open. Light in stable on again. Voices. Music downstairs. Voices in the bedroom. Quilt moved again.* "What the hell," she said aloud.

She heard a crack behind her, turned and saw the family portrait had fallen over again. "Absolutely," she said. Retrieving it, looking at Ellen and Howard she was overcome with rage. "Sorry, Howie," she said to it. "It's not you. It's the company you kept." She opened the window and flung it, frame and all, out against the side of the stable, where it shattered on the metal trashcan.

"Hey, watch out up there!" came a shout from below.

Janet looked down and saw Mike standing with the rest of the condo crew and Archie. "What the hell are you all doing here?"

"We were called in," Mike said. "Reinforcements or something."

Janet knelt down and leaned on the windowsill, holding her aching head.

"You look like hell," Sam said and Mattie smacked him. "Well, she does," he insisted.

"Go home! All of you." Janet shoved the window closed, stood up a bit too quickly and lost her balance. She tried to brace herself on the wall and knocked a painting off its hook. It fell, flipping as it landed revealing a photograph taped to the back. It was Max standing with Anna holding an infant. Janet touched it and began to sob again.

Archie stood below, looking up at the window, silent. Everyone else looked at Mike. "Yeah, I got this," Mike said.

Upstairs, from the hallway, Mike could see the top of Janet's head on the other side of the bed. "Go away, Mike." Her voice was thin. He walked in and sat on the floor against the wall facing her.

"Having a fun summer?" he joked.

"What are you doing here?"

"Archie called when he found you passed out in the grass yesterday. Said it looked like you'd done a face plant."

"He what?"

"Said you were belligerent as hell before you passed out. He carried you up here."

"He carried me?"

"Said you were in crisis."

"So, you all came to manage my crisis."

"That's what we do. How many times have you rallied the crew? When Mattie's mom died? We were there. When we had to move Carmen out of that big ass house after Jack died? You saw the guilt trip she took when we didn't see it."

Janet sighed.

"Got to Mackinaw City late and caught the first ferry this morning. Well, not the first. We had breakfast, then caught the next ferry."

"So, breakfast before crisis management?"

"Priorities."

They sat together in the kind of silence most people can't endure. He waited.

"I'm just so angry," she finally said. "All my life. So angry. Never felt like I belonged anywhere."

"You belong with me. With us," he quickly added.

"Oh, Mike. Don't you see? I couldn't give you something I didn't have. Still don't."

"You're wrong."

"Would you please stop arguing with me?" she snapped. "My whole life has been a farce. One lie on top of another on top of another. No wonder there was no love in that house. Do you know what it's like to look at your mother and see no love at all? And have people say I looked like her and think I might become her? That horrible bitch of a woman? To look at your father and think to yourself, how could I have come from that?"

"No, but --"

"Just shut up, would you? You know what Ellen called me when I visited her in the nursing home? Sissy. She called me sissy. I thought it was just some derogatory slam bullshit, but it was because I was her sister, not her daughter. Did he tell you all this?"

"Yeah, he gave us the general theme of the thing."

"The general theme." Janet smirked. "Ellen may not have remembered much but she remembered that. Can you imagine how she must have felt? And I didn't help the situation. I never gave her anything. Not one shred of kindness or consideration."

"Did she show you any?"

Janet tried to catch her breath. Her chest was tightening, her throat felt raw.

"What are you doing, Mike?"

"I'm defending you." She started to cry again, and he gave her a moment to move through the wave. "Would it have been any better if you'd known you were adopted?"

She looked up at him in shock. "Yes! It would have given my life some context. Just to know that I wasn't the product of Ellen and Howie's crappy genes. That they froze me out for some better reason than my worthlessness."

He picked up the photo. "Is this her?"

"Yeah."

"She was beautiful. Just like you."

"I am not beautiful."

"Oh, my dear, dear friend. You have no idea."

"About a lot of things! I have no idea about a lot of things! What does it say about me that this is the first moment in my life that I felt anything for my mother but contempt?"

"Maybe because that's all you knew. Look. One way or another, in all this mess, you have to figure out how to forgive. Everybody. This beautiful young woman who fell in love with the wrong man and gave birth to you. Howie, for whatever. Ellen for taking her pain out on a girl who was there every day to remind her of her father's cheating. Forgive anyone who was too chicken shit to tell you the truth. But mostly, and this is important, you have to forgive yourself for whatever you did in response to it all. Look. You made a life in spite of them. We all love you." He glanced up to the window. "Nice aim, by the way."

"I've got it from here," Archie said from the doorway.

Mike turned, looking at Archie like an intruder.

Archie stepped into the room, his presence saying more than words could.

Mike stood up.

Debbie appeared at the top of the stairs, looking at Mike with hard eyes. "That's enough, Mike," she said.

Mike reluctantly stepped out to the hallway and turned to Janet. "We'll be downstairs."

Archie took hold of the door and slowly closed it.

"There's two Tylenol if you want them on the dresser," Mike said as the door clicked closed.

Archie slowly made his way to Janet.

"I'm sorry about all this," she said without looking at him.

"I'm the one who's sorry," Archie said, holding his hands out to her. "Let's get you off the floor, shall we?" She took hold and groaned a little as she stood up. He piled pillows against the headboard, got her situated, and gave her the Tylenol and water. She downed them, and he climbed up next to her.

"You smell like a distillery. Been drinking?" he joked.

"Stop yelling," she said with a vague smile. She gave him back the half full glass of water.

"I'm actually whispering. All of it. Drink it all."

She drank it, and they sat there, silently, until another wave of tears hit her. Archie put his arm around her shoulders, and she rested her head against him. The wave passed.

"I thought you were maybe a closeted lesbian."

Janet laughed a little.

"I mean, I'm a charming guy and you never . . . well, now I know there is more to your story."

When he began to speak, it was in soft, low tones so comforting she could have listened all day.

"Genevieve knew she had cancer a full month before she told me. She started to withdraw from me, and I thought, well, I thought she was done with me. I saw a bit of that in you, just never imagined the fear you've lived with all your life. And that notebook? Holy shit, woman. Thinking what you must have thought?"

"I couldn't tell you. You watched your wife die a horrible death and I wasn't about to put you through my insanity. I just wanted one good summer, just one more."

"How about we have a lot more good summers? What do you think?"

She raised her face to his and they kissed, a soft, loving kiss, the first kiss of the summer, the first kiss of their new life together. They lay entwined for nearly an hour before he reminded her the crew had gone through a lot of effort to be there for her.

"I forgot they were here. We should go down," she said but did not budge.

"Come on," Archie said, stretching. "Besides, you really do reek."

Janet went downstairs. Archie retrieved the photograph from the floor and followed her.

"You were right," Debbie told Sam. "She does look like hell."

Archie stepped to Janet, wrapping his arms around her, rocking her gently back and forth. She melted into him. The condo crew stopped and stared. They'd never seen Janet accept close personal contact with anyone.

"This one has been through the wringer the last couple days," Archie said. "Anybody ready for a Bloody

Mary?" He released her, and Janet noticed the slack jaw gallery.

"What?" she said to them and headed to the bathroom with a mug of coffee. "I need a bath."

Placing the photo on the dining room table next to a stack of pictures he'd brought in from the chest, Archie went to the kitchen, pulling out spices, tomato juice, beef broth, and celery. He delivered a pitcher of the mix to the table, then went upstairs to collect fresh clothes and took them into Janet.

As he stepped out of the bathroom, she invited him back in. When the bathroom door closed behind him, all eyes fell to Mike who watched with a scowl.

Sam gave voice to what they were all thinking. "Looks like you're officially off duty there, Mike." No one laughed. It was a statement long overdue.

Archie took a washcloth, soaped it up, and washed Janet's back, having no idea it would trigger a new round of tears. "I remember this," she said through sobs. "I remember baths where my mother washed me and sang to me."

"I'm not going to sing," he said.

She laughed through her tears. "How much can one person cry? I mean, this is nuts."

"You're grieving. This is good," he said, rewarming the washcloth. "This is your adult body catching up to that three-year-old who lost everything." That, of course, brought on another wave. "Your body has years of toxins to flush out." He told her to tip her head back, and he washed her hair.

"No one's done that since I was a child," she said, surrendering to the comfort of the moment.

Archie left her to dress. When she finally emerged, she walked past the crew directly to the porch.

Carmen stepped out to her, but Janet waved her off Martin style. She silently obeyed.

Janet listened from the chaise as everyone hashed over the historical transformations to her life. Mattie attempted a recap. "So her grandfather was actually her father, and her mother was her sister, and Martin's boyfriend pretended to be her father until he died, and his family disowned her because she was a bastard and her real name is Katherine."

Then Carmen chimed in, "And Ellen was just some crazy woman she had to put up with all her life?"

"Sucks to be you," Mike hollered to the porch.

Martin wandered in through the kitchen. "Where is she?" he asked, and they all pointed to the porch.

"Uncle Martin?" Debbie asked. Archie nodded.

Tears streamed down Janet's face, but it was difficult to discern exactly what they meant. She yearned for the life she should have had and resented the hell out of those who'd stolen it from her. She heard footsteps at the doorway and waved off whoever was there.

"That doesn't work with me, Kitty Kat," Martin said.

She could barely get the words out. "I remember you calling me Kitty Kat."

Martin sat on the chaise at her feet. Janet wiped her eyes, and half smiled.

"How could he?" she asked.

"Who?"

"Max. How could he let me live in that hellhole?" The tears poured out, her breath coming in starts and stops. "Why didn't he rescue me? He should have loved me enough to get me out of there."

"He did the best he could."

"It wasn't enough!"

"Well, my dear. It rarely is."

The tears subsided. "What I don't get is why didn't Max and Anna . . . "

"Raise you? Different times, Pumpkin."

Janet smiled. "No one's called me names in a really long time."

"Oh, my darling Katherine, I never could get used to calling you Janet." That set off new tears and he plopped the tissue box in her lap. "Anna wanted to keep things from getting messy. I suppose we were all cowards. Scandal averse. Too much to lose."

"So I was the sacrificial lamb."

"I take offense at that," Martin scoffed.

"So do I!" Janet shouted. "It wasn't my fault I was a love child!"

Martin laughed out loud. "Hey!" he hollered inside. "She's a love child!" Janet laughed and cried as the crew started singing Diana Ross's *Love Child*.

"I'm so happy you all think this is so entertaining," she called out, "because if I wasn't fucked up enough before, I sure as hell am now."

Martin drew close and gently poked her in the chest, holding his finger on her heart. "You are no longer predestined, my dear. You, we all, have a choice. I believe the sins of the parents reside within us for as long as we live, or for so long as we choose to carry them." He leaned back again. "Shake it off. Become who you want to be. Live. Love. Laugh."

"You do realize you sound like a Hallmark card, right?"

"Darling, your life is what you make it. Listen to those people in there. *They* are your family. You created that for yourself." He patted her legs and went back inside. Janet collected herself and joined them.

Mid meal, Janet stood up from the table. "In honor of my true parents, Anna and Max, I am going to have my name legally changed to Katherine Post Crawford. Janet Granger is dead," she said boldly. "Long live Katherine Crawford!"

"To Katherine," Archie toasted. "Long may she rave."

"I have another toast," Mike said.

"Oh, please, I think we've about done me enough already," Katherine said.

"Oh my dear girl," Uncle Martin chided. "How you do think the world revolves around you. In fact, from what I hear, there's more afoot here than you know. Raise your glasses high."

Debbie glanced to Sam with a big smile.

"In one sense," Mike said, "Katherine, formerly known as Janet, but loved equally by any name she chooses, is the catalyst for more than one life-altering decision."

Debbie interrupted. "For the love of god, Mike! We sold Casper's Cove!"

Glasses clinked all round the table, and Katherine shouted her approval. "I hope you got a shit load for it!"

"They did," Sam said. "Somebody wants to put in a condo development around it. They made a killing."

Mattie told Sam to deliver his news.

"OK, OK," he said. "Much to the chagrin of my clients, I'm selling my practice."

"You what?" Katherine shouted. "Holy shit. All this happened in the week since you were here?"

"A national conglomerate has been hounding him for the last six years," Mattie said. "It was time. See what you started, Janet?"

"Katherine!" they all shouted.

Mattie said she was keeping the kitchen shop. "I'd drive Sam crazy with nothing to do. But I've given the new manager more responsibility. Being out of touch for that week was hard as hell, but I got to liking it."

Sam said she discovered having a life outside of work was kind of fun.

"So there," Archie said. "You've all made your little fortunes."

"Not me," Carmen said. "I'm not getting any windfall. I feel sidelined."

Debbie said she recalled Carmen's portfolio was quite comfortable last time she reviewed it. "One year later and you'd have had nothing."

"How considerate of Jack to die in '07 right before everything went to hell," Sam said. "You made a fortune on his house."

Carmen hung her head. "Yes, I did. Would have been so much better if I didn't feel like I killed Jack to get it."

"Jack drank his own self to death," Sam said.

"You just made sure he had fun doing it," Mattie added.

Debbie nudged Carmen. "And . . . there's nothing you'd like to proclaim?"

Carmen feigned ignorance then belted it out. "I'm seeing someone. Lenny. He has a boat."

"Do we like him?" Katherine asked.

Archie bristled. "That's a little callus. Do *we* like *me*?"

Everyone chimed in that they liked Archie and Uncle Martin, and yes, so far they liked Lenny.

The table was cleared and all the photos were spread out. "This one, the one you found upstairs, I took that in Baltimore," Martin explained. As upbeat as he seemed, he was not immune to the tragedy of it all. Describing the stories behind other pictures, he slipped into a melancholy. He looked at Katherine with weary eyes. "Nothing was the same up here. After the accident. The whole Annex felt it. Trixie Baldwin didn't last the week before she offed herself. Said Jimmy was still here. She heard him playing the piano at night. Said he was living in the stable. The light would go on and off out there."

Carmen and Mattie exchanged glances, holding up their goose-bumpled arms.

"Senior called the island police to guard the house. Said people were breaking in at night. Of course they thought he was nuts. One day, Trixie ate a bottle of pills, and that was that. And James's horse," Martin choked up a bit, struggling to get the words out. "Such a beautiful animal. An Andalusian warmblood. Regal Fellow. He kept acting up, kicking the stall, agitated all the time, calling out. I suppose he was grieving like the rest of us. He used to be so gentle, but something happened to him when James died and no one could get close to him. In any case, Senior had him put down. He's buried in Astor Meadow."

"Was he pale gray?" Katherine asked and all eyes fell to her.

Martin looked at her and smiled. "Yes, dear one. You used to feed him carrots and sit in the stall with him. You loved that horse."

"I've seen him. And all those other things?" Katherine said. "They still happen. All the time." She looked up and saw Mr. Harris in the kitchen.

"Did I miss anything?" he called in.

"Only everything," Katherine chided.

"What?" Archie asked, but Katherine was already up and headed to the kitchen. He reiterated that he told them the place was haunted, and everyone started in, talking over each other about the possibility of actual ghosts.

Over the laughter and speculation in the next room, Mr. Harris asked if Martin was setting them all straight.

"Did you know? About me?" she asked.

"Oh, I had my suspicions, but that's all. You look just like your momma, just her hair had a different cast to it."

"It's all so sad."

"That it is, young lady. That it is."

"Is it true Mrs. Baldwin went crazy? Thought her son was still here, like a ghost."

Mr. Harris glanced into the next room. "People see what they need to see, I guess."

"Today is the anniversary. Of the accident," Katherine said.

"Going out to the cemetery then?" he asked.

"Yeah. Are you coming with us?"

"Naw, I'm not much for groups." He looked out the screen door. "Haven't seen a sunflower grow on this property for forty or fifty years. And this year? Everywhere. They just came up everywhere. You should take a bunch with you today. Anna would appreciate it." Katherine was called to the other room as everyone was heading out to the porch. When she turned back to invite Mr. Harris, he was already gone.

At precisely three o'clock, the procession made its way to the cemetery. Each of them carried a massive sunflower.

Katherine stood at her mother's grave, surrounded by her friends, her true family, and felt connected to something greater for the first time since Grandpa Max died. Martin raised a bottle of Champagne in tribute. "To truth," he proclaimed, and took a swig and passed it on. It went around until it was drained dry. They left it leaning on the gravestone in the midst of the sunflowers. They left the cemetery chatting up a storm, planning the next meal, and talking about the coming winter. In only a few short weeks, autumn would be upon the island, and Katherine would be heading back to the condo. Archie invited them all to New Orleans for as long as they could stand it.

The crew left the island, returning to their new lives. Katherine stayed on, settling into her new identity. Martin took up residence most days on the porch of Baldwin Cottage, reading and napping. Archie became a permanent fixture. Katherine found comfort in his embrace, something she never expected to be capable of. She enjoyed falling asleep next to him and waking up wrapped in his arms. She even let him be on top when they made love.

CHAPTER 31

Stardust

Pink House residents cleared out mid-September. Martin stayed behind. When October winds came on cold, it was time to close up for the winter. Mr. Harris stopped in to go over the arrangements with Katherine. He said he was sorry to see the season end but was content to know the next summer would bring life back to Baldwin Cottage again. Katherine joined Archie and Martin on the porch. Mr. Harris went to the stable, looked at the trunk, and called out to Katherine, saying it should be put in the cottage. "I'll take care of it for you," he said, adding it to the list on his notepad. "Got things to do at Pink House first, get her ready to close up."

"I'll be staying on a bit longer," Martin said.

"You should leave with us," Archie urged, but Martin waved him off, dismissing him.

"I'm not ready to leave here. Not ready," Martin mumbled.

The night before Katherine and Archie were planning to go, Martin took them for dinner in town. It was a cold and blustery carriage ride there and back. Archie walked Martin into Pink House, stoked the fire, and poured him a glass of sherry before heading over to Katherine. "Are you sure you won't come with us tomorrow? I don't feel right leaving you up here alone." Martin gave him the wave, and Archie obeyed, leaving his uncle to his thoughts.

Katherine was sitting on the floor of the living room surrounded by the contents of the trunk when Archie came in with an armload of wood. "Look at all this stuff," she said to him. That's when he noticed her tears. Spread before her were not only more photographs, but books, and a scarf, a couple hats, and a beat up pair of women's keds.

"Martin kept all these things," she whispered, her voice having abandoned her.

Katherine held up a book of hand written poetry. "I've been reading them. They're utterly beautiful," she sighed. "James wrote them. They're about the woods here and nature and the intricate connection we each have to each other. He must have been a beautiful soul."

Archie sat down next to her and asked her to read one.

Beauty in silence

a current of stardust

filtered through sunlight

Breath of a giggle

takes hold of my heart

running

tiny toes through dew laden grass

"I bet that's about you." He kissed her and suggested they go to bed. He took some wood upstairs and stoked the fire in the bedroom as she crawled under the covers. The wind howled outside, rattling the windows, and the power cut off. Archie lit an oil lamp.

The woodstove snapped in the corner of the room as Katherine read another poem aloud.

Heart swells

breath pauses

eyes well

from a smile

"And I bet that was about Martin." Archie blew out the oil lamp and pulled her into his arms.

⌘

An argument drifted up the stairs. Katherine sat up, surprised to feel warm sunshine. She padded down the hall, trying to make out what was being said below, but the voices were muffled at first.

Mother . . . to stop this . . . What are they . . . changing everything . . . isn't yours anymore . . . mine. Who do they think they are . . . so angry all the time . . . I'm grieving . . . lost my boy . . . grandbaby and . . . left alone.

The words suddenly became clear.

"We're right here," a young woman said.

"Mother, it's Katherine," said a man.

"What? How can you be such a cruel boy?" said an older woman. "Katherine is gone!"

"No, Mother, she's back. Katherine moved the furniture."

"A toddler can't move furniture!"

Katherine stopped half way down the steps when she saw three people at the bottom. She knew her mother instantly, and just as quickly realized she was dreaming, and knew she had to take in every detail because dreams were fickle, appearing and vanishing in the space between heartbeats.

Anna whispered to the older woman, pointing to the steps. "Trixie, look. She's all grown up now."

Katherine watched Trixie's face soften.

"Katherine?" Trixie asked, her eyes glistening.

Katherine nodded slowly, unsure what was happening.

"Yes, Mother," the man said, hugging Trixie from behind. "The crash didn't take her. She's the one moving things. She's in our cottage now. That should make you happy."

"She didn't die?"

"No, Mother. She's happy. She found us. So, no more grieving," he whispered. "No more grieving. You can go now. She's fine. We're all fine."

Katherine watched the old woman walk toward the kitchen, the sound of her hard shoes fading before she had time to reach the door.

Katherine looked to Anna who now held a tray of cinnamon rolls, with a blue and white striped sackcloth towel draped over her arm.

"Good morning, sleepy head," Anna said, urging Katherine downstairs with a smile. "About time you got up."

Katherine descended the stairs and Anna gave her a kiss on the cheek before going through to the table.

"Hey, baby girl," Max said, stepping into view. "We've been waiting on you."

When he gave Katherine a big hug, it felt so real and warm she wouldn't let go until he chuckled and told her to lighten up. "Go get yourself some coffee, sweetie."

She looked him in the eyes. "Dad," she whispered and he grinned.

"You two straighten Trixie out?" Max asked the young man standing behind them.

"She won't be interfering any more."

"James?" Katherine asked and he smiled. He was everything she'd heard of him, dark curls falling over his brow, pale blue eyes.

"So sorry she frightened you, K. She didn't know."

Max pulled another chair up to the table, dragging it across the floor and plopping it in place, and Katherine recognized the sound as what she'd been hearing all summer.

"Honey," Anna said to Katherine, "would you go call James in, please?"

"He's right here," Katherine said, but he wasn't, and she knew exactly where he was. She stepped outside. From the middle of the yard, where she had stood as a small child, she looked up to the hayloft and saw James sitting in the chair at the table. "Breakfast is ready," she called out.

He looked out over his notebook, his face drenched in a golden glow. "Just a moment," he said. "One more thought escaping here." He scribbled something onto the page, clapped it closed, and smiled. "There it is then! Coming right down."

Anna and Max were already sitting at the table when Katherine went back in. Max pulled out the chair next to him for her. He asked about her summer and about Archie and her friends at home. "I like them," he said as if he'd met them.

"So do I," Anna agreed.

It struck Katherine that she was having no ordinary dream where things appear random and ethereal. Everything about this was vibrant and almost linear. James walked in through the kitchen and turned suddenly, surprised by someone walking in behind him. It was Martin, no longer old, but young again, sauntering in for breakfast. He went straight for James and they embraced, arms gripping tightly. James buried his face in Martin's shoulder. "Oh," Martin laughed. "I've missed you so much!"

From the corner of the room, Katherine glimpsed Mr. Harris. He raised a mug and smiled at her.

⌘

Katherine awoke to cold darkness. She sat up with a shiver.
"What is it," Archie whispered.
"It's Martin. We need to check on him."
Archie didn't question her. They both bolted out of bed, pulled on some clothes, and ran to Pink House. The fire was out and Martin sat in the dark, the glass of sherry still balanced in his cold fingertips. "He's home," she said, kneeling next to his chair.

Archie and Katherine postponed their departure until Martin was laid to rest in the Thorn family plot across the path from James and Anna.

Mrs. Cecelia Coventry approached as Katherine was loading the last of her luggage onto a dray behind the cottage. It was a bright day and the air was fresh and cool. Bare branches clicked overhead in the breeze. Katherine gave the driver a twenty. "Thanks so much," she said to Mr. Harris who sat on the back, his legs dangling off. The driver hollered a sharp *Hep* and the team stepped out, the harnesses snapping taught against the Clydesdale's massive bodies. Mr. Harris waved as they disappeared around the hedgerow.

Cecelia called out to Katherine. "You'll be fixing the Baldwin nameplate, won't you, dear?"

Archie appeared from around the corner. Katherine glanced his way then back to Cecelia. "Not a chance," Katherine told her. "Not a chance in hell."

Once again, this outsider had shocked Cecelia. People didn't talk to her that way. Ever. She looked at Archie expecting a noble defender and found only a smirk. She backed up a step and stumbled before regaining her footing. "I presume you've made plans to close up for the season," she said.

"Mr. Harris is taking care of it for me," Katherine told her.

Archie looked at her with a cockeyed grin. "Mr. Harris?"

"Yeah. He said he'd do it right after he's done with Pink House."

"Well, I don't see how that's possible," Cecelia argued.

"Why?" Katherine asked, a little annoyed.

"Well, for one, because he's been dead for decades," Cecelia said.

"Forty-one years actually," Archie said. "I was thirteen the summer he keeled over."

"But, he's been here all summer," Katherine insisted. "You've seen him, Archie. He was just here. And that morning we all had breakfast. He was right there in the stable last week when Martin told him he was staying on. You were there. You have to remember."

Cecelia chided them for trying to make her look like a fool and she charged off in a huff.

"You're pulling my leg," Katherine said. "Maybe there's another Mr. Harris?"

Archie took her by the hand and they sauntered down the lane to town. "Mr. Harris was in everybody's business as I recall. Spent his whole life here, caretaking the Annex."

"He's dead," Katherine confirmed.

"Very dead." Archie laughed, put his arm around her, and pulled her close as they walked. "I tried to tell you," he said.

They walked a bit further.

"Oh my," she said with a spark of concern. "If Mr. Harris isn't winterizing, then..."

Archie grinned. "It's under contract."

"I have a contract?"

"Yes. No worries."

The island seemed to sigh in relief as the last of her summer people sifted down to town and were ferried away.

There was no one left to hear the slamming of Trixie's bedroom door in Baldwin Cottage.

The End